SOUL HARVEST

R. C. Thom

Books by Rachel C. Thompson writing as RC THOM

SOUL HARVEST
in print ISBN 978-1-7321459-1-7 or E-book ISBN 978-1-7321459-0-0

DRAGON FIRE
in print ISBN 978-1-7321459-2-4 or E-book ISBN 978-1-7321459-3-1

STALKING KILGORE TROUT
in print ISBN 978-1-7321459-4-8 or in E-book ISBN 978-1-7321459-5-5

AGGIE IN ORBIT
in print ISBN 978-1-7321459-7-9 or in E-book ISBN 978-1-7321459-6-2

AGGIE IN SPACE
coming late 2019 or early 2020

PERSIDECIAL THREE PACK Amazon exclusive

BOOK OF ANSWERS due late 2019

ANTHOLOGY TWO coming in 2020

INTRODUCTION

I ask myself a lot of 'what if' questions, that's what we sci-fi people do. After all, we build worlds from scratch and dive into rabbit holes to do so.

In this near-future story I asked what would UFO disclosure look like and how will it happen? The people that know about aliens, if anyone knows, aren't saying. If it's true that they are here, it's not the 'Powers that Be' who will tell us.

Here in *Soul Harvest* I explore how and why this unlikelihood happens. If disclosure happens at all, my guess is it will come unexpectedly. Someone like Aggie Piper will smash into it headlong and be forced to face the impossible. How will Aggie and the world fare? Read on and find out

PRELUDE
25 Years Ago

Bob Callahan never saw anything like it. Previously as a detective in Philly, he had seen a lot; too much, too many bloated bodies and shot off faces. Philly made Iraq seem safe. Nothing ever changed in Philly but everything turned on a dime; disrespect came fast and furious.

But now things were too slow. Bob became Sheriff of Cryersville, a small town in north central Pennsylvania, to heal and live a normal life. He got his wish, but normal didn't last.

Cryersville was a peaceful nineteenth-century-built village where dairy farmers, carriage-traveling Mennonites and people from Brier Air Force Base gathered. Everyone got along just fine. With Briar closing soon, the peace could only grow. Bob's main worry; he was getting fat. In Philly, his nerves were too raw, he couldn't eat. Adrenalin and whiskey provided sustenance. Pennsylvania Dutch comfort food became his restorative medication. Mennonite baked goods regularly appeared on his desk. Respect tasted good.

Trouble was the last thing he expected in Cryersville.

Hell broke loose on September 6th while standing on the porch of Myer's Old Time Hardware & Drug with a young Mennonite farmer named David. It was a fine Indian summer day. Folks were outside eating lunch on the town square's lawn, or under old-growth oak trees on vintage benches. The antique park's fountain gurgled its usual lullaby.

Looking over David's shoulder toward the park, he saw jaws and sandwiches suddenly drop. People jumped up from the old wrought iron benches like their seats were on fire.

"What is that?" Bob said.

David turned, saw, and nearly collapsed but only David's sack of horseshoe nails hit the porch deck. David held onto the porch rail like a sailor fighting wind. Bob stepped past him and moved to the street covering his eyes Indian style. A soundless, shiny disk, thirty feet in diameter, floated slowly down the middle of Main Street fifty feet off the ground. The thing was hard to make out. It moved at a fast-walk pace.

The light was blinding. It went down Main a few dozen yards, and back again just below the roofline. Centuries old brick buildings and three-story clapboard Victorian houses glowed yellow as it passed.

Pandemonium broke out on its return. People ran from the park in every direction, others burst out of doors, cars stopped dead in the street while other drivers raced off wildly. Robert Crain's horse and utility wagon flew across the park driverless bucking off produce as it went.

Bob's detective mind clicked into overdrive. He was trained to ignore disaster and keep his wits. Mostly, he was fascinated. He loved puzzles and that was one hell of a puzzle. He stood there thinking until David shook his shoulder.

"Aren't you going to shoot it, Sheriff?" David cried. "It's the devil come to take our souls!"

"It's trying to hide," Bob said, walking out into the middle of the street. David took off, accidentally kicking his bag and scattering the nails. The object wobbled slightly as it moved between the Widow Maker Saloon and the blacksmith's pole barn. There it hovered and glowed less.

A faint thumping sound like a distant machine gun report grabbed Bob's attention. He spun on his heel, keyed for action. Between buildings he saw three black cobra-jet helicopters coming over the rise of low hills perpendicular to Main Street. They were half a mile away and closing fast.

The Village was situated in a little valley. The choppers descended toward town. There was a distant whoosh. The object reacted and shot straight up one thousand feet just as two sidewinder missiles spiraled inbound. The craft streaked away north. The missiles twisted crazily and followed. The choppers veered off after it.

Stupid bastards, there're civilians here!

Bob jumped into his patrol car and stomped the gas pedal launching the Crown-Vic. He sped up Main with heart pounding while dodging abandoned cars and carriages. *They can't shoot rockets here.* He damn near hit a little girl standing in the road. He stood on the brakes. His guts twisted. It was a near miss.

"Get a hold of yourself, concentrate, you fucking idiot!" *Protect and serve.*

He made sure no one else was in the street before hammering it. At the end of Main Street, he hung a sliding left onto County Road 420. The light was before him, now miles away, it made an impossible ninety-degree right turn, but another pair of missiles cut it off. The Cobras had spread out and launched more sidewinders, projectiles flew in every direction, smoke trails crossed the sky like drunken spider webs. Bob made a hard right onto a dirt road.

He couldn't believe the government would fire rockets here. He had to stop them.

"Bastards! Nobody fucks with my civilians!"

The craft boomeranged and flew right over him. The Ford stalled going full bore down the dirt road. He jammed on the brakes thanking God police cruisers have power reserve braking. Stuck, he jumped out.

Adrenalin pumping, angry as a hornet, he drew his revolver, cocked the hammer and aimed it at an oncoming chopper but he didn't fire. Instead, he lowered the gun's hammer back to rest.

"Never resolve this from a Federal Pen. God damn Feds."

There was an explosion, then thundering cracks and snaps behind him. He spun and witnessed it plowing through a patch of trees. It went down on Appleton's farm.

He reached through the open window and jerked the microphone off the dash. The radio screeched with static — that never happened. He shouted over the noise.

"Dispatch, it's the Chief, get fire and ambulance over to Appleton's, fast."

"Chief," Mildred replied, "You better get back here, the people are all... David Horsum..."

"Never mind that: Handle them, get that equipment going. Call Brier, tell them, tell them..." Bob didn't know what to say. He needed the Air Force on site, that much he knew. "One of their airplanes got shot down, no...make that crashed. I want them here pronto. Somebody's getting an ass chewing for this."

He got back in the Vic and tried the ignition: nothing. He punched the steering wheel and tried again and again. It started just as the fire department's WWII air raid sirens began blaring.

He flew down the track kicking dirt all the way to Appleton's farmstead. He didn't stop at the wrought-iron gate; rather he crashed it at speed. A row of trees lined either side of the farm road. The trees of one section of Appleton Lane were chopped off at twenty-five feet and the treetops were laid in the cornfield. *What, the Jolly Green Giant's harvesting broccoli?* A debris field of branches led on toward a cedar tree patch within the hollow. Bob picked up the radio.

"Mildred, it's in Appleton's swamp, tell rescue."

"Got it, Chief."

He checked his mirror; black helicopters were landing well behind him in the cornfield. There wasn't any flat ground near the crash site. The last hundred yards of field sloped steeply into a wetland. Appleton Lane was too narrow for choppers. He was ahead of them.

He didn't wait; seconds saved survivors. He stopped his car where the track turned away. His cop brain screamed warnings. *The pilot might be dangerous, the Feds have a reason to act so goddamn stupid.* He pulled his beloved Remington 1100 shotgun off the rack, and hurried into the cattails pushing his way blindly through six-foot tall stalks.

He cleared the muck and made the cedar field. A thirty-foot wide scorched path was cut through a deep thicket of tall trees and low junipers. Eighty yards ahead, was a domed silver pie plate on-end buried halfway into the loam. The thing wasn't badly damaged. He expected twisted wreckage smeared with blood and guts.

A shiver went up Bob's spine. *This just ain't right.* He checked his revolver and chambered a shell into the Remington with a one-handed pump and proceeded on slowly, alert, ignoring the water squishing inside his chukka boots. The smell of wood-rot mixed with ozone was unnerving.

He stopped mid step, the hairs on his neck hackled. At a hundred paces he saw a small, pale, hairless, naked figure. Its back rested against a stump, its large head down between scrawny white knees. It just didn't look right. He choked down fear. He had to get closer, a better look. He moved ahead slowly, felt like he was wading in molasses, knees barely holding his weight. His nerves rode on coiled springs. The creature's head snapped up: Its big black eyes, like pools of crude oil, drilled a hole into his soul.

"Hold it, CIA," from behind. "Drop your weapon."

Bob's hands shot up, his shotgun flew and splat-landed in the mud. He hadn't lost his Philly cop-sense; someone had a gun on him. He turned around slowly. Two soldiers dressed in black had AK-47s trained on him. He almost shit with relief.

Several more soldiers ran up with rifles pointed at the kid, or whatever it was. They advanced with extreme prejudice. The other two didn't lower their guns. *NATO guns; why not M-16's military standard.*

"Come with us. Mr. Black will debrief you."

Two men grabbed Bob and forcefully spun him around. They marched him away from the scene. But, from behind the Sheriff heard, "It's Karnack's, fire!"

Bob tried to turn but his escorts tighten their grips. Each man was a vice. They jacked him straight like a naughty rag doll.

"Karnack, you sure?"

"Shut up Archer, shoot!"

Guns fired. The men in black ignored it. Bob felt sick but he was too outraged to puke. His adrenalin withdrew and weakened him further, too weak to fight for that albino kid. All he could do was choke down his bile and let those government goons drag him away.

Back in the field, he recovered his wits and took a good look at those black choppers. No markings, they made little engine sound although rotors were spinning under power. The air was thumping but not the motors. He craned his neck; his guards had no name tag or insignia. Bob had seen their type before. *Better not fuck with them—not yet.*

Two matte black box-trucks with multiple antennas were lined up behind his patrol car. Three all-wheel drive military trucks were parked in the cornfield splattered with black loam—they had come cross-county. Heavily armed men in black military gear were scattered around watching the sky. A two-rotor chopper from Brier had landed, heat distorted the air above its' motors but it wasn't running.

Pay attention Callahan. Where'd they all come from so fast?

There weren't any other marked military vehicles in sight. One of the box trucks was set up like a camper. It had blacked-out windows and an air conditioning unit on the roof. Bob was brought to the truck's rear. A rifle pointed him up a folding stairway. The inside was a padded jail cell lined with benches. On one bench sat two USAF chopper pilots in full gear and an officer in formal attire sporting a chest full of medals.

"What the hell's going on here?!" Bob demanded, putting a hand on his revolver, surprised he still had it.

"I'll be damned if I know," said the officer, standing up and thrusting his hand out. "Major Roger Dent, Chief of Security, Brier. You called?"

The events of the next few days were a succession of debriefings for Bob and the gathered populations of Cryersville and Brier Air Force Base. Speeches about national security were made, along with threats of ruined lives or death.

The men in black uniforms (Bob never did see any CIA identifications) said the craft was a top-secret remote-controlled air target drone that malfunctioned. It had to be brought down before more people were hurt. Money was paid, oaths were administered and fears were expertly instilled.

Bob didn't buy any of it and either did Roger Dent. Bob and Roger had business together setting up the meetings. They got chummy fast.

The last time they met formally at Brier was in Roger's office. Only Roger wasn't seated behind his gun metal desk. A man wearing a black suit, hat and sunglasses sat there instead. Roger was in one of two drab metal chairs set before Roger's WWII-era desk.

"Sit down, Sheriff Callahan," The man in black said. "I've studied your backgrounds and I know full well men of your caliber aren't easily swayed by our ... techniques. As you probably know we have the ability to destroy your lives. No one will ever believe the stories you'll tell. I'm sure you've seen the papers."

The man tossed a newspaper to Bob, a well-regarded rag out of Harrisburg, Pa. Bob unfolded it and read an outrageous headline about this UFO sighting. It said, 'UFOs, What's Next Big Foot?'

"We are very good at...co-opting the media. You two know what you know, but it will do you no good. So, save me the trouble of disappearing you, tell me you will cooperate with the U.S. Government, to which you swore your allegiance, and forget what you saw. Understand?"

"Of course," Bob said through gritted teeth. Roger's knuckles were white on the chair's armrest; he didn't like it either.

"Yes, Sir," the Security Chief said.

"We'll be watching you," the man in black said.

Bob boiled within but he didn't let it show. Maybe Philly wasn't for him. Maybe country living wasn't either. This high strangeness shook him out of complacency. He needed a challenge, something that mattered. He decided right then he was going to solve this puzzle if it's the last thing he ever did. *Look out project Karnack, here I come.*

After Mr. Black left Roger said, "You going to let this pass?"

"Not on your life."

"I'm with you." Roger said.

Bob and Roger went to the empty Officers Club and spent the rest of the day getting drunk.

ONE

Monday, December 10, 3:15 P.M.

School was letting out, but not for Aggie Piper. She sat in Key West High School's main office reception area pushing her long blonde bangs over her face; still, she could not hide. The front office had big windows. It should have been really hot but the air conditioning was blasting. A sunbeam lit her sundress but all she felt was cold. Mrs. Preggey's wrath seeped into the waiting area like a melting slushy. Aggie sank deeper into her steel chair; she was five foot ten tall but managed to scrunch down to three feet small.

The dismissal bell rang. Billy Barns strutted out of the hall that led to Preggey's office. He had that annoying bounce in his step. *I hate jocks.* Billy opened the door and shot her a smug look that said, 'You're in for it now, bitch.' He flipped her off and left. As usual, nobody saw it but her. The hallway was a river of kids; Billy slimed in and swam off.

Ten minutes later one of the secretaries leaned over the orange Formica counter and announced, "You're up, Ms. Piper."

"Mrs. Preggey's going to kill me," She whispered.

She hesitated, brushed her dress, stood taller, raised her shoulders, and pushed the hair out of her eyes. *Keep it together, you need that scholarship, bad.*

But, by the time she arrived at the principal's open door, her hair was back in her eyes, shoulders re-slumped. Mrs. Rich Parent-kiss-ass was a tiny woman with short brown hair, an English accent, intense hazel eyes and a serious small-man-complex. Preggey motioned her to take the hot-seat.

"Agatha Piper," the Terminator began. Don't say a word. I don't care who started it."

"But, Mrs. Preggey, Billy tripped Jimmy and — ."

"Enough!" the principal said. "First, although Billy is admittedly a bit rough about his perimeter, that doesn't give you a constable's license. He is not an expert in karate or whatever fighting art it is that you do. Do you know I could have you arrested?"

The Terminator leaned back in her chair and crossed her tiny arms. Preggey looked like a T-Rex considering her next meal. Aggie bit her lip...hard; she wanted to say how much T-Rex hates push-ups.

"Remember all the trouble you started this past time? If there hadn't been witnesses…"

Aggie remembered it all right Billy took a swing at her. She caught his fist and slung him into a locker and broke his nose. *It wasn't my fault.* She was trained to react, just reflex. Too bad it was the day before the Thanksgiving football game. Billy didn't play well at all. Who would with a busted face? Everyone hated her for that one.

"I should have had you arrested, if not for that confounded lawyer mother of yours."

"But I didn't attack him! I deflected his blow, that's all and—."

"It doesn't matter what he did," Mrs. Preggey said standing up. "Every time there is a spot of trouble you are in the thick of it." She leaned forward with knotted hands on her desk. "Why must you reside within every quagmire? You with an unfair advantage ought to know better…"

Aggie stopped listening. *Unfair advantage! Billy's parents have the PTA bought and paid for. He gets away with everything!* She bit her lower lip drawing blood. Anything to keep the wise-ass remarks inside her head from spilling out. *Why'd I have to clock the big-deal football guy?*

"What have you to say about that?"

"I should have learned how to throw a football…Oh crap."

Mrs. Preggey did a classic double take. *She got the sarcasm. Crap, crap, crap.*

"It's a bloody shame you don't apply yourself. Your teachers complain that you barely engage in class activities. Best test scores in school. You should be a lock for the Scholarship Program, but…"

A scholarship that Billy's parent's support; I'm so doomed.

"I have a responsibility to this school…"

Mrs. Preggey droned on and on. Aggie knew the speech by heart but something new got her attention. Preggey suddenly stood on her tiptoes and leaned way over her perfectly ordered desk. Aggie squiggled deeper into the leather chair and pushed more hair into her eyes. *Here it comes.*

"You leave me no alternative; if you touch Mr. Barns once more, in or out of school, consider yourself expelled. Furthermore, I've stricken your name from the Scholarship Program until you demonstrate avid participation in class. Do I make myself clear, Ms. Piper?

Aggie almost choked. *No way! It's social suicide.*

"But, but, I know more than my teachers. The kids will think I'm showing off. Everybody hates a know-it-all…" The facts were useless. Aggie shut herself up for a change.

"I see. Shall I expel you now, then, if you like?" Mrs. Preggey voice was cold acid. "You have credits enough to graduate. Your expulsion won't upset my graduation ratings. As for the scholarship, there are other low-income students qualified. And I dare say, more deserving. What will it be? File in or file out?"

Aggie was crushed by the weight of unfairness. She had no options.

"I'll do my best, Mrs. Preggey, I won't cross the line."

"See that you don't. You are dismissed."

She slunk out of the Principal's office feeling lower than whale poop. Mom's voice echoed in her head, 'head up, tall girls shouldn't diminish themselves, be proud.'

"Yeah. Right."

She didn't go to her locker — she never carried books — read them all sophomore year. She headed directly to student parking. She walked across the lawn, head down, counting blades of dried grass. Hitting the pavement, she looked up. Her pride-and-joy scooter had been tipped over again.

If it were some ordinary old scooter she wouldn't have cared. But Daddy had fixed up this '62 Vespa just for her. It was really cool. Made in Italy, the Vespa had a 125CC two-stroke motor and a three-speed transmission. It was the fastest scooter in town. Of course, it was illegal, but it looked like a 50CC and Daddy and she kept that fact secret; Daddy loved putting it over on The Man. He'd have been the greatest dad ever if he wasn't so stuck on his stupid flying saucer crap.

She up-righted her scooter while pushing thoughts of rightful vengeance down.

"If I didn't want college Billy Barns, I'd mess you over so bad."

She kicked the motor over. Despite being flooded, Robin started right up. It smoked a lot; it always did when first started. She checked it out while warming it up. No new damage. The robin's egg blue bodywork was already full of dents and scratches. But she was still mad as hell. *Rich kids and jocks get away with everything.* Billy had both categories covered.

She pulled in the clutch, twisted the gearshift grip into first, revved it up, dumped the clutch and shot off. She stood up on the floor boards and pulled the front wheel off the ground riding a wheelie all the way across the parking lot. She glided Robin's front tire down before hitting the apron, slid the rear tire sideways and fishtailed onto Flagler Avenue launching herself south toward Melissa's leaving a trail of hot, blue, oily smoke.

TWO
Monday after School

Mel's house was only a half mile away like everything else in Key West because the whole place was only a mile square. Aggie turned right off Flagler, went two blocks and turned south. She stopped at the next intersection even though there wasn't a stop sign. She didn't need traffic laws. Stopping here was for pure survival. A scooter rental store was just up the block. The cross streets were loaded with clueless tourists on rented scooters zipping around like they had sand crabs in their shorts. The cops didn't mess with local bikes unless the riders were like the tourists; really drunk.

She reached Melissa's place in two minutes. Not enough of a ride to cool her temper. So, she sat across the intersection facing Melissa's house calming her mind like Mark taught. The Van Ness estate always made her feel small. In a town where most homes were tiny and a shotgun shack cost half a million, the Van Ness family had bought up half a city block. The house looked like a series of glass blocks stacked randomly on top of each other. It looked pretty cool. She liked it despite the opulence and felt bad that she did. So much ruined land, but Mel's mom did have a nice garden. The property was like a nature reserve. She took a deep breath inhaling a mixture of tropical flowers and Vespa smoke.

Feeling better, she slowly rolled along Mel's six-foot-high pink stucco fence wall. Many tropical flowering vines clung to Mel's wall. Palms and other trees towered overhead. The trees were full of singing birds. Lizards darted everywhere. Mel's place was an artsy Eden. Even Mom would have liked the Van Ness place if she didn't hate wealth so much.

Aggie pulled up to the wide wrought iron gate in the middle of the property. She showed her face to the camera and stuck out her tongue. The gates slid opened. Weird, the security guy didn't even say hi. She followed the gray paving stone driveway to the right-side garage and stopped next to a black Bentley. Her faded blue-green scooter blended in with the foliage that was reflected on the Bentley's mirror polished door. She killed the Vespa's motor quick so no oil smoke would get on the car.

Mrs. Van Ness was picking flowers in a tiny black string bikini. She got up and strode past the antique Rolls and around the Bentley to greet Aggie. Mel's

Mom looked like a runway model; tall, thin, bleach-blond and tan. Not your average Goth geek's mom. Like many rich women on the Key she passed for a Nordic Goddess. Aggie wondered how she and pale, nerdy Mr. Van Ness got together. They were madly in love, too. *Maybe money does buy love.*

"Hi, Mrs. V. What happened to the security guy, the gates just opened?" She said putting the Vespa on its center stand.

"Agatha, don't scratch the Bentley with that thing you ride," Mrs. Van Ness said with a condescending tone but Aggie took no offence, Mrs. V always talked that way.

"Albert is on duty; Melissa is testing some new toy. Some sort of face recognition system. That child is so much her father. I just adore how they do things together. Melissa is in the lab."

Mrs. Van Ness pointed the way with her long, straight nose. Aggie rubbed the bump on the bridge of her own nose; a remnant of kickboxing.

The garden path went along the north side of the garage. She followed the paving stones to the pool. Behind the Olympic sized pool, half hidden by tropical plants, there was a pink stucco pool house, which was Mel's makeshift lab. Aggie ducked through the arched portico and found Mel hunched over a fold-out table strewn with all kinds of electronic parts. Mel wore big, weird magnifying glasses fastened to her skull by a leather T-band.

"Hey," Aggie said, "You look like a geek-punk scientist in a brain tourniquet."

"I'm hoping to go blind and grow hair on my knuckles like you Kung Fu dudes." Melissa pulled off the goggles. Her short black hair spiked every which way. She tossed her nerd glasses onto the bar, which was also covered with gizmos and gadgets.

"Put them back on," Aggie said. "Works for you, matches the black T-shirt you wear every day."

"So, I'm a fashion plate, shoot me. Why aren't you at work? I thought Mark wanted you to paint rowboats? You never miss work."

"I'm so screwed, Mel."

"Dude, what happened this time?"

Aggie didn't bother with how Billy did it to her again; rather, she reported her meeting with Mrs. Preggey. The wheels turned behind Mel's blue eyes as Aggie spoke. *She's got pretty eyes. Mel should lose the black hair.*

"Only one thing to do," Melissa said, "Let's geek-over his ass."

"Geek power's your answer for everything. When you hacked the school computers, changed his grades, it didn't matter at all. They had to know it was you. If your parents weren't big shots, you'd be toast. I can't take any risks."

"Dude, that's not where I'm going," Mel said, "We go high-tech surveillance. I got a phone that's wired big, GPS, full-on computer, Sat-linked or cell tower, software to track anything, remote Bluetooth, voice command cam. We'll catch him in the act, won't even know he's on cam. We'll bug his scooter and track him with this sucker." Mel held out chewed gum.

"Yeah right, gum him up, that'll slow him down." Aggie said pushing hair behind an ear.

"Look at this crap. It's magnetic; it's a tracking bug, Dude."

"How's that going to help, you're losing it Mel."

"If you know where Billy is, he can't mess with you. This is my Dad's stuff; it's not even on the market. Too advanced for civilians. I got more."

"What if your Dad finds out you were in his stuff?"

"He doesn't care, I'm Daddy's little girl. Check this out."

Mel's dad was in the defense industry, he specialized in surveillance junk and Mel had a history of helping herself to it. She pulled a slim, red cell phone from her pocket and slid it open revealing a keyboard and screen. She pushed it across the table to Aggie. Aggie pushed it back.

"I can't take it. You know how my Dad is. I don't make enough to buy a phone. Crap, Mel if he sees this he'll flip. He'll think I've sold out to The Man."

"Tell him it tracks UFOs he'll love it. Besides, look at how small this is. Just keep it in your pocket, yeah. He'll never see it. I'll give you an in-ear Bluetooth. We'll setup a micro cam in your earrings."

"Mel, look at my sundress, I don't have any pockets! I wear a sundress every day. They'll know something's up if I'm all commando-outfitted."

"Lose the bathing suit and wear shorts under your dress instead. Come on Ag, lets geek-over Billy Barns. All we got to do is record him and put a bug on his scooter, maybe one in his backpack."

"I don't know. Spying's dishonest. You can't record someone without their permission, its' illegal."

"When'd you start supporting the police state, geezs. OK, don't cam-him in the act. They'll take his side anyhow. Just track him. Dude, it's not spying, its survival."

Aggie wasn't one to run from a head-on fight. Sneaking around to avoid Billy was way weird. Too much like what cops do.

Yet going to college relied on that Scholarship. Mom and Dad didn't have money. They wouldn't even let her call filthy-rich Grandpa Branford to ask him for help. No, if she wanted college, she had to do it herself. If that meant eating Billy's crap for six months; bring on the ketchup. She hated ketchup. It really was better to avoid him altogether.

"I'm in Mel, hook me up."

"Dude."

Mel showed her the ins and outs of the spy phone. It was coolest device ever. Too bad it had to be secret. People weren't supposed to know anything about the National Security Agency's junk much less have it, or use it to mess over the town bully. Mel brought out the fake used-chewing-gum transponder, brushed Aggie's hair back genially and tried to stick it to Aggie's forehead. Aggie shivered at Mel's light touch.

"You removed that iron plate from your skull, bummer Dude."

"My scooter needed parts. Check the school Secretary's computer. If the Terminator sends a letter home, I'm crisp. Mom will bust on the school board again, they hate her."

"Dude, they don't just hate her, they hate all lawyers, and her being an Earth Priestess doesn't help either." Mel's fingers were flying over the keyboard as she spoke.

"Mom's not really a lawyer; she quit practice to be a professional hippie."

"Got it. Intercepted." Mel started retyping the letter. It would go out but not as dictated. Preggey would sign it without looking. They see her do that on cam all the time.

Aggie wasn't so sure Mel's high-tech solution would work. She had a low-tech problem to solve first; plant the bug. She had to get at Billy's scooter without him freaking out. She decided to wait and see, think it out. Like her karate instructor, Mark, says, 'Observe the enemy before you strike.' She couldn't afford another run-in with Billy blow-hard; that was for sure.

THREE

Monday afternoon

Bob Callahan and Roger Dent started a UFO newsletter that grew into a national volunteer investigative reporting organization and website even before Bob retired. The thing took off, data poured in. Inside their office their original newsletter cut-sheets still plastered the walls but they published it electronically now, so computers hummed everywhere, a server occupied one corner with racks of hard-drives blinking madly. A folding table against one wall held stacks of printed research materials.

Twenty-five years after the Cryersville UFO incident the organization's co-founders still hadn't found definitive proof, but they were getting closer. The National UFO Reporter (NUFOR) had a quandary, incidences were breaking and they needed more volunteer reporter-observers.

Bob Callahan, gray haired and a lot fatter, leaned back in his chair causing it to crack in complaint. He looked over the piles of papers stacked on his desk; Roger Dent was still lean and straight, only a touch of gray at his temples; he looked too young to have retired from the Air Force. Roger had taken the only chair not stacked with books and set it before Bob's desk.

"It's big, maybe disclosure," Roger said, "I feel it. Why else would the Navy allow so many orb fly-bys near their air space? We must move on this now."

"The evidence looks good," Bob agreed. "But we can't keep up with all the other reports as it is. Our volunteers have their hands full."

"We must confirm Key West," Roger said, "it's imperative."

"How? Our nearest…acceptable volunteer is in Miami and Phil has a job, can't expect him to drive all the way down there. We can't afford to put another nut-case on." Bob said thinking of the scandal where one of their marginal reporters had trashed the organization on The National Press TV show. The media piled on NUFOR; it was Gulf Breeze all over again.

"What about Sonny Piper? I gave you his info. You checked him out." Roger said.

"He's married to Charlotte Branford, calls herself Sky-flower or some other weird name nowadays; her father's an R&D defense contractor. Branford's strictly black-ops. No help."

"Branford's an interesting connection. Can't we use it?"

"The Old Man never leaves his ship. I can't blame him. Branford Industries is bad news; every peace-nick in North America wants his hide and likely why he's estranged from his hippie-dippy daughter. None the less, I'd bet the Feds keep an eye on her. No good, too many eyes on the Pipers."

Roger drummed his long fingers on Bob's desk a few minutes. He leaned toward Bob.

"Look, his email is sincere."

"He's a nut job," Bob said.

"How crazy can he be?" Roger said. "He's got a bright daughter, name's Agatha; they don't let mental cases raise gifted children."

Bob's old detective mind clicked in and he said. "I'm not convinced, wasn't he arrested for protest trespassing?"

"Ok they are a little nutty, hippie types to be sure. He hates 'The Man', so he's motivated. Look, he's keeping an eye on them anyway. Paranoia is his friend. Think of this: If Old Man Branford is involved in reverse engineering, Piper might just step on the inside track."

"I doubt it. Piper isn't in Branford's good graces," Bob said, "Daughter hates the Old Man. It'll be slim pickings. He can't write worth a damn; you saw his application sample."

"Slim is better than none," Roger said. "We need someone in Key West. His place is next to the base. He runs a charter boat right past it. He's the monkey in the middle. We might get lucky."

"Piper has no credentials."

"Admiral Sanderson's down there."

Bob and Roger had long known of Sanderson. Wherever Sanderson was, strange things happened. Media got shut off or put on a tight electric leash. Sanderson's op-eds, publicly critical of NUFOR's alternative news reports, had dogged them after Gulf Breeze. Disinformation followed Sanderson like a pull-toy.

"Piper's close to the action, I'll admit." Bob said it not believing his own words. He didn't like it, but Roger was hot on this guy and he learned long ago to trust Roger's instincts.

Bob caved. "I wonder if he has a camera."

"I'll send him a cheap camera." Roger said pulling Piper's printed email off a stack of papers atop Bob's desk. Roger scanned through two pages. "He's definitely an interested party. He's in an ideal place."

"We need all the…legitimate…investigators we can get." Bob said. Either indigestion or excitement kicked his guts, either way Bob took it as a good sign. "He had better follow protocol. We can't afford another debacle."

"Call him; make sure he understands he can't screw this up. I'll overnight the camera and investigator's kit."

"I'll call in the morning." Bob said reaching for a bottle of antacids.

Roger took a box off the stack on the side table. Bob looked at his desk phone thinking sometimes something is not better than nothing. Roger better be right. Bob had had his fill of bad publicity. He popped three tablets into his mouth.

FOUR

Failing to participate Tuesday morning

Mrs. Preggey's warning was fresh in her mind when she entered Mr. Beal's first period Western Civilization class. Aggie was determined to 'participate' as ordered. She took her usual seat in the back row along the windows not exactly sure what to do. She must have read a hundred books on history, religion and anthropology just to keep her brain from spinning. Beal wasn't teaching cutting edge stuff. 'Beal's babble' was so hard to take.

Aggie loved scholarly non-fiction books and hated internet junk like flying saucers, Big Foot and conspiracy crap. *Why did other kids read it?* Non-geek kids were way misinformed. School didn't help, way boring. She needed material with bite, new stuff, deep and real, stuff that meant something. For entertainment, she wanted exceptional fiction. Her English-lit class was mostly crap. If it weren't for Kurt Vonnegut, she'd have gotten a D last year. *I'd lose it for sure if I didn't have good books*, Aggie thought as she gazed out the window yawning and wishing she had something interesting to read.

"Are we disturbing you, Ms. Piper?" Mr. Beal asked.

"Oh crap, class started?" She popped up in her seat like an eager cork.

"Ten minutes ago," Mr. Beal said with a hint of humor. "Care to join us?"

She liked Mr. Beal; he was smart and sort of cute. Beal was five six, trim for an old guy, curly brown hair like Frodo the Hobbit from J.R.R. Tolkien's books. If he wasn't like thirty, he'd be hot. *I wonder if he'd go for a bi girl?* It wasn't his fault he had to teach to the lowest denominator; that's how school worked. Be nice, she told herself.

"I'm sorry, just thinking, where were we?"

Mr. Beal's bushy eyebrows rose up. She broke custom by refraining from her usual wise-ass answer. Active attention and cooperation felt really weird. The class murmured in surprise.

"We were discussing the Roman Empire, and how Constantine's conversion to Christianity affected the development of Europe. Care to comment, Aggie?"

Mr. Beal took a step away from the blackboard. The class took a breath. Aggie glanced at his diploma on the wall behind him. He graduated from

Fordham University; Mr. Beal was hardcore Catholic. She had to be careful. She always avoided Constantine; it was Beal's open sore.

"It's obvious," Aggie started, "when the Empire collapsed in the fifth century, some say the sixth century, depending on whose scholarship you accept as constituting the actual collapse, the Emperors took advantage." She bit her lip. *Constantine followed standard practice.*

"Political manipulation of the Orthodox Churches was already the standard to consolidate power. Because government had consolidated the various churches' infrastructures, it made it easy for the strongest church faction to emerge after the collapse, and absorb the weaker factions, and take over the government's roll."

"Very good Agatha —."

She just couldn't help it and said, "Of course the power-hungry Church then went on to terrorize and plunder Europe, especially after the eighth century when the Roman Church truly consolidated its power under Charlemagne. They controlled everything well into the enlightenment period and —."

"That's enough, Aggie," Mr. Beal said raising his right hand. "Thank you."

Once she got rolling it was hard to stop, especially mid-stride. Thoughts flooded her mind.

"They even destroyed the Cathars, a Christian sect from the south of France…"

"Thank you, Ms. Piper!"

"But, Mr. Beal, I forgot to mention the Knights Templar." She was revved up, her mind whirling with historical facts. "But getting back to Constantine, He never actually became a Christian, that story about his conversion was State propaganda, a ploy to help —."

"That's enough, Aggie!" Mr. Beal said. His face flushed.

The class erupted with laughter and taunts. "Where'd you get that, that's not in the book, what a geek," and other insults.

"I can't believe you people buy this crap!" Aggie said to the jeering.

"You're out of line Ms. Piper," Beal almost screamed it.

"What? You think the Roman Catholic Church formed the day after Jesus croaked, give me a break. The idea of a Holy Church is ludicrous."

The entire class inhaled at once, followed by a few whistles. She and Beal had had this argument about Church history before and it always flustered Beal. She suddenly realized she'd gone over the cliff…again.

"Outside, now," Beal said pointing a thumb at the door.

"Oh, crap."

She jumped straight up and proudly walked to the door puffing out her small chest. *I know I'm right!*

Outside, Beal's nose flared. His brows furrowed in a peculiar way. His Hobbit face became an ogre's. She had never seen him so mad. Beal wasted no time.

"You're undermining my lesson! Why?"

"No, I'm not, Mr. Beal. Mrs. Preggey told me to participate in class, so I am." She was trying to control her temper, but the edge of her voice was still sharp. "I'm telling the truth."

"You are confusing my lesson," Beal said hotly. "We stick with the book, the text that's issued."

"But its way behind, it's full of errors!"

"It's the approved text."

Beal exhaled and let his shoulders drop a little. She smelled bad breath and bit her lip to keep the comment inside her head from spilling out. He walked back and forth until his jets cooled. After a few long minutes he moved in closer and lowered his voice.

"You must understand advanced scholarship doesn't apply to high school. I like you, Aggie, I really do but I can't have you disrupting my class."

Frodo is back.

"You can't go over my head, it's counterproductive. I don't disagree with your assessments, the book is behind the curve, but it is what we must work with..."

Yeah right, capitalist control propaganda.

"...Aggie, you have got to learn to play by the rules or you'll never get anywhere in life. Do you understand?"

Suddenly filled with shame, she looked down at the terrazzo floor and let her bangs fall over her eyes. She didn't mean to mess over one of the few teachers she really liked. He's just doing his job. Worse yet; *What if he sends me to the office, I'll be roasted alive.*

"I understand, Mr. Beal, I'm so sorry, really, I'll chill, can I please go back to class?"

"Look Aggie I know what Mrs. Preggey wants, and that's order. Refrain from disputing my lessons, and I'll consider it participating. Keep your comments short and relative, without sarcasm. Can you do that?"

"I'll try, Mr. Beal, thank you for giving me a chance."

She shuffled back to her seat. Mr. Beal went into his lesson as Aggie's gray-blue eyes clouded over. Before long, her head was down on her desk as usual.

Machinegun knocks on Beal's door caused her head to snap up, but not fast enough. The door swung open and Mrs. Preggey made a beeline to Aggie's desk. Preggey had to have been watching through the door's small window. Everyone's a spy.

"Crap."

"I see your class effort is less than ideal, Ms. Piper," the Principal said, her teeth clenched. "I'm losing patience with you. Better shape up and be quick about it. Got it?"

The Lord of Mordor didn't wait for an answer; she spun on her low, square Terminator heel and briskly walked out of the room. Mr. Beal shrank back as she passed.

"I'm so doomed."

Aggie ignored the hoots and jeers of her classmates. She pushed her hair over her eyes, sat straighter, and pretended to pay attention thinking maybe what she really needed was a T-rex detector rather than an outdated textbook.

FIVE

Karnack and Mr. Black

Karnack walked the long plasma-steel gantry way that ran bow to stern through the belly of his Ionian base-ship. First Mate, Moby, followed close behind. They wore green insulated jumpsuits. Each alien sported a wide, black control belt worn at the waist with a gold pyramid-shaped buckle that blinked with multicolored lights. Karnack's buckle was larger than Moby's.

Although Karnack was seven feet tall, he stepped lightly. His home planet, Ishtar, was a low gravity world. His wings and hollow bones would fly him back home, that is, if he were ever allowed to return.

Moby was also an oxygen-breathing humanoid but of the opposite sort; his home world was high gravity. He was five Earth feet tall, beer-barrel stocky, long, thick arms that hung ape-like to his knees, his neck wasn't discernible. He weighed five hundred pounds on Earth. His high biological density would make him into an unstoppable deep-sea anchor planet side should he ever try to swim.

Karnack called him Moby after his planet's name. It wasn't a proper name. Moby's real name was unpronounceable by way of Earth's languages. Karnack thought of him as a high-density leprechaun. Even in low Earth orbit, Moby's magnetic boots rang the gangway like a bell. It suddenly occurred to Karnack that he had been on Earth far too long, he was thinking in Earth English again. *I'll soon break that bad habit.*

"Karnack, look," Moby said in his deep voice, "We should get out of here. Our holds are full, we have copper, gold, enough Life Force to jump three galaxies. I lost count of how many Earth humans we milked. Every time we abduct another, our odds of getting caught increases. Earth's military knows about us… Staying is too chancy. The Galactic Trade Organization (GTO) is all over this system. We can't stay cloaked forever."

The giant craft shifted. The artificial intelligence, which was flying base-ship, was constantly dodging space junk and the gravity generator always lagged. The equipment was worn out. Karnack didn't care; he didn't lose balance or focus as the ship groaned.

Karnack addressed Moby without turning. "I want it all. The GTO must suffer."

Karnack's sweet voice was absorbed by the magnetically charged hull but Moby heard him well enough.

"A chain reaction: We'll wreck the planet." Moby said.

"And with it, the Galactic Trade Organization's lucrative new market," Karnack said.

"Look, we could get caught in the reaction. We'll be destroyed."

"I know what I'm doing," Karnack said, the sing-song sweetness of his voice faded into monotone.

"Look, the American military now has magnetic aircraft, you know."

"Earth MACs can't keep up with ours." Karnack flexed his wings, a sign of pride.

"I don't understand. Why go after the Trade Organization. It's been five thousand Earth years since they—."

"Since they stranded me, made me a pariah."

Karnack spun around, his wings trembling. His golden face whitened. Gold hair-like appendages on his head stood up like crown feathers. His electronically enhanced eyes clicked. Any sentient being would know better than to speak again. Moby couldn't hurt him. Karnack always wore a force skin. Karnack walked on in silence. They reached the shuttle. It was an old disk-shaped magnetic craft sixty feet in diameter; Karnack couldn't wait to get his hands on one of the new, roomy triangle MACs. *All in good time.*

They entered and the lights came on. Two androids seated at the controls with their heads down came to life. Karnack touched his belt buckle. The androids turned to face them. Their liquid-black eyes blinked; confirmation they were back online. The androids' three-fingered hands danced over touch-light controls. The ship's magnetic motor began to hum.

Karnack took his seat forward of the center of the circular craft. Moby's chair was just behind the shorter, slightly built grays on the perimeter. Flat translucent trays descended from the ceiling on a spindle-like articulated metal arm, one at each station and a dozen holographic screens shimmered on the air, the largest front and center. Moby examined his control display.

"Anti-gravity's go, magnetic is go, cloak running, clear to launch," Moby said.

"Probes," Karnack asked.

"Two on standby in the hold."

"Very good, launch," Karnack intoned musically, his voice sweet again.

The androids ran shuttle's controls. Human reflexes were too slow. On screen, base-ship's side bay door opened and the shuttle slid out. Once clear, the small ship shot off. The androids were programmed to avoid radar and human flight; thus, the shuttle's path was chaotic. Speed also varied as they zigzagged toward the target. With gravity shielding, there was no inertia effect. Despite aversion tactics, they arrive at Edwards Air Force Base within minutes. Karnack telepathically ordered the ship to hover just outside the Base's perimeter. They parked mid-air one hundred feet above a furrowed farm field near a tree line and well below radar.

"Pilot," Karnack said so Moby would hear the order, "Send an orb. Buzz the main base, do not collide with Earth humans, let them see you, go slow. On my mark, you will rush away and crash in that field," Karnack pointed at a holographic screen with his chin. "Understood?" Karnack's belt blinked confirmation received.

"This is crazy," Moby said. "We've played cat and mouse with Majestic sixty years and now you're giving them exactly what they want?"

"No," Karnack said. "They have MAC tech. A gift from the GTO, I'm sure. What we don't have is adequate information in order to conduct our final operation and how do we gain superior intelligence?"

"An MJ-12 operative," Moby said miserably.

"For one so dense you are not so thick," Karnack said with a bird-like cackle.

Karnack touched a light on his armrest and a control tray folded up and out of the chair's side. Karnack expertly handled the manual controls moving the shuttle toward the tree line as seen on the main view screen. The craft simmered in the sun blinking in and out of Earth humans' visual spectrum. A few moments passed before Karnack had his ship situated within the shade of the trees' canopy, adjusting hover mode Karnack reset to fifty feet above the ground. There were few leaves but it was enough. They would not be seen.

On screen, the orb appeared over the base. Karnack switched view to the main forward holographic and had it project in 3-D. The orb slowly descended toward a six-story glass facade building near a runway. It circled the building slowly paralleling the fourth floor's continuous windows. People poured outside. Other nearby buildings emptied as well.

The parking lots were filled with people pointing up. Karnack had it swoop low and stopped between two large buildings just ten feet off the ground. It glowed less making its flattened egg-shape hull distinguishable.

"Pilot give people time to use camera phones, then a few times around the airfield." Karnack said.

Moby bolted out of his chair and stood square-legged with hands on hips — a command challenge on his planet. Karnack smiled open-mouthed showing perfect white teeth — on Ishtar it indicated annoyance.

"If pictures get back to the GTO, they'll see it's us!" Moby cried.

"Think me stupid?" Karnack said. "I had base-ship hack every phone within twenty miles of here; they'll get nothing. Shut up and stand down."

Moby slid back into his seat putting his elbows on his armrests in protest. Big hands covered his broad, square, chin. Moby didn't sulk long.

Only a few seconds passed before the monitor showed a black unmarked helicopter move in and start chasing the probe. They flew around the airfield in a game of hawk and sparrow. Air traffic was being cleared and missiles would soon fly.

"It's Navy Intelligence," Moby said checking one of his displays. "MAC killers are on board."

Karnack thought a command and the probe moved between the helicopter and a group of people on the ground. It couldn't fire its rockets. Karnack relished the human pilot's frustration as was indicated on the human emotional response detector. The pilot had no fear but the ground people radiated with it.

"Oh, how amusing," Karnack said with a bird-cackle. "However, let us proceed to business."

Karnack touched his belt and the orb shot away toward their position. It bounced once off the top of a concrete barrier, tore through a high chain-link fence, and flew a low arch one mile before crashing into a field exactly where Karnack wanted it. It rested a hundred yards from their position.

"Perfect, self-destruct is still operational."

"Waste of a good probe," Moby said. "When my contract's up — ."

"Shut up Moby."

He had heard Moby's complaints before. His chin jutted forward and back several times like a pleased cockatoo's beak. He intended to suck every bit of Life Force off this planet. He would be rich beyond empires; he'd buy an entire fleet of the best probes available. Thus, Karnack was without worry as he ordered the probe to explode once he reached a safe altitude, of course.

"Farewell faithful servant," Karnack said in a low sing-song of mock empathy. "I do believe that helicopter is coming this way. We needn't wait long for our prize."

"Two more coming in, it's Majestic," Moby said, "Mr. Black, himself."

"Excellent," Karnack sung. "Should one go fishing, by all means, catch the biggest fish."

The single-android MAC had plowed perpendicular across a newly turned field; the little ship was cracked wide open. A ruined android hung limply half out of the opening with eyes dulled. It was staring at the invisible shuttle.

Karnack cackled laughter. Moby lowered his eyes; Karnack well knew how Moby, as primary android controller, never found dead androids amusing. That too, for Karnack, was quite humorous. Such love for a machine was ridiculous, even more so than love itself. *And to think I once loved Earth humans.*

*****

Two silent Cobra Specials, lacking registration numbers, landed to the right and left of the ruined Earth where the gouge began. *Nothing will grow there for years.* Mr. Black, a tall strong-built man in black suit, fedora and sunglasses got out. He ordered the others to stay inside with a hand signal. He slowly walked the gouge with his head swinging left and right. He stopped when he came upon the MAC. Nothing moved. *Good.* More helos zoomed in — local military. Mr. Black didn't need to see; he knew that sound.

He spoke, tilting toward his breast pocket. "Keep the regulars back."

He did not react to the dead gray; he had seen such things before. He bent closer and looked over the wreckage. He wiped mud off the craft's silvery side with his handkerchief. No markings.

This bothered Colonel Archer. *Privateer? Karnack's supposed to be gone; what the hell's going on here.* He pulled the radio out of his jacket's pocket as two regular Cobra helicopters touched down behind his boys. *It's going to be one of them days.* The Army flew in against orders.

"Get those regulars out of here, fast. Is this channel secure?"

"Yes sir."

"It's not ours. No GTO markings, either."

"What do you want us to do Colonel?" The radio said.

"Deploy teams. Set up road blocks, have the Army do that. See if any civilians saw it and get a recovery team down here ASAP. Gather up everyone that saw anything…don't call me Colonel, it's Mr."

"Yes Sir! What about the witnesses on base?"

Black considered that problem for a moment. The witnesses worked flight line. They had security clearances. Standard procedures applied.

"They took the oath, set up a debriefing and remind them of their confidentiality agreements. Make them understand talkers get a free ride to Gitmo."

"Roger that," the radio said.

As the Army birds flew out, ten of his body-armored men jumped out of Black's personnel HE-3 gunship and spread out. They wore black military uniforms without markings and were fitted with top secret rifles; infrared sights, laser scopes, daylight vision enhancement, computer Smart-aim and explosive rounds.

The men aimed their weapons in every direction seeking survivors, or witnesses.

Another of Black's choppers came in, didn't touch ground, dumped five men and jetted back to base for damage control. His ride rose slowly and started a circular search pattern. Black's second-in-command would watch the regulars work the road. He didn't need to micro-manage, his team knew the drill.

He crouched down near the alien and put his hand under the dead thing's chin lifting a limp, waxy head; the gray's eyes were fish bowls of cloudy black ink. Green, oily blood dripped from its small, lipless mouth. Active green foam bubbled out of every rent in its body.

"Dead androids can't upload," Black said. "You're about as useful as tits on a bull."

Black let go; its pseudo-organic head thudded against the ship's hull like a sack of hamburger meat. Majestic Twelve wasn't going to learn anything new today.

Why would anyone pull a stunt like this? Who crashed this probe? It sure as hell wasn't a U.S. mission: Too sloppy. It had to either be a moon student or the U.N. playing games. Someone at the U.N. was trying to force disclosure and the new president was seriously bucking for level twelve clearance info, too.

Black had this uneasy feeling. This kind of vintage MAC was too familiar. *Haven't seen one in field since Cryersville.* He was just a soldier then and didn't know what he had seen, but now, he knew all too well.

"Couldn't be?"

A soldier came running up, looking past Black, the private turned a little green.

"New to this? You'll get used to it, kid. What is it?" Black asked.

"Red Team spotted two farmers who may have seen the crash, Sir!" the soldier said.

"Easy kid."

"There's a house over there." The soldier pointed.

To Black's left was a rise leading up to a tree line. As he recalled, on the other side of the line, the ground dipped. A farmhouse was located on the far side of that field; maybe a mile. No one could see the crash site from there. *Good, we got lucky.* An access road, not likely used after harvest, was further on. Only the tree line had a direct view. Farmers didn't work this time of year. But it was goose hunting season. Hunters could be sitting on that tree line.

"Tell Red Team to hold the farmers. I doubt anyone saw, but if they did, mind-wipe them. Secure the perimeter, no one in or out. Block the farm roads. I'll check that ridge."

Black turned from the crash and walked up slope toward the tree line ignoring the mud accumulating on his Italian-made patent leather shoes.

He stopped on the far side of the trees and surveyed the expanse. Red Team's chopper was grounding at the farmhouse. No farm equipment or four-wheelers in the field. *It's never this easy.*

Black's thin suit jacket did not protect him from the wind, rather it was designed to repel radiation and was no help in this weather. He ignored the cold, but it wasn't the weather that caused a sudden shiver to race up his spine. *I'm being watched.* He looked up. There was a hole in the sky and inside it was an angel-like face looking down at him.

"Son of a bitch."

*****

Karnack watched Mr. Black from the hatch with amusement, his wings vibrated so much a feather dislodged and fluttered down to the dark soil below. The shuttle's sensor array picked up every word, even secured radio. When Black looked up, Karnack touched his belt. He then got up, backed away, and took his seat. Moby joined him peering at Black on the monitor. Black was immobilized.

"Open the hatch wider." Karnack said. The floor became an eight-foot diameter hole. "I like this Mr. Black. He will be useful."

"Look, Karnack, you've done it this time."

"Oh quiet, don't ruin my fun."

Karnack touched his belt and a bright white-blue tractor beam shot from the outside perimeter of the hatch. The light surrounded Mr. Black and lifted him; he hung immobilized three feet above the ground while Karnack took a moment to gloat. Moby's teeth started chattering.

"I suppose, I should bring him up before they start shooting," Karnack said calmly. "Oh, but what fun!"

Moby rushed to his control tray and manually operated the anti-gravity tractor beam. Androids were not permitted to tractor-beam live cargo. They tended to work too fast and cause damage.

Karnack turned to the monitor array. The nearest group of Black's special-ops soldiers stood motionless a hundred yards off with mouths agape as Mr. Black slowly ascended. To the men on the ground, when their commander entered the ship, he simply disappeared.

"So much for Special Forces," Karnack said, "Pilot, remove us from here, best evasive course."

The shuttle de-cloaked for maximum power and shot straight up. The new kid on Black's team dropped his custom-built gun in the mud.

SIX

Confrontation Tuesday noon

Aggie made it to lunch without running into Billy but, the day wasn't over yet. She spotted Mel and Jimmy at their usual place in the back of the cafeteria and as far from the jocks' table as humanly possible. Aggie slid into her spot without a food tray. She was low income and ate for free, but grilled cheese and rice pudding was the last thing on her mind. Besides the cheese wasn't really cheese and the rice was genetically modified. It tasted like dishonesty.

"Bitch, you're too damn skinny, go get you some food," Jimmy said, flipping his long, braided hair aside.

"Stomach's too twitchy," Aggie said.

"You don't want a free sandwich? Oh no, no, no, you didn't." Jimmy said mimicking wide-eyed surprise. "I'd take it home for Moms."

"Why, so she can beat you for forgetting the pudding?" Mel said.

Aggie pushed her bangs into her face. For once in her life she couldn't think of a comeback. She internally kicked herself; should have gotten that sandwich for Jimmy. He didn't get fed at home. *No wonder he's a size one.*

Thoughts of Billy Barns had her distracted. The Winter Dance was Friday and going was asking for it. Yet she had to go. Everyone was going. Not going was like saying, 'Hey everybody I'm a bigger dork than you thought'. She reached under her sundress and touched the phone stashed in her cut-off denim shorts. The bug was secure in her change pocket.

"Girl, this is no place to feel yourself up." Jimmy said.

"Best place," Mel quipped, "They fear what lurks within a nerd's panties. Miss Kung Fu might be growing a dick."

"She ain't got no anaconda up in there," Jimmy said. "That's my department."

Aggie just sat there. It was her turn. And, she normally would have trashed both of them on cue. Jim and Mel held their breath a long second. Aggie held her tongue.

"You didn't plant the tracker, did you?" Jimmy said.

"She needs to grow balls first."

Aggie shot Mel the look. "What, everyone knows?"

"I told him. Come on, Dude, you got to do this and you need help." Mel said.

"You guys can't," Aggie said. "Especially you Jim-Jim, you can't afford to get into trouble."

"Like you can?" Jimmy said.

"That's the point dumb-ass, "Mel said, "This will save us all," Mel did her Mrs. Preggey impression, "One for all and all for one and all that rot, pip-pip, what, what?"

"When, how?" Aggie moaned. She slouched deeper into her seat.

"Now," Jimmy said. "Back door, I'll go with you."

"My problem, you two stay here, I'm going."

She slid off the bench seat and remained crouched at table level. Mel had disarmed the cafeteria's fire alarms long ago. Aggie quietly opened the fire door directly behind them and slipped into the hall. The parking lot exit wasn't far. She prayed to the Goddess that no one was watching the security cameras.

Once outside she ran to the scooter parking area but pulled up short halfway there. Billy and his bandits were holding court around Bill's scooter. They weren't supposed to be outside either.

If I get caught, they get caught too. Fine by her, she preferred a frontal assault anyway. She pulled the bug out of her pocket, closed her fist around it and got between Billy and his fancy Aprilia scooter. It cost more than a good used American car.

"Hey dick brain, you pushed my scooter over yesterday."

"Fell over by itself ass-wipe."

She checked. The closest rotating security camera wasn't on them. She pushed Billy with two closed fists. *That had to hurt.* She knew what was coming next and she uncharacteristically let it happen. Billy pushed back. Aggie faked losing balance, stumbled backwards, and fell on his bike knocking Billy's scooter over. She went down with it and slapped the bug under its rear fender. Billy's bandits swooped in to upright the bike. Aggie rolled away and bounced up.

"Lucky, you caught me off guard. We're even. I'm out of here."

"You did it on purpose," Billy said behind her. "I'll fix you. No cameras at the Dance. I'll flatten you."

"Better bring an army." Aggie said over her shoulder. She took off for the building with her flip-flops beating time like a rapper on crack.

One of the security guys stopped her in the hall. She lied and said she left her lunch money in her locker—he couldn't know she was a free lunch kid but she felt like crap for lying anyway. He led her back to the lunchroom ten minutes before the bell rang. She grabbed a sandwich for Jimmy on the way to her seat.

Aggie got away with it, but she felt crappy. It was like what Dad says, 'Don't pig tussle, you'll get dirty and the pig likes it.' Dirty tricks just weren't her style. She looked forward to taking a shower after gym.

SEVEN

Alien bullys

Karnack had Mr. Black of Majestic Twelve suspended in an extraction chamber, the same type he used to relieve his victims of Soul Energy. This force-field was projected aft and starboard of his command chair away from the main hatch. He had once accidentally dropped a body on top of a skyscraper. The tabloids had a field day with it. It still made him laugh. Such was an inconvenient jail, however. Immobilized prisoners could see and hear. If one escaped unprocessed it could be a problem. He always applied mind-wipe if they survived extraction. None of that mattered now.

Earth was catching on as his archaic equipment became dysfunctional. Many publications wrote of his handiwork. Alien abductions were constantly in print because of mechanical inadequacies, especially the faltering mind–wipe device. Getting caught, and the equipment, was Moby's worry and not his, not now. Moby's fears and complaints would soon be moot; they were about to become very rich, and no one would be left to accuse them of the crime. *No witnesses, no conviction.* Then he would return home a free Ishtarian.

Karnack moved the shuttle to the center of Lake Erie and well away from shipping lanes. They hovered a hundred yards above the water yet under radar. Cloaking used a lot of LF. Karnack wouldn't waste Life-Force energy, why tap his commodities horde unnecessarily? He had the ship de-cloaked.

"Moby, check Mr. Black's condition."

Long-term total immobilization could damage a person and he needed Black alive, although a man such as Mr. Black was best kept immobilized. Black was a statue under glass with darting eyes. The Earthman was no doubt taking it all in.

Moby was standing at the enclosure focused on his control belt when Black tapped on the shield. Moby jumped back, startled.

"Look, he's got a limiter, he's moving, how the heck, where'd he get it?"

Karnack sprang lightly from his seat and faced the prisoner. Black pressed his hand on the shield and spoke but his voice was muffled. Karnack took note of the wristwatch. The man was fully functional and only trapped for the moment. Karnack wasn't at all frightened. He chuckled like a pigeon cooing.

"I see Earth's elites are in league with Moon Base." Karnack said as he circled the shield with his hands behind his back and under his wings. The man turned and likewise studied Karnack. "We'll get what we need from him. Our time to strike is now."

"Let him go," Moby said in a voice like grinding train wheels showing his alarm. "He'll get out, power's climbing; beam him out. He'll short the field in two minutes. We can't use him; scanners say the brain-bender won't work. He's shielded. Let'm drown."

"Moby, Moby, Moby, such a worrying fool. I must know more. It's time for drastic measures. Start the generator. I will bleed his soul. All of it."

"Look, I didn't sign on for this. Bad enough soul-sucking without their permission, that alone gets us a thousand cycles in lock-up. What if I kill him? This guy proves it—the Galactic Trade Organization made terms with Earth. They're involved. Let's take the booty and run while we can."

"Start the LF generator," Karnack said with clenched teeth and clicking eyes.

"I won't do it. He's human. We're all human. I don't care if he's a primitive."

"I'll override your belt," Karnack threatened.

"Look, you can't run this fleet with one control belt. You can't override without my permission, not while I'm alive. I won't kill this man's soul."

"Perhaps you are right," Karnack said thoughtfully. "It takes two to run an operation such as ours. I can't make do without a living partner."

He put a long, thin arm around Moby's shoulder and walked him toward ship's center. Karnack touched his belt and the hatch suddenly retracted. Moby teetered on the edge with nothing below except a deep lake.

Karnack grabbed for Moby hooking his talon finger under Moby's belt and pushed with his other hand in quick succession. Moby toppled but his belt remained in Karnack's hand—its' leather strap cut though.

Karnack said, "Beam on," as the First Mate cleared the hull. Moby fell a hundred feet in a split second before becoming suspended. On the world where Moby was born nothing was more fearful than water. High-density people can't float. Moby would die in seconds under water.

Karnack turned to Mr. Black.

"Shall we allow him a few minutes rest?" He said caressing the cracked force bubble with an extended talon. He retracted the claw. "I am now the master of all facilities."

He walked around the force shield another lap before facing Mr. Black whom had stripped a piece of shield away like a translucent banana peel. The man reached outside with one arm attempting to grab the alien. The shield was near collapse. Karnack, quick as a raptor, deposited a silver control bracelet on Mr. Black's wrist. It morphed to fit tightly. Black froze.

"This device, Mr. Black, is designed to control biological robots. You know the type, the little gray beings you previously stole from me. You have them on ice at Groom Lake. Dead, I'm sure."

Karnack bent lower to look Black in the eyes. The usual fear he found in Earth's people was not evident. Karnack resumed pacing.

"Android controllers aren't healthy for sentient beings. It is not one hundred percent effective, unfortunately, on humans. Oh, you could resist commands, it takes a strong mind, but you'll find it pleasurable to cooperate. Resisting will eat your Life Force faster, that's how we power it you know…So, then, if you obey, you live longer. If you fight control, you die fast. Try it."

The force shield fell away. Black reached for his pistol but he could not move quickly, the more he tried the more pain was evident on his contouring face and the slower were his movements. He shook all over with the effort. Black stopped. Like all persons under a bracelet, he knew he'd die by resisting it.

"What do you say, Mr. Black: join my crew?"

"I'll help you," Black said, his face was red, the muscles along his jaw pulsating.

"Welcome to my crew Mr. Black. If I recall correctly, I believe you Earth-lings call this…what's the expression…a Shanghai."

Karnack had the ship pull Moby back on board. He did not give Moby back his facilities belt but rather Karnack gave Moby a subservient secondary belt of his own. Moby could still control robots but Karnack had override powers. He dropped Moby's personalized belt into the lake. The Captain wasn't about to let anyone interferer with his plans, not even a longtime First Mate still under contract.

Moby, simply put, had a conscience and such a primitive state of mind was simply intolerable.

EIGHT
Home Tuesday afternoon

Aggie parked her scooter at Mark's Marina, where she worked. Mark's place was two hundred yards down her sandy, overhung driveway and just across Geiger Avenue. Parking at Mark's gave her time to fix her hair, which was a mess, as usual. She hated motorcycle helmets and ponytails or anything that screamed geek. Riding the Vespa was a hair-disaster. Mom or Skyflower as she insisted everyone call her, forever hassled Aggie about doing dreadlocks. Ok, it made sense, but the last thing Aggie wanted was to look just like her mom. She liked her hair straight. *Maybe I'll chop it when I get to college. That'll piss-off Sky.*

Aggie felt like if she had to hear one more dumb-ass lecture about natural hair…a lecture which always started Sky preaching about the Earth Goddess and pot…her head would vaporize. It sucked being an Earth Priestess's daughter.

All she wanted to do was go online, but that required going through the front door. Aggie brushed out her hair with her fingers while walking down the lane. The Pipers lived, squatted really, in Grandpa Branford's old marina, which he abandoned long before Aggie was born. They were squatters.

Aggie arrived and checked everything out. Sky wasn't outside picking stuff for dinner in the garden. The only sound was the wind generator Dad had salvaged from a shipwreck. Even the stupid wild chickens that Sky and Po-boy, Dad's nickname, refused to eat were quiet. *All we eat is veggies and fish, veggies and fish; I'd kill for a bucket of fried chicken.*

Maybe she would get lucky, maybe Sky was out in the mangroves tending her hanging pot plants, or maybe Sky was beach combing for her dumb found-object art projects.

After Mel's place Aggie could barely look at her crappy home. The house, if you could call it that, was the old marina office; just a gray wooden saltbox structure with tall old fashion sash windows and a rusted tin roof. At least they had a porch. In south Florida, shade was everything.

Po-boy had converted the tackle store area into the living room. The original ugly green tiled bathroom was untouched. Mom and Dad's bedroom, the former tackle repair shop, was behind the living room aside a galley kitchen.

The common space was "L" shaped. *Mel's pool-house is bigger.* No place to hide. No wonder the kids rip on her; living in a bait shack was embarrassing.

Her bedroom was OK just off the kitchen. Po-boy took a sea container and attached it to the house. He fixed it up pretty nice; wood floor and walls made from refinished pallets and he had cut off the metal top and put on a high, steep roof made of wood. She had massive screens on each roof end with a whirly roof thing for air circulation.

The only problem was the windows between metal ribs were too small to crawl through. Not that it mattered. She didn't need to sneak out like other kids; her folks wouldn't mind her drinking or sexing. She wanted to sneak into her bedroom not out of it.

Sky and Po-boy didn't believe in The Man's rules. Aggie had her own rules, rules The Man would like. Number One: No dating boys or girls, and no pot or booze until college. Dating girls, she wasn't sure about.

She swung the crooked screen door open. Sky was home. *Oh crap!* Sky sat in the lotus position on the floor, she was meditating naked again. Aggie blew air with an upturned lower lip; her bangs were too tangled to move off her forehead.

"Agatha just look at your hair. Why won't you let it go natural?"

"Because, Mom, I want to go to college. Hello! You know, make a good impression at the entrance interview…if I ever get there." She couldn't keep the exasperation out of her voice.

"If the Universe wants you in college, it will happen," Sky said. "Trust in your Karma, Mother Earth loves you. She will provide."

"Yeah right. If Gaia loves me so much, why doesn't she bend over, crack a smile and suck up Billy Barns?"

"That's the type of thought that pollutes Karma. Please, put aside negative vibrations, free your soul."

"Bunch of crap. Vibrations can't pay tuition. *If I don't get this scholarship, I'm toast.* You're too broke to help."

Aggie flopped down on the tattered loveseat near the front door and crossed her arms over her chest. The sofa smelled like burnt rope. Sky's bong was on the orange-crate end table. She wanted to kick it across the room. *I hate pot smell.*

Sky stood, dropped a tie-dyed sundress over her head and took the beat-up recliner opposite Aggie. Aggie stewed. Sky waited.

I deserved college, good grades, no drugs, no boys, no parties. I'm focused. I already have the grades to graduate. That'll impress admissions.

But now she was on the edge of blowing it. *Why can't he just leave me alone? Because my parents are social drop-outs living off-the-grid and out of touch.* The thought stung. It wasn't totally true. People hated anyone different. Her parents were weird, OK, but they didn't hate, not even The Man, not really. They also helped a lot of people, especially homeless people.

"I'm never going to get to college, am I?"

"Your father and I went to college and where did that get us? Nowhere. We opted to do what we truly desire. Follow your bliss. College may not be right for you either. Agatha, college isn't that important."

Aggie jumped out of her seat. "It wasn't for you, but it is to me. Grandpa paid for yours. You graduated law school! OK, Dad injured-out of his basketball scholarship, but at least you guys went!"

"I understand." Sky said, "But, you don't need a degree in order to help better the world. The Universe provides opportunities for good. Just yesterday I helped a homeless man avoid arrest and — ."

"Mom, I want an important job. A job that requires education, get it? If I blow this scholarship, I'll ask Grandpa. He's rich, he'll cover it."

"Don't you dare!"

Sky never raised her Zen-like voice. Aggie's back stiffened with tension even as curiosity filled her. The elephant in the room just stampeded.

"Don't sacrifice your karma," Sky cried.

"What's so bad about Grandpa?" Aggie asked quietly, still shocked. "Haven't seen him since I was little? You must hate him."

"No, I don't." Sky's tone became somber. "It's time you know more. He isn't just an industrialist polluter working for The Man. He is The Man. Agatha; Branford Industries is a primarily defense contractor. They do secret covert government work. They deal in death. He became wealthy killing people. He's heartless."

"Oh crap, really?" Aggie felt like she got punched in the stomach. She kind of knew that, and in the back of her mind she thought it was kind of cool. Some-one had to make warriors' stuff, but she never thought about what his inventions actually did or considered the wider ramifications.

"That's why I turned my back on him. He demanded I work for him. Once I found out what he really did, I couldn't accept it. He's a government murderer."

Aggie slumped back into the loveseat. "But he does good work too, right? Sometimes war is necessary. Look at history, and..." The set on Mom's face stopped Aggie cold.

"His money is blood money," Sky said with wet, green eyes, "My love child, accepting blood money is very bad karma. I won't have it. It will ruin you. His money isn't free; he'll demand reciprocity."

Aggie didn't buy Sky's weirdo spiritual ideas, not completely, but she sure didn't want to get involved with the defense business. She wasn't sure what she wanted to do but it had to be something for the greater good, something that mattered. She just couldn't work for a weapons manufacturer. She hated guns but didn't mind an honest fight. Aggie squirmed internally. Sky was right. The cost of his money was too high.

"Ok, Mom, I get that, really."

A fishy smell appeared on the air. Po-boy was back from his charter run. She didn't want him to see Sky so upset. Aggie quickly changed the channel.

"Mom, how'd you do at Sam's Thrift Shop? Find anything cool for me to wear at the Winter Dance?"

Sky immediately brightened. She dabbed the corners of her eyes with the hem of her sundress. Skyflower delighted in lost objects. Dad said recycling was her middle name. She found really cool stuff, even in people's trash cans. Mom had the artist's eye. The clothes she made, or found in junk shops, rocked. Funky was way cool.

"Have I got something for you. Thank the Goddess." Sky said.

Sky sprung lightly from her chair like a kid on sugar drops. *That yoga stuff pays off, I guess.* Sky headed into her bedroom just in time. Dad was washing up outside in the old porcelain sink along the side porch. He'd be inside any second.

"Thank the Goddess," Aggie repeated.

Sky, in the bedroom, was cheerfully singing a Grateful Dead song. *Better get on line and check Mel.* Aggie was dying to know if the Billy finder worked. She booted up just as Dad came in. He still smelled like sardines.

"Scoot on out of there," "Po-boy said in a thick Louisiana accent. "I expect I've got some files waiting. I've been dancing on fish hooks all day." He put a scratchy, rough hand on Aggie's shoulder.

"Dad, I'm doing stuff for college."

"Sorry Honey Pie, this here's important. The National UFO Reporter called me this morning. I'm officially a UFO investigator. They're sending me stuff on the internets. I got this here report to make. They'll want me to write up everything I've seen."

Aggie hated Po-boy's obsession. All he ever read were stupid conspiracy books, mostly about aliens and now he wanted the computer, too? This was her domain.

"Daaaaad! Give me a break!"

Sky came out of the bedroom with clothes wrapped in white tissue paper and said, "Po-boy that's wonderful. They finally accepted your help. I'm so proud of you!"

"What about me?" Aggie said, "I got school stuff to do." She wasn't budging from the computer desk.

"The National UFO Reporter," Po-boy said pushing out his skinny chest, "they need me Honey. Now, get on up, I got Nu-for work to do."

"He's right this is important," Sky said. "Come on, Agatha I'll show you…"

"Important!" Aggie sprang up. "I'm working on college; you know college, real stuff. UFOs are a bunch of crap!"

"Well that's not true, Agatha, according to Shaman Edgily they are multi-dimensional spirits…"

"I don't think so Honey Bee," Po-boy interrupted. "They may shape-shift but I think…"

"ARRRGGGHH! That's it I'm out of here." Aggie twisted around in her office chair stood and knocked it over, blowing past Po-boy. She stomped to the screen door with a final, "ARRRGGGHH," went outside and slammed the screen shut.

She had heard it all before. She was sick of Mom and Dad discussing spirits and aliens and Earth changes and sociopath politicians and reptilians and the police state and the secret government and all kinds of crazy crap. The only thing they never discussed was reality, her reality, like how was she going to get to college. Aggie pulled Mel's phone out of her pocket. She had the answer right in her hand but she was too pissed off to figure it out. She needed to blow off steam first.

NINE

Aggie hits the bag

Aggie, still steaming, walked to Mark's thinking the last thing she needed was more adult advice, although, she liked him a lot she was in no mood for another lecture, not even from Mark.

Mark Levine, owner of Mark's Marina was the Pipers' nearest neighbor on Geiger Key and a trusted family friend despite his background. The friendship between Mark and her folks was kind of weird. He was a retired Navy Seal and well loved by her peace-nick hippie parents. Who would have thought? No way would it work if Mark acted hard-core military. She saw how Mark won them over. He was free-giving and full of love.

First off, Mark let Po-boy dock his boat for free and slips were outrageously expensive in the Keys. Mark had an old messed up Vietnam war Navy riverboat that he made into a fishing vessel. He sold it to Po-boy for next to nothing; more strangeness. That twenty-eight-foot Uniflight drafted shallow and its jet drives ran her fast. It was perfect for tarpon fishing, Dad's specialty.

She couldn't fault Mark, he taught her his special brand of karate, and gave her a part-time job. She worked the counter, or ran the grill, or washed dishes or painted rental boats and did whatever odd jobs he had around the marina. Once in a while he'd even tell a war story.

Right now, Mark's place was just the place to get away. Late afternoon, things were slow because Mark wasn't about money. He let young Navy dudes hang out for free. His place was popular with Navy guys. They were always hanging around, drinking discounted beer, and hitting on her. *They're so annoying.*

Squids sometimes rented boats or booked charters, but mostly they just hung out and bugged her. Thank the Goddess the place was empty now or she'd clock the first one that's opened his mouth.

She made a beeline to Mark's unofficial dojo. It was nothing more than a 20X20 tin-clad boat shed with a heavy bag hanging from a ceiling beam, a couple of speed bags and old wrestling mats spread over a sandy floor. It smelled like dead fish packed in gym socks. OK, sometimes what she liked best about Mark's dojo was beating the hell out of smart-assed Navy guys, but right now she was in no mood to spar.

She split open the old wooden doors. No one was there. It was closed all day and hot as hell and just perfect for cooling her temper.

She skipped the padded gloves and foot gear. Still in her sundress, she smashed into the rough canvas bag with a right jab, a spinning hammer fist, and a left leg front kick all in a flurry. She kicked it so hard the bag jumped straight up. Then she went to work. The bag folded on every punch. Dust rained down from the rafters and coated her with black powder. Her yellow sundress turned midnight gray. She didn't care.

When her knuckles began to bleed a lot, she changed stance and planted solid roundhouse kicks with her left leg, one after another. She was right-handed but favored southpaw. She considered her left leg her best weapon. Her sweat-soaked sundress turned into a mud compress.

"Ags, you got to use that right leg, you know it, come on."

She spun around in a defensive position. With a puff she blew at her wet bangs but the hair didn't move. Aggie raked the plastered stands off her face. Mark was short but his well-developed body and big brown afro-hair filled the doorway.

"I know," she said taking a few breaths, as Mark stepped in. "But...that scar...it still hurts."

"It's in your head, Ags, not your foot. If you don't work through it, you'll never master it. Face your fear."

"Oh Yes Obi Wan, should I embrace the Force while I'm at it?"

"Funny. We'll talk more when you're in learning mode. What brings you here? You're not scheduled."

"I'm almost kicked out of school; my scholarship is practically history." She punched the bag leaving a smear of blood, she didn't feel it. "My stupid folks aren't helping at all."

"Ags, I agreed to teach you the arts to improve your self-control. Your parents would never have let you work out with me otherwise. Haven't you learned anything? What did you do this time; sock another bully?"

"It's nothing like that," she said glumly. "I kept my cool; it was Jimmy. Billy was about to trash him. I took the heat. Jimmy's got enough trouble."

"I see," Mark said. "At some point, Jimmy must learn to take care of himself."

She burst into tears and plopped down on the dusty mat cross legged. She hung her head but the wet hair remained plastered on her face. She wanted to crawl into a coconut crab hole and die. One more screw-up and her life was over. *But I can't let my friends down.* Mark stood near and waited. She forced herself to stop crying.

"What am I going to do?"

Mark squatted down on his hunches facing her, reached out and put a finger under her chin and lifted her head.

"Go to college, that's what. You want it, don't you?"

"Yeah, but how? My folks can't afford it, where am I going to get the money?"

"You'll find a way," Mark said, "and I'll help you. The only way you can fail is if you decide to fail."

"That's Kung Fu Yoda crap, that's not a real answer. You sound like Mom." Aggie imitated Sky's Zen-voice and said. "'Let the Universe show you the way,' that's a pile of crap."

"Come on Ags. If you want it, you'll figure it out; use your head. Stop emotionalizing. You'll find an answer. Trust yourself. College is closer than you think."

Mark had that all knowing look in his eyes. And, he was right. Getting twisted up inside never helped anyone. He wasn't into mystic mumbo-jumbo like Mom and Dad, either. The guy survived horrible things and still had his head together. Mark had citations all over the office walls, Medal of Honor, Bravery under Fire and more. He was no cornball. *So, what's wrong with me?* All she'd ever done was what's right. She felt like her life was a crap magnet.

"So, what do I do?"

"Apply logic and fortitude," Mark said, "Think it out and don't give up."

She sat up straighter and pushed the tangles back and applied the relaxation technique Mark taught. She pushed her emotions out of her mind with concentrated breathing. Possibilities flowed into her as the negativity left. After fifteen minutes a logical move popped into existence. *Maybe Grandpa can give money without conditions, it couldn't hurt to ask.*

"Grandpa," Aggie said. "My folks won't talk to him, but what's stopping me? They won't give me his phone; I bet Mel can find it. Mel's dad builds government junk, Grandpa's in the same business. They must be connected. Gramps might even sponsor a scholarship. There're all kinds of scholarships out there. My SAT scores rock."

"Branford Industries," Mark said. "Good idea. But forget normal communications, the only way to get to the Old Man is the direct approach."

"You know about him?"

"In a way, everyone in special-ops brushes up against him one way or another. Scuttlebutt says the Old Man is anchored off Fort Jefferson right now. He's doing research out there, overseeing it personally. Take one of my boats and go. It's not far."

Aggie's heart sank. She was a good swimmer, an asset to Key West High's swim team, before they kicked her off the team for insubordination, but she swam in a nice, safe pool. She hated natural waters. She had been terrified of it ever since that time while fishing with Po-boy and Sky. She shivered.

"I can't, I just can't."

"It's that stingray scar. You avoid water like an acid bath. What happened?"

The reminder caused Aggie to shiver all over. She felt like a clam on ice and just as tight-lipped. All she could do was squeak out one word, "Sharks."

"Most sharks are harmless; your fear is unfounded. Odds of an attack are very low."

She knew that, of course, but her fear was stronger than that reality. She was a total water bug back then, a sailing champ at age seven. But she had not been in a boat or otherwise on the water since it happened. Shallow or deep, the sea scared her senseless.

"If it's all the same to you," She said, "Think I'll try calling first."

"He won't be easy to reach; direct is your best approach. If you can't get through, let me know. My offer stands. Don't wait too long; he'll be shipping out soon."

"Thanks," she said, "I'll think about it. I better get home I need a shower, later, K."

Aggie took off for home. Another hippie kid might have got naked and dove into the lagoon to wash off. Walking through the marina clothed in dirt and sweat was way more embarrassing. If only the squids saw her now, then, maybe they'd leave her alone. *No such luck.*

She hated herself for being so chicken-shit. Face any three bullies, no problem, nude beach, no problem, diving off the high board, easy. Sail out to Fort Jefferson, no way. So much for fortitude she thought, as she walked her driveway in misery. There had to be another way.

Another idea popped into her head. She stopped halfway down the lane, hiked up her dress and put a hand in her short's pocket. She still had the phone. She flipped it open and pressed the Mel key. It was time for Billy tracker 2-0. Double the odds in my favor.

That scholarship wasn't history yet.

TEN

Bugging Billy Wednesday morning

One day at a time was the goal, but; *I need two more days Billy free*, Aggie thought as she rode her Vespa down a side street south of school. Mr. Osborn, the head of the Scholarship Committee and the school's guidance counselor, always chaperoned the Winter Dance. It was her best chance to talk with him privately and convince him she deserved that scholarship. She had to see him unofficially. His office was wired, Mel discovered he recorded everything and shared it with the Terminator. Aggie couldn't let the principal see how desperate she was.

She found a good spot, pulled over and shut the motor down. She didn't dare park anywhere near the crowd. She checked the phone. The Billy-tracker found his scooter in student parking. She started the Sat-link. An orbital camera zoomed in on the parking lot. There was no sign of him. She put the cell away and sat on her scooter for a long minute biting her lip. Jimmy was enthusiastic about the plan, Mel less so.

"Could be anywhere; my idea better work."

Aggie was dressed for action. She pulled all her stops and scrapped her usual clothes. Commandos don't wear sundresses and flip-flops. Denim shorts, oversized white t-shirt, and skateboard sneakers, was her uniform. She needed easy access to pockets. Grabbing the bug from under a dress was too complicated. The sneakers were for sneaking, and running like hell.

She still didn't know exactly how she would do it. Her plan wasn't very specific. Mel and Jimmy offered to help, of course, but she didn't want to get them in trouble. Of course, Jimmy wouldn't take no for an answer.

"I can't believe I talked them into this. I'm so retarded," She said as she pulled Mel's cell and checked the time. "It's too late to call it off now."

Mark says, 'surprise works to the weaker force's advantage. Strike and run; that's the mission profile of underdogs' He should know.

But knowing about Mark's spook-tricks, and doing one, were two different things. She hated sneaking. She justified it inside her head, it was reasonable, and she couldn't afford an honest battle. Her stomach hurt: It couldn't digest logic.

She headed for the south entrance with crossed fingers. The plan was planting the transponder unseen while Jimmy's diversion played out. She pulled the little device from her pocket; it was the size and shape of a marble cut in half with a wax paper peel-off back. *Just peel and stick simple right?* She stuffed it back into her vintage 501 cut-offs and opened the fire door. The south wing didn't have homerooms, just industrial arts and music studios.

She slowly made her way toward Billy's homeroom. It was just off the intersecting wing. Her guts tied another knot. A hungry bull shark waited around the bend. Every step down this long passage felt like dragging an anchor.

She stopped at the intersection. Billy was within earshot just around the corner holding court in front of homeroom. *Freaking jocks.* She checked the phone. One minute before the bell. She plastered herself against the locker-free wall listening for Jimmy's entrance. Billy wasn't ten yards away. She peeked. His backpack was on the floor. He was bragging about how he lined up a dance with every hot girl in school. She felt a weird pang of jealousy.

"I'll be busy tomorrow night," Billy said. Cat-whistles and hoots followed.

She cringed. *What an ego! But he is cute. What am I thinking?*

She didn't know what sickened her more, spy-craft or Billy's bravado. He was cute, OK; tall, that hot athletic V-build, long curly hair, chiseled face. He didn't even have zits. Too bad he had the brains of a caveman. She saw that crooked smirk of his inside her head. She wanted to punch his lights out.

"Yeah, I'll be busy," Billy said.

"Busy!" Jimmy said loudly. "With girls? Oh no, no, no bitch, that's not what I heard. I heard you gave pedophile Pete a blow job behind the Rainbow Club."

"What're you talking about," Billy demanded. "Shut your pie-hole before I drop-kick you!"

"Everybody at the gay youth house is talking about it."

"Shut up!"

"Make me, bitch."

Jimmy's book bag went flying past the intersection and slid out of view. Jimmy threw his books at Billy! That's asking for it. Pandemonium broke out. The sound of kids scattering and Billy's cronies dropping their backpacks was followed by the sound of sandals slapping down the hallway, away from her. Somebody was chasing somebody and no telling who was doing what. Everyone wore sandals. She froze in amazement. Jimmy never started a fight before. Mel rounded the corner.

"What are you waiting for?" Mel hissed.

"Crap!"

She snapped out of it, peeled the backer off, and jumped into the main hall.

Billy's backpack was ten feet away on the floor in front of his locker. She ran a few steps and pretended to trip and fall over it. From the floor, she quickly stuffed the bug inside the phone pocket on his pack's shoulder strap. Billy always carried his phone in a belt holster. She rolled away and jumped up. Knowing how to fall came in handy.

A few kids near laughed at her falling. She didn't even hear their insults. Looking past them, Billy had Jim-Jim up against the wall, his fist drawn back. Meat Head was about to bust Jimmy's jaw. *I can't let it happen!* She bolted.

Someone cried a warning, Billy turned, his fist ready. Aggie slid under the swing like a baseball player, and swept Billy's legs. The bell rang. Billy was down. She popped up as if nothing had happened. And just in time. Billy's homeroom teacher stuck her head out of the room.

"What's going on out here?" Miss Thompson said with suspicion plastered on her face.

"Nothing, I tripped," Billy said as he righted himself. He pressed closer to Jimmy as he did so. Aggie was further down the hall but she heard what Billy said under his breath.

"Set me up you little faggot," Billy seethed. "You're going to pay."

Billy stormed off toward his homeroom. The crowd quickly dispersed. Mel caught up with them and the three walked off toward their homeroom further down the hall.

"Dude, that was close," Mel said. "Another second and Miss Thompson would have seen how you spilled that shit-bag. Game over!"

"You do it?" Jimmy asked a little short of breath.

"Of course, she did," Mel said. "Think I saw it, right?"

Aggie ignored the question. "You OK Jim-Jim?"

Jimmy was the target of bullies all his life. He was short, petite, gay and black. Even in the Keys it wasn't easy to be him. Pushing gender buttons was his main talent and problem. An effeminate gay-boy who loved to flaunt it invited disaster, even in gay-OK Key West. Aggie admired him. In drag, Jimmy wore size one and looked stunning, just amazing. But now he was three feet taller and outright butch. He led the march to homeroom with a confidence she hadn't seen before.

"This is the best day of my life! The power of three will set you free!" Jimmy beamed.

"Shut up," Mel said poking him in the side, "you sound like Aggie's Mom."

"Naw," Aggie said, "Sky isn't half that butch."

Jimmy laughed with a girlish squeal. Aggie decided Jimmy might be OK, but then again, he was a good actor.

Aggie managed to avoid contact with Billy the rest of the morning although she hadn't activated the new bug yet. She needed to get on her desktop at home to do that. She saw him a few times before lunch but he wasn't interested in her. He had a new focus, or so the tweets said.

Lunch break took forty-five minutes. She decided to skip out, zip home, and activate the bug. As Aggie kicked over her bike it sank in; Billy wasn't after her, he was now gunning for Jimmy *Oh great, some freaking plan I made.*

She took off for home. Now she had to keep an eye on Jimmy even more, for a least the next few days until Meat Head got over it. He didn't have enough gray matter to hold a grudge long.

She paused at her driveway. She hated riding the scooter down the lane; the dusty track wasn't good for the bike's air filter. She rode on anyway, slowly, eager to get on line. She was barred from the School's library computers. The Librarian thought Aggie was the school's in-house hacker.

Why does high school have to be so complicated? She thought as she parked at the house. She entered. Po-boy was on the computer.

"Dad, I've got to get on line," Aggie pleaded.

"It's got to wait, Honey Peach, "I'm plotting a course closer to the Navy air field. Those boys be getting buzzed by grays. I've got that Google thing going; look at all them little channels running through the flats."

"What are you talking about?"

"Aliens, Honey, I'm going to get me some first-rate pictures." There was a camera she had never seen before next to the mouse pad. Po-boy clicked and opened a minimized window. "Look here; they got some good ones on the New-for website."

She didn't argue. He liked to say about himself, and it was true, 'I'm a dog digging bones, once I get the scent there's no stoppin' Po-boy's tenacity was usually reserved for bone-fishing or finding grouper. Once he set his mind on something, forget it. *Aliens, yeah right.* She didn't bother to look at the screen.

"Whatever."

She stomped out of the house. When Mel and Jimmy come over later, she'd make Dad get off the computer. Democratic Dad wouldn't have a choice, he'd be out numbered. She had just enough time to get back before lunch bell rang. She had to warn Jimmy; Billy was after him, for sure.

ELEVEN
MAC flight Wednesday 1 P.M.

Seaman Jon Colbert ran checks for the third time. Predator control stations were like most advanced aircraft indicator clusters. If anything was wrong the computer would chime alerts, but he fiddled with his console anyway. It helped his unease. It didn't need adjustments, but he did. *All remote airframes are basically the same.* Yet, this station had stark differences; a 3-D tactical screen and a three-hundred-and-sixty-degree joystick. It was just like a space game console.

He was technically ready, just needed his flight partner, Sam Shuto, and a green light from Sanderson. He didn't cotton to working with a full admiral. He never rode with high brass before. On the thought, his leg started pumping like an oil derrick; he hummed an old Oakridge Boys tune in time. Music always corralled his nerves. *Wish I didn't leave my guitar in Texas.*

New to Key West, he liked it just fine, but this duty station, and all the extra security that went with it, just didn't set right. *Maybe I'll get used to underground flying.*

He had a lot of adjusting to do. Back home he was surrounded by cows and dry, open land, here land was crowded and water was everywhere. *Maybe I ought to learn how to swim.*

Sam blew in and plopped down in the other air-padded flight chair. The seat automatically adjusted to fit Sam's bony ass. Jon figured the seat's air rushing out smelled like a Naugahyde fart. Sam spun and faced his console and ran his flight-check. Jon had met his North East nerd padre in the briefing and he didn't much like Sam Shuto's attitude right off. *More balls than brains.*

"What's up Cowboy, you look tight, yo. What gives?"

"Ranching boys flying six stories underground just ain't right." Jon said. He stopped his leg twitch. "Ain't natural is all."

"Why'd you join the drone program? Should-da stayed down on the farm."

"Ranching ain't farming," Jon muttered between tight lips.

He clamped his mouth shut to stop the next word, asshole, which brushed against his teeth. No sense starting up. He pushed his service cap back on his head like a cowboy movie lawman sizing up a rustler.

"The Navy volunteered me. They must-a caught wind of my license. I flew Cessna and biplanes back in Texas driving cattle. Hell, I can fly anything with wings. How'bout you?"

"Video games," Sam said with his slightly bucked teeth front and center. Sam was locked onto his screen. "Three-D's my game and Sam Shuto's the name!"

A stiff-necked marine MP came through the small room's hatch and shouted, "Attention!" Sam and Jon bolted upright. Jon's ears hurt. *Ain't no need to shout in this dog-gone tin can.*

"At ease," rang out equally loud as Admiral Sanderson shoe-horned his mass through the bulkhead hatch and into the little metal cube. Sanderson looked like a man that could make a wild bull into ground beef with his bare hands. The ropy muscles of Jon's gut tied three new knots.

"Listen up, listen good," Sanderson boomed. "This is a top-secret project. You are flying the experimental MAC. You are not to tell anyone…ever. And, you are not to ask any questions as to the details of its operational configuration. You will obey my orders without reservation. Understand seamen?"

"Yes, Sir!" They said in unison.

"You will launch from a ship anchored off the Key West National Wildlife Reserve, Fort Jefferson. You have the coordinates. Your flight path is already programmed. Do not deviate from that flight path. You will ditch the aircraft if I give the order. When I clear you for free flight, I want razzle-dazzle. Show me what the MAC can do."

Sanderson didn't wait for a 'yes, Sir,' rather he charged off like a prize bull after a sow. A few seconds later the battle stations light blinked green. Sanderson came over the com. "All go."

Jon and Sam were assigned to fly tandem. Their flight plans were displayed on one of six screens each pilot enjoyed. Orders came over the com headset and across a smaller screen dedicated to text. The flight controller, a female he hadn't met, came on the com.

"Blind take off," she instructed. "No eyes on the platform. Bird One first, one second delay, then Bird Two. On my mark."

"Fly by graphics?" Jon voiced his internal question aloud. All his Predator take offs had real-time cameras on board and on flight deck. How else would he know if his instruments were calibrated? He could fly right into a deckhand and never even know it. His leg started up a new ho-down.

"That's right sailors," Sanderson cut into the com." This is a secret airframe, and that goes for the launch platform as well. Get going."

"Yes, Sir," both men squawked. Jon put a hand over his headset microphone. "I hope this bird is healthy."

"Go in three," the female commander said. She counted down. Jon, then Sam, was off and flying. This wasn't any Predator Jon had flown before. What-ever it was, it was way too fast. Almost instantly, he was at three hundred knots and twenty thousand feet elevation. Sam was on his tail in the blink of an eye.

"Level off. Switch to auto."

Jon switched over and crashed back into his seat. He had been sitting on edge. According to flight plan, the autopilot would take them to the proving grounds, an empty Atlantic Ocean location far away from shipping lanes and deep inside the Bermuda Triangle.

The nearest inhabited island was far away. Jon figured, at a Predator's rate of speed, he'd have an hour to cool his jets. He checked. Flight path graphic said he didn't have time to take a fast shit. Jon's leg started another ho-down.

Jon and Sam looked at each other. Jon covered his microphone.

"Has to be radar malfunction," Jon said, "I'm reading three thousand five hundred knots."

Sam switched on his downward and side scan cameras; his Asian eyes popped wide-white like a horror movie victim. Jon switched on his cameras. The ocean blurred. Little coral islands came and went in a flash. The other craft was pixilated. A quick glance at the altimeter confirmed his fear: he was flying thirty feet above water. The auto took it down too low. No jet could go that fast so close to water, air pressure would make it unstable. This bird flew like an arrow. *What in the hell's a MAC, anyway?*

"Command," Jon said, "This is Bird One. I have three, five, zero, zero knots. Altitude thirty feet. Confirm?"

"Confirm," the com said. "Destination twelve minutes." Then Sanderson cut in and added, "You haven't seen anything yet."

"Damn," Sam said with a hand over his mic.

"Shit," Jon said.

"Cut the chatter," com demanded.

Jon was so flummoxed by the MAC's capabilities he forgot to cover his microphone. Not ten minutes into the flight and he had broken discipline...and got caught. Duty in Key West was going to be like dodging cow-pies in a shit-storm.

TWELVE

Wednesday after School

Jimmy and Mel pulled a pair of chrome chairs away from the Pipers' 1950s Formica-topped kitchen table and set them either side of Aggie's latest computer desk. She had a nice modern Ikea desk. Like everything else around there, Sky got it out of someone's garbage.

"Dude, nice. Lots of room, plenty of bookshelves Mel said taking the center chair.

"Too bad Dad's hogging all the shelves with his stupid conspiracy books."

She could almost tolerate the shelf invasion; it wasn't a bad trade. Mom and Dad had little interest in computers. Dad used it to check the weather before fishing. That was about it, no problem. But, lately, when she really needed her space, he was acting like a total butt-hole.

The computer case was junk, just a 1990s tower with an old-fashioned deep monitor. Everything was covered with Hot Wheels and Power Ranger stickers. Aggie paid three bucks for it, but what was inside it was what counted. Mel's rejected parts were better than anything in the stores. Aggie liked the sticker encrustation too; it reminded her of fossil beds.

"Think this'll work?" She said as Mel install the new software, "I got to get to the Winter Dance OK. I got this awesome vintage outfit." Last year, Billy dumped a milkshake on her before she got inside. She had to go home and change and missed half the dance. "The jock squad would love to mess me over."

"They can't screw you if they can't find you." Mel said without looking away from the screen. Her fingers flew over the keys. "With this, you'll avoid him better than a cloistered monk hiding from the plague."

"You're such a Goth bitch" Jimmy said. "Nobody loves the Black Death like you."

"Dudes, check it out." Mel said pointing at a skull and crossbones icon with the curser. "Just click here. I pre-set the tracker. Just open the Sat-link page. This is way better than that one-stop uplink I started with."

Mel clicked. Aggie moved her chair closer. A password window opened and Mel typed in, 'Billy sucks ass'. A split window opened, one screen was a map of Key West showing a blinking light on Duvall Street, and the other screen was a satellite view. Mel zoomed in. An aerial view of Billy sitting on his scooter at a traffic light appeared.

"Google," Aggie asked?

"Better," Mel said. "I…er…sort of barrowed this from my Dad. It's a military system access program. You can use Google Earth too, but that's limited and not real time. This is accurate, any time, any place. It gives you the closest satellite available; we're tapping into everybody's hardware."

"Bitching," Aggie said.

"Don't use it too long," Mel said, clinking to kill the Military Satellite Link's live feed. "Every few minute's security checks the loops. They'll think it's a hacker if they trace it here. Takes like two minutes for the NSA to trace an MSL."

"MSL?" Jimmy asked.

"Military Sat Link," Mel and Aggie said together.

Mel opened Google inside the program and got a picture of where Billy was but he wasn't there.

"It's memory not real-time, see?" Mel said. "Sometimes it's old so you have to check."

"Cool, I can confirm if it's really him. I'll use the MSL just for a second, right." Aggie said.

"That'll keep that creep off you." Jimmy said.

"I'm more worried about you, Jim-Jim." Aggie said.

"Access it from your phone… as long as this desktop is on and the software is running." Mel added. "Your home unit acts like a remote-control hub."

Aggie pulled her cell phone and keyed in. The Google image appeared on her phone. She switched to MSL mode and typed in Billy sucks ass. The tracking program instantly opened with the top of Billy's head center screen. She exited the MSL and wrote the password on the green desk blotter underlining it three times so she'd find it easy. The blotter was already a maze of scrawls and doodles, Dad will never see it.

"Keep this software running in the background," Mel said, "But, operate it from the phone, it gives another layer of protection. Welcome to government surveillance land."

"As Sky once said, 'far out'," Aggie said crinkling her nose. By the look on their faces, Mel and Jim-Jim smelled it, too.

"Fish, I hate fish." Jimmy said.

"Dad's home," Aggie said.

"I'm glad my Dad's into engineering. He mostly smells like ozone aftershave." Mel said.

"On the right man, aftershave works," Jimmy said batting his eyes.

"At least my Dad doesn't make beer farts." Aggie said. "Sorry Jimmy, I know you like that."

Po-boy burst through the door. Everyone twisted in their chairs. Po-boy's easy, southern demeanor was gone. Sweat on his brow, face tense, he was in a hurry and he was never in a hurry. It shocked them all.

"I got to get on," Po-boy said a little breathless. "Something big is happening."

He held up the new camera. Aggie's pocket digital was in his other hand. *My camera too!*

"I saw them off Jefferson. Flying saucers. Let me in there Melissa."

"Dad! I'm using it now." Aggie yelled. Jimmy cowered in his chair like he was getting hit.

Mel stood and backed away. Jimmy bunny-hopped his chair back.

"Mel! Help me."

"I'm pulling rank," Po-boy said taking Mel's chair. "This here's my chance to do good by you Honey. This works out; I'll have your college money lick-it-tee split. Now you girls run off, I got me some Nu-for work here."

"But Dad," Aggie exclaimed, "I'm on here every day after school. I've got schoolwork—."

"Hush now, got to file this here report," he said, "Them boys up in Atlanta got to see what I seen. With all this UFO activity going on round here, I'll write up a bestseller quicker than a mud-bug jumping off a hot plate."

Mel reached over Po-boy, grabbed the mouse and clicked to minimize the sign-in page. "Mr. Piper, please don't close the programs I'm running, K? Updates," Mel lied.

"Don't you worry your pretty little head Missy. I just got a few things running here; I won't touch it, no how."

"I GIVE UP," Aggie said as she rolled out of her seat.

With a huff and a look of disgust at Dad's collection of books, she marched through the front door. *That's my desk.* Mel and Jimmy hurried after.

"Just what the world needs, another stupid UFO book," Aggie said. "I can't believe he takes this crap seriously."

"Dude, he better not mess with it; the MSL is still running. If he tries signing on with a bad pass word…"

"Don't worry; Dad wouldn't know what to do with it, even if he found it."

"I hope you're right." Mel said.

"My ass is on the line, too. Can they trace it with the software just open," Jimmy asked?

"No way," Mel snapped. She looked like she had seen a ghost. "Think I'm a moron?"

Aggie freaked out a little. Mel only spit out prissy answers whenever she thought she had screwed up. But Mel hardly ever screwed up…But, she never admitted it when she did. Aggie was just going to have to trust the Goddess of technology, or the next best thing, Melissa Van Ness.

THIRTEEN

Black and Sanderson Thursday morning

A dmiral Sanderson was six foot five, rotund, had a weak heart and high blood pressure. He would not have been allowed to continue in the Navy if it weren't for his rank and special clearances. He looked fifty but he felt like a hundred. The secrets he harbored scared enough people to ensue job security. His position warranted an alien-built artificial heart so his secrets couldn't die with him and he was still waiting.

The Joint Chiefs insisted a Ship Group Command wasn't an option for him. They said, 'the stress of high command was too great.' They offered him, 'a job with less strife,' or so they sold it. Sanderson knew it was bullshit even before he accepted. The Chief's Galaxy Project was a slippery deck over a stormy sea, and that was exactly what he wanted; nobody that mattered kept track of a drifting skiff on boiling seas. *I'm in Key West surrounded by water, and without a fleet…But not for long.*

The base wasn't his responsibility. Sanderson's only concern was the U.S. Navy's space operations and the kickbacks he'd get out of it. But things weren't moving. Negotiations with the aliens had stalled. *Goddamn GTO.* He wasn't sure what the real problem was, but it was his job to fix it.

At least a lucrative side project dropped into his lap. The Magnetic Aircraft Project was a license to print money. He didn't mind putting it over on the Galactic Trade Organization while getting rich, either. Sanderson would build an American space fleet one way or the other.

"Fuck the GTO, if they won't help me, I'll do it myself."

The MAC's drive system and its capabilities were understood for forty years, but it took this long to develop fly-by-wire control systems that humans could operate without android pilots. Androids were better but the very idea of making robots out of bovine and human DNA discussed him.

Sanderson's wall clock said six a.m. He adjusted the monitor on his desk and leaned back in his leather chair. Seamen First Class Jon Colbert and Sam Shuto were below decks flying MACs, and doing well. They got a little too close to that Uniflight but it wasn't their fault. His men had no idea what they were flying. He'd have them work on reaction time.

Sanderson's intercom blinked. "Admiral," A young women's voice said, "There's a Special Agent here for you, Sir."

"How special Yeoman?"

"His identification places him out of the Pentagon's Majestic section. He's with the Navy Recovery Office."

This gave Sanderson pause to consider. He should send this agent packing. MJ-12 was the invisible sand in the crack of his ass. Always plucking his dingle berries but they never say why. Yeomen Nostrum's intercom was secure so Sanderson spoke freely.

"How the hell does the NRO even know I'm here?"

"He didn't say, Sir."

"Hold him, let me think."

The Joint Chiefs and MJ-12 were not usually on friendly terms. Majestic was far too autonomous and always at odds with the Chiefs. Majestic rolled over any compartmentalized departments that got in their way. Even though one of MJ's boys sat on the Secret Security Council, and one with the Joint Chiefs, non-co-operation was MJ's standard operational procedure.

The Chiefs' interest was to obtain the Galactic Trade Organization's technology, then, eventually, membership in the GTO for America. But MJ was still doing it the old way; shooting down alien ships, stealing their technology, and screwing up progress. What were they trying to do? Start a galactic war?

Majestic was currently increasing their forceful gathering of alien materials for reverse engineering. *Goddamn unnecessary: They're getting nowhere fast.*

Cooperation wasn't forthcoming between any top-secret departments; only a handful even knew about the Navy's MACs. The President didn't even know. *What does anyone really know?*

"Goddamn need-to-know bullshit—I need to know what the goddamn NRO knows."

Interstellar flight by dimensional shifting was the big nut and unreachable thanks to Majestic. *Worse, the goddamn aliens gave the U.N. magnetic drive.* The pressure was on. Sanderson wouldn't be prematurely testing MAC controls if the GTO didn't cut the Navy's balls off. Majestic was why the GTO gave MAC-drive to the U.N. in the first place; he was sure of it. *What bullshit.* The Navy had the jump on everyone but MJ-12 wouldn't play nice.

"Fucking Majestic."

On top of everything else, the President was bucking for answers, too. She'd disassemble the whole goddamn security culture to get in on the game. Sanderson didn't even know who the NSA worked for anymore. Something had to give. Nobody was telling anybody anything straight. Maybe it was time Project Galaxy kicked Majestic in the balls.

"Yeoman, let his sorry ass in."

It took a few minutes for the guest to arrive. He had to pass screening, give up his weapons. This gave Sanderson time to calm down. MJ wasn't worth shorting-out his electronic pace maker. He'd go get a lab-grown organic heart from the aliens on Moon Base once the dam broke.

Security buzzed his door. Sanderson blanked his monitors. The door swung open and a tall man in a dark suit and sunglasses came in. He sat down opposite Sanderson without ceremony and took off his fedora. Sanderson recognized the scar high on the man's forehead. Archer was waxy and pale. He used to have more muscle.

"Colonel Archer, well I'll be damned." Sanderson put on his best fake smile. "Last time I saw you; you were running special ops in Kuwait." Sanderson extended his hand and Archer took it. "What in the hell are you doing with Majestic?" MJ and the NRO were known to be linked.

"Admiral, that's a long story. Let us just say the Pentagon wasn't ready for me to retire. Please, call me Mr. Black, that's my official rank."

"Suit yourself. I have a few questions for you...Mr. Black. Why is MJ-12 at my door, and how the hell did you know where to find me? The Galaxy Project isn't exactly happy with your NRO operations."

Black took off his sunglasses. Archer was a cool fish before, but now his eyes had no spark, nothing but pools of dusty brown sad sack surrounded by yellow-white. Not a glint of humanity. He had seen too much action, Sanderson guessed. Archer was just the right kind of operative to tag and bag dead aliens.

"Admiral, I've come to you without Majestic's knowledge. They would not have me share what I'm about to tell you. As you know, MJ-12 prefers conquest over trade. I find myself...forced to...disagree with MJ's philosophies," Black said putting his glasses back on.

"You're selling out?" Sanderson was incredulous.

"Not at all — what's good for Earth is good for Majestic, even if they can't see it now."

"Agreed, what've you got?"

"I didn't learn your location through Majestic. I'm here on my own. I won't tell them your whereabouts, either. I was recently contacted by a third party whom was willing to share information; this independent entity is monitoring the GTO/Earth situation. This free-trader, one of many operating in local space, revealed you. He says the GTO is playing you."

"Son of a bitch!" Sanderson said standing up too quickly. "Independent entities, what are you talking about? GTO says Earth's off limits, secured. They ran off the buccaneers thirty years ago."

Of course, Sanderson knew there were other factions although the GTO would never admit it. He didn't tell the GTO what he knew about independent alien activity nor would he tell Black.

"Despite the GTO, others are making deals, possibly with our country's enemies." Black said.

Sanderson felt his blood pressure shoot up. *Trying to cut me out — them bastards.* He suddenly felt lightheaded and slowly let himself back down. He took a few slow, deep breaths. Black poured him a glass of water from the pitcher atop his desk. If that were true, it was bad news. Sanderson was an opportunist but, more so, a patriot. 'A workman is worth his wages.'

All the new sightings and abductions fell into place. The GTO was lying and Black confirmed it. Moon Base had lost control but they had to know who else was flying. It pissed Sanderson no end that they wouldn't tell. *Who, pirates, smugglers?* Had to be bigger; perhaps the GTO was a small fish in a huge sea trying to gobble bait-fish before the whales swam in. Mistrust flooded Sanderson like water through an un-caulked wooden ship. *More setbacks! Goddamn GTO.*

Sanderson got his chest pains under control and asked. "What do you propose? What should the U.S. Government do about it?"

"Honestly, Admiral, I'm not at all sure I can trust my source. We need to know more and we need to keep this quiet or we'll look like fools. Let's work together and find the answers. You have means I don't have at your disposal."

"What means? I'm not a spy," Sanderson lied. He was intrigued. Black made sense.

"I need to get onboard Branford's ship. Majestic knows he's building and launching your MACs. My source has Branford playing two ends against the middle. You know full well Branford can't be trusted."

"Why board his ship?"

"If he has technology that shouldn't be there," Black said, "we'll know he's dealing with independent traders. Think of this; do you want a guy like Branford controlling intergalactic trade, scooping the U.S. Government? He'll do it, given the chance, and you know it."

"He's had his hand in Uncle Sam's pocket too long." Sanderson had to admit. "I can get you on his ship, but I'm not convinced I should."

"There's more, Admiral. I'll need further help."

"Depends, I don't trust Majestic."

"The GTO is close to terms with Earth, closer than you know, that's good but they won't sign your Project Galaxy proposal. They're going over your head to the U.N. I need time. If we expose the deal, show the U.N.'s involvement, the GTO will be forced to sign with the U.S. You're on the team. Disrupt negotiations. Give me time to get the evidence out of Branford."

"Majestic isn't supposed to know about the Joint Chief's access!" Sanderson barked.

"They don't, but I do and I'll keep it to myself; good faith between us," Black said. "Tell Branford that Majestic and the Galaxy Project have come to terms and I'm coming over to inspect the operation. We don't know who is dealing behind our backs or what faction, if any, is behind the GTO. I for one am not willing to let private industry get the golden ring when our Government is near collapse for lack of cash and oligarch's greed. We must get to the bottom of this so America comes out on top — without the defense industry's controls."

Sanderson rocked in his chair while weighing his options. Either Majestic is playing dangerous games or Black is telling the truth. Black wasn't asking for contact, only time to figure it out. Archers' bosses wouldn't do that, but the Archer he once knew did the right thing every time.

Sanderson didn't trust the aliens, hell he trusted no one.

Black didn't know Sanderson's real mission to secure a trade contract for the U.S. alone, no international corporations or U.N.; that was the real game. *Goddamn U.N.*

If Branford was into something better, screw the GTO. He would go around them all. One way or the other, he was going to get a trade agreement with aliens for the good and glory of the U.S. and its military, and his Swiss bank account. Most important, he needs that alien heart.

Sanderson's love of Country, which meant the Armed Forces, stirred in his chest. He respected Archer's service. In the Gulf Wars Archer proved a patriot many times over.

"Mr. Black, I think we can work together for the good of our Country. Give me a few hours to make the arrangements. I'll get you cleared to board Branford's ship."

"God bless America," Black said.

"Goddamn right."

After Black left Sanderson felt something wasn't right. He was no spy master but he was just as paranoid. He'd spy on his spy. Sanderson already planted an informant among Branford's mercenaries working on board the Contention. *We'll see what we see when we see it.*

*****

Black drove his Ford Crown Victoria north up Route 1 and into Key Largo where he parked his unmarked police-interceptor under a closed bank's drive-up canopy.

He parked in a safe zone and out of NSA range. It was a CIA communications hole he had used before. He took a pen out of the glove box and twisted it back and forth three times. A voice sung out of it.

"Yes?"

"Karnack, it is as I thought, Branford Industries is building MACs for the Navy. Branford has the facilities we need. It's a covert ship with MAC support systems. If we cloak it, and move it, no one will know it. I can get there in a day or two. Sanderson is making arrangements."

A cackle came over the pen. "What about the GTO?"

"You were right; the Navy is working with them. The program director, Sanderson, also happens to be the Joint Chiefs' negotiator. He's the only one that can stop us and he will soon be busy delaying the GTO's intervention for us. I projected doubts regarding the integrity and motivations of the GTO. We'll have time before anyone reacts. While Sanderson is in transit, we'll take the ship."

"Very good, Mr. Black, now report to your office and send them chasing their tails, won't you."

"Yes, Master."

"I love when you say that, Karnack out."

Black drove back south a few miles and turned into a little private airfield that hosted sky diving. The gate was locked. The sign said closed. He got out and went to the gatehouse. Homeland Security had a TSA man at every airfield, the guard here was a local and non-professional. Half the guard's face was melted away like a burned plastic doll, which explained why Karnack used the older grays for this mission: Easier to override the no-harm setting.

Black took the keys off the dead man, went inside, and relocked the gate. He proceeded to the back side of a hanger where two NRO helicopters sat—the same two that went missing three years ago. They were rigged for remote flying. Black sat and waited for Sanderson's call. Mr. Black would not eat although he needed to, to stay alive, he wasn't ordered to eat so he would not. He still had that much control over himself, if he was lucky, he might starve himself to death before Karnack made him do too much harm.

FOURTEEN

A dark sunny morning, Thursday 6:45 a.m.

Aggie wheeled her Vespa into student parking before school. She parked next to Mel who was sitting on her bike texting. No one missed Mel's ride; it was the only scooter in the Keys painted pearl-pink with fist-sized laughing black skull polka dots. The paint job cost more than Aggie's bike was worth.

"Hey," Aggie said, "I just figured it out, the reason you ride at all is so you have an excuse to wear that nasty bomber jacket."

"Not so. Dude, I'd wear it riding my brother's big wheel. It's way too cool not to wear."

"Only Goths wear black when it is eighty degrees and say it's cool."

"Brains, fashion, weird friends, I've got it all." Mel said.

Aggie pulled the phone out of her yellow 1950s pedal pushers' front pocket and cleaned the screen with her Grateful Dead dancing bears T-tank.

"His bike isn't here; let's see where the Brainless Boy Wonder is." Aggie started the phone's tracing software. It loaded fast. She tapped on the tracker icon.

"Nothing," she said.

"Let me see." Mel snagged the phone. Her thumbs flew over the key board. "It's off, home base software is off. You shut your computer down?"

"Freaking Po-boy was online when I left.

"Never let a non-geek near a computer," Mel said somberly.

"How am I going to track Billy?"

"What, with that?" Billy said coming from behind. "I thought you were smart; Google isn't real time asshole: Can't find me with that." Billy whipped out his I-Know phone. "This is a real phone. I've got real time webcam access all over the island. It's not a piece of shit like that thing."

Billy held his phone out. The school's main parking lot security cam was on screen. He brushed the screen with a fingertip. The next security cam shot rolled in showing Flagler Ave. from the school's viewpoint. Mel had hacked school's security two years ago. The geeks had security cam access since then. It was a huge secret. Billy flipped pictures in fast succession.

Panic almost choked her. *Think Aggie think.* Billy had public access only, must be, not the student parking cams. He didn't show her the bike lot. Billy slung his I-Know phone back into its belt holster. Aggie took a breath. She wasn't sure what his capabilities were.

"You can't hide from me," Billy said leering at Aggie.

"Ok, I'll kick your ass right now. Let's stop dicking around." She said viciously.

Billy laughed, "No way, I don't want you thrown out of school, not yet. We'll have some fun Friday night, first. I'll spank that fag, and you too, Melissa, saving the best for last."

"You don't have the balls. There'll be teachers, they'll call the cops."

"Cops? No problem. Dad gives them tons of money. They owe him big."

Billy swaggered away. A couple of his friends fell in behind. Aggie sat side-saddle on her scooter and pushed hair into her face.

"Forget him, he can't do shit." Mel said.

"He's right, he can attack anytime. Between Dad messing with my desktop, and Billy's army of rat-finks, I don't have a chance." Aggie stretched out a long leg and stuffed the phone back into her skintight pants pocket.

"Dude, he can't do anything once you're inside, you got to get to Osborn," Mel said.

"Even if he misses me at the dance…what if Billy gets the security code? I bet he has it already. He'll find all the blind spots. He'll jump me. I'll have to take him on and his bandits, too. But if I touch him…How'll I keep him off me until graduation?"

"We'll form a geek patrol," Mel said.

"Yeah right," Aggie said between gritted teeth. "That's a big help. I'll just stay home."

"Dude, we can't let that pea-brain scare you off the dance. We'll hookup after school and plan some rock-in Kung Fu sneaky mojo stuff. Don't worry, this'll be great."

The ten-minute bell rang and they started toward the building. Aggie knew Mel meant it but she couldn't let Mel and Jimmy get into trouble for her sake although Mel could take the heat. Mel's folks were rich, too. If Billy messed with Mel, her folks would sue the crap out of Billy's folks and the school, too. Billy knew better than to mess with Mel.

Jimmy was another thing. His Mom was broke, stoned, and stupid. Who'd look after him? Aggie felt she had to do the dance. Jimmy was going in drag. Someone had to watch his back.

A sunny morning never looked darker. Win or lose, she just couldn't drag her friends down her rabbit hole. After the dance, maybe she'd quit school, or go on home study, or figure something else out. She hated not knowing what to do, and her supposed 'highly functional' brain didn't help at all. Maybe she should, 'trust the Universe.' *Yeah, right.* With every step toward homeroom, her thoughts turned darker and college slipped further and further away toward the shadows.

FIFTEEN
Flies in a web Thursday afternoon.

After lunch two dead-serious and heavily armed MPs met Jon and Sam in the foyer of the little one-story brick building where Sanderson's office was located. One military policeman silently searched them, while the other watched. They were then escorted to the hidden elevator, which was behind a closet in the conference room. The elevator lobby was well hidden. Each pilot had to walk through a metal detector, like the one at Sanderson's door. One MP carefully checked the lift before Jon and Sam were allowed in.

"Christ on a cracker," Sam said once the elevator doors closed. "Paranoia will destroy ya."

Jon didn't say squat. Video cameras were in the elevator pointing down at them like a couple of stagecoach shotguns. *Paranoid's the right word, ol' padre.* He swore he was being watched twenty-four seven but he couldn't prove it. *Looks like MPs are everywhere.* That creepy gringo in the black suit out front of Sanderson's door yesterday didn't set right either. He sat there stiff as a corpse dipped in wax.

Jon was brought up on straight honesty and he was proud to be an honest man, but he wasn't getting any return here; truth wasn't regular Navy issue. He tried talking to the gal sitting behind the reception desk the other day real friendly like but all he got was a heap of hostile. Whenever his flight cam fell on Sam's MAC, he got pixilation and reprimands. Curiosity was kicking a hole in his gut but his clearance wasn't high enough to get any medicine.

He hadn't even met his flight team, or flight commander. Hell, he didn't even know what he was flying. The whole posse was just Sanderson, Shuto, a bunch of Marine MPs and a voice on the com.

His flight station was starting to feel like a closed coffin; working six stories below sea level just didn't set right. He didn't even know how to swim. *I expect swimming don't matter in hell.*

Jon and Sam took their seats. The twitch in Jon's leg tapped S.O.S. Today they were scheduled to execute extensive free-flying.

"Chill, Cowboy" Sam said. "Yo, after work, hit the gym, burn off that rocket fuel."

"Naw, I'd sooner get me a posthole digger and set a line-o-fence." Jon rolled up a short sleeve and brandished a ropy bicep. "Ranchin's all the workout I need. Got me these here guns from it."

"If I see any loose cows around here, I'll let you know." Sam said putting his headset on. Jon did the same. "I'd pay to see you wrestle a cow."

"Rope a steer, you mean."

"There's a difference?"

Jon tied his tongue. No point starting up. You can't fix ignorant.

Orders came over the headset, it was the usual: Take the MAC up blind, put it on auto, arrive, run it through paces according to Command, then auto back to a no-name ship and a fly-by-wire landing.

The MAC's incredible capabilities filled Jon's head with questions, some fighting to spill out into his mouth, but he wasn't allowed to talk about it, not to anyone, not even Sam. He just had to know what in the hell he was flying.

Once in the test zone Sanderson came over the com.

"OK, Boys, do what's on the flight plan. No hold-back. I don't give a damn if you wreck. We're here to test capabilities. After the general run, when you get the green for the head-on, crash the son of bitches. Got it?"

"Yes, Sir," they replied.

Jon and Sam ran the maneuvers as ordered; a series of impossible dives and right-angle turns — maneuvers that would kill a pilot. The G-forces were stone-cold ridiculous yet the hardware took it all unaffected.

Jon was confident in his craft's capabilities; his ability to fly it improved more than he figured possible. He felt good flying it, too. Even his leg relaxed. He hated to see it splashed, but if Sanderson wanted it wrecked, he'd give him a dog-gone good one. Then maybe he'd get himself duty somewhere top-side. With the MAC in pieces, he'd be out of a job.

Sanderson came back on the com. "OK, Boys, approach head-on ten miles out, ten feet elevation. Forty percent throttle, last half mile."

"Ten feet, Sir," Sam asked.

That was the lowest elevation they were yet to fly. Hardly anything except a biplane going really slow could fly that low. Forty percent was too damn fast.

"If they blow, I don't want to send up a flare." Sanderson said.

"But Sir," Sam said. "On board radar is ten foot plus or minus accuracy and worse over the water. What about reflective distortion?"

"Use your eyes; manual, forward visual. Do it."

Sam tended to over-check all his screens when he was nervous; his head was on a swivel. While the crafts flew out to line up Jon covered his microphone.

"I could use a day off: Let's shove these here MACs up his ass."

"I'm with you Cowboy."

They lined up according to radar and started their approach slow, only thirty knots, as instructed. If they came at it too hot, too soon, they'd never adjust manually in time and radar was already bouncing altitude. Jon needed a good fix before hitting the gas. This far out, Jon had a hard time drawing a bead. The pixilated imagine on his targeting screen was hard to zero in on. Sam was listing side to side too much. Jon was used to brush flying, hopping over cows, sage bush, or coyotes in the middle of landing, but this weren't that.

"Hold her steady, Sam, it's just dodging doggies, I'll aim, you fly straight."

Sam locked in auto. They both hit the gas pedal. Their crafts came together. Jon blinked expecting nothing but blank screens. That wasn't the case. His nose cam was pointed at blue sky. A glance at the flight profile monitor showed two dots climbing straight up like an oil gusher. Blue sky was going black fast.

"Level off, level off, goddamn it I don't want another MAC in orbit. Shit!" Sanderson shouted into the com.

Jon was still able to control it. He curled a big loop and was back in the test zone in thirty seconds still going mach six.

"Slow down, slow it down!"

Jon brought the craft down to forty knots in a matter of seconds. Sam was able to do the same. He couldn't believe it was still flying. *What the hell.*

"Form up, back in formation" Sanderson barked. "Hot damn, that's what I'm looking for."

"How's this possible," Sam muttered.

The blood had drained from Sam's face. Jon's restless leg turned into jelly. The scent of his sweat mixed with Sam's made Davy Jones's locker smell like a rodeo dressing room.

"Dog gone," Jon said into his mic. "How the hell?"

"Magnetism," Sanderson said sounding well pleased. "Don't forget, you boys are sworn to secrecy. Officer, take over, I need a martini."

The very business-like female voice came back on the com. "Prepare for return flight."

She had them key the auto return command. Jon realized the Flight Commander had to have high rank or Sanderson wouldn't up and leave. She could make decisions.

Jon recalled a fact from high school science: Like charged magnets repel each other. This gave him an idea. He put a finger along his nose and turned to Sam.

"Com, we should go manual, make sure we got no damages before landing, Sir."

"Affirmative. Stay on flight path, no deviation. Stay alert for evasive action. If eyes get near you, bug out, copy."

"Yes, Sir," the two flyers said in unison. "Elevation twenty feet, confirm?"

"Roger that."

Sam covered his microphone, "What're you thinking, Cowboy?"

"Let's say we're off Key West and this here big ol' fish goes a-jumping up and makes me jerk the stick, I might just react, bounce off you. I might go flying into them live webcams over there on that there state beach. How far you reckon we just bounced? What was it, three hundred nautical miles? I'd sure like to know what in the hell I'm flying."

"Copy that, Space Cowboy."

Jon figured there was no way they'd get roped. Accidents happen all the time with experimental aircrafts. After the chewing out they had gotten about better reaction time, he had himself a handy reason to react too fast. He might even get lucky and get fired.

SIXTEEN
MAC attack

Po-boy was getting the hang of it. Back in college it took him a year to learn the word processor. Nobody then, poor folks like him, had a personnel computer. He mostly used a manual typewriter and it worked just fine. Electricity was hard to come by on the bayou. He'd grown up not much liking technology, didn't trust it, but then again, he didn't get to use it much. The more he played with Aggie's computer the more he learned and the more he liked it.

"Po-boy," Sky said, "Don't you have a charter, it's eleven already."

"Noon, Honey Peach, look at this. I got the webcam over at Sunset Pier."

Sky came over and put a hand on Po-boy's shoulder, she leaned over to look at the screen. He slipped a hand behind her and cupped her naked butt. *Firm as can be, all that beach walking.* She wiggled in acceptance. But, Po-boy didn't have time for it now. He had to go and get the boat ready in a few minutes.

"Can you get the State Park?" Sky said. "I need more driftwood. No point in wasting gas if there isn't anything on the beach today. They clean the beach tomorrow, should be loaded."

"Sure thing, Honey Peach."

Po-boy searched in the browser, found the site, and brought up the live feed at Fort Zackary. The beach was empty, typical for a Thursday. The tourists were hung over and the locals were either working or in school.

"Looks like good pickings today," he said.

"Far out, I'll walk with you to the marina. Mark said I could take his pickup. I must shop today anyway. I'll ask if he won't mind me stopping at the beach, too."

"Well go on and get you some clothes, times running late."

Sky laughed and headed into their bedroom to get dressed. "I better find a bra, might take a little while. Where did I put it?"

Po-boy had to wait so he explored the other cameras. One was facing out to sea. He figured he'd check the conditions and see if they were fishing. If so, he might go down there and try it. He started recording to mark who fished where. He'd radio on the way out and check on the catch. He didn't see any boats, not one charter. Maybe it wasn't good fishing there today.

"Dang this is handy."

He was about to shut down when he noticed a little sliver speck. It got big fast. It came at him like a swordfish. Then it stopped. It hung there a split second and then streaked away. Po-boy nearly fell out of the chair. *Flying saucer?*

"Mother of god!"

His heart raced. Po-boy had quick eyes; thought he saw tiny lettering. He backed up the recording with a trembling hand and zoomed in. He found the writing. It read, 'Branford Industries.'

"If that don't beat all."

Po-boy's hopes collapsed all at once. He couldn't send this to NUFOR. They were after real UFOs. Publicizing the Government's secrets would ruin them, and him. *Mess with The Man and The Man will ship you to Cuba.*

He couldn't tell Sky. Her Old Man was worse than she ought to know. He wanted them to patch things up and this was a deal breaker.

Fighting reeling thoughts, he accidentally clicked on Melissa's skull and cross bones icon. An NSA sign-in page popped up. He panicked. He fumbled on the keys trying to make it go away. But asterisks appeared in the long-in box. He felt like the National Security Agency was looking right at him. *They got me.*

Po-boy clicked around until the browser closed, but the sign-in page remained. He grabbed the power cord and yanked it out of the wall. The monitor went dead but not the PC. He couldn't reach the PC cord. Stomach acid burned his gullet.

"You ready Honey," Sky asked coming out of their bedroom. Po-boy snapped up from under the desk. "You look pale." She said.

"Watching that dang webcam made me sea sick, that's all, come on let's go."

Once outside, he immediately shut down the wind generator. Nothing odd about that. They didn't run power when nobody was home. For once he was glad the house batteries were shot. *The Man can't get me now.* The computer's power was cut off for sure.

*****

Sonny Po-boy Piper didn't know the desktop was still running: Its internal power supply held power longer than two minutes. All over the world security operatives were wondering how anyone but an insider could find the military's spy satellite sign-in hub. Government computer spies got busy pinging.

There wasn't enough time to find the exact location before the PC died. But this much was confirmed: it didn't come from the Navy base; the hack was at another location and very near. Many agencies concluded independently that someone outside of the club was spying, but as that was nearly impossible, the idea of success was discounted; the Navy Air Station likely had an attempted electronic intruder. Spying was expected.

Where Sanderson went, eyes followed and ears projected. The question was: whose eyes? Sanderson wasn't above hacking his own government, either. Very few knew how to access the hub. If Sanderson used his own sign-on everyone watching would know what he was up to. No one would move on Sanderson too quickly; none had enough grit in hand to catch this slimy eel although more than a few had previously tried unsuccessfully.

SEVENTEEN
Jon late Thursday

Jon rode his 1985 street and trail Yamaha XT350 up to the officer condo complex gate. He swiped his card. The gate slid sideways by way of cupped wheels riding on salt encrusted galvanized tube stock. The rusted screech became a slow crunch as the gate retracted inside a doubled chain-link fence. The odor of salt, flora, and WD40 smelled good. Back in Texas, oil and dirt was always in the air but never mixed with flowers. Flowering vines covered everything but the gate. He idled past the fancy condos and through the back lot, down an access road to an isolated row of WWII bungalows. His place was almost hidden by a little jungle.

Except for the peeling blue-green paint, the place was OK. There were only two others living among the dozen cottages, single officers. He wasn't allowed to mix with them and that suited him just fine. *Good thing about special-ops, they issue nice berths.* Jon wasn't that far from other seamen his rank, but far enough. He was used to going it alone; it was peaceable. Best part, Sam lived somewhere else.

Out on Daddy's cattle range he never felt lonely. But this was different; Key West was living under a honeycomb: Things were buzzing and you never knew when you'd get stung. Local folks and officers treated him the same, that is, like dirt. They must have figured low rank squids are from another planet. *Must be how Daddy's Mexican ranch-hands feel back in Grainger; disrespected in plain sight.*

Jon stepped up onto his porch and startled a black scorpion. The arachnid slid off the edge of the porch and disappeared in the brush.

"Reckoned I'd left your kind in Texas, ol' Pard."

There wasn't much to his place: Navy issued kitchenette, an island partition, two bar stools, a cheap flower-patterned couch, a dresser, his bunk, an old TV on a munitions crate. Only things that belonged to him were his civilian clothes, a computer, and a folding card table he bought at Sam's Thrift.

Jon grabbed a Budweiser. He took a creaky wooded chair over to his little table and started the computer; he went directly to the State Park's webcam. Webcams were how he got around Key West. The Park's camera looped footage every hour. He had five minutes to review it before the footage changed. Jon watched scrolling the fast-forward and sipping beer not sure when or if the MAC would appear. Toward the end, he let it run naturally. Suddenly, there was a little dot on the horizon. It grew fast. The damn thing stopped just short of the camera. It hovered for a second or two before it shot off like a Winchester round after a galloping buck.

Jon spit beer. He backed up the footage. It was so dang fast. He wasn't sure what he'd just seen. As he played it again and saw something, an airframe like a disk, maybe ten-foot around, shiny on top, blue underneath.

"Dog-gone it if that ain't a cotton pickin flying saucer."

He ran it again and slowed it way down. *Yup, that's how I flew it.* He stopped the recording just as he had turned the craft to rejoin his mission. He blew up the image. 'Branford Industries' was stenciled on the edge between disk halves.

Jon tried to run it again, but the loop had turned over. He should have had another three minutes but it switched out early. Sailboats were floating past that weren't there before.

"Dog-gone-it, I hope nobody else seen it, Sanderson'll skin me like a mule."

His leg started tapping 'Save Me Jesus' on the yellow pine plank floor. Jon sucked down his Bud and cracked open another. He didn't drink much and never this early, but he felt like getting a drunk on.

After an hour and four beers, Jon figured things were doing all right. He'd checked on line, nothing on the Key West Electric Bulletin Board, nothing in the news, he checked NUFOR's website: nothing there. *I missed a bullet.* Figured he was safe until someone banged on the door.

"Seaman First Class Colbert," a hard voice called from outside.

Jon heard familiar sounds; an M-16 rifle's action slammed shut. Someone cocked a 45.

"Military Police; show yourself, hands up, come out or we'll come in shooting."

Jon complied. He was searched, cuffed and put in the back of a Humvee faster than a diamondback rattlesnake crossing a hot blacktop road. A marine sat on either side of him while one drove. Jon was so out of sorts, his twitchy leg forgot to dance, or maybe it was the beer. Even so, his curiosity got the better of him.

"What I'd do?" Jon twanged friendly-like.

"Damned if I know," the driver said, "Admiral Sanderson's orders."

Jon instantly sobered and his leg resumed duty.

*****

Sanderson's office was better than the Base Commander's. His was more spacious; walls lined with teak bookshelves stuffed with antique books and his collection of vintage Navy manuals. His desk was made of teak and rare South American rosewood, couches and chairs were fitted with the finest black leather.

The main differences between his office and the Base Commander's place were twofold; location and technology. Sanderson's hole was a nondescript bomb-proofed building out on the edge of a secondary, little used, flight line and far from the normal buzz of base activities. From the outside, it was nothing special.

"God bless black-ops," Sanderson said as he pushed a hidden switch. He relished the show; his bookshelves came forward, spun 180 degrees and retracted back into the wall without a sound. A bank of flat computer screens replaced his books, lit and ready. With the laptop on his desk he controlled everything.

"Let's see you boys in Base Operations do that."

'Real power,' he often told his High Command equals, 'was in black operations.' Most of them, generals and admirals alike, had no idea what he was really in to. Not even the President knew what he knew. On reflex, Sanderson sucked up his gut while sitting in his chair.

The intercom sounded. "Mr. Black is here, I have him on the outside camera, Sir."

"Send him right in."

"Sir, do you need time to retract your equipment?"

"No, Mr. Black has the highest clearance."

"Yes, Sir."

Black entered without greeting, ignored the equipment, and immediately took a seat in front of Sanderson's desk. Black appeared relaxed...or was he weak, or sick? *Maybe Archer had cancer, could be motivation for selling out, like a regular E. Howard Hunt.*

"My intelligence has it your man Colbert just took the MAC for a joy ride. You want me to take care of him?" Black said in monotone.

Archer sure wasn't the chipper guy Sanderson knew in the old days. Black's condition was disturbing but he was really taken aback by Black's intelligence. Sanderson didn't dare show it.

The Admiral's mind switched into hyper-drive: How can Majestic know that? It was conceivable. After all, Majestic's Naval Recovery Office (NRO) provided crashed alien crafts, make that shot down, for research contractors. Maybe they were duplicating alien technology on the side? Anything was possible in the spook universe. What else did they know? What do they really have? They must be holding back, Black knows more than he's saying, Sanderson decided. *Goddamn need-to-know policies. I better be careful.*

"I should take him out."

Sanderson straightened in his chair. "I have it covered; it's handled."

"What about that webcam? One or more civilians saw that feed. I had better step in."

"You are out of your parameters, Mr. Black. First one is handled and I'm working on the other. You do your job and I'll do mine." Sanderson said feeling irritated. *Goddamn, where is he getting this intel? He doesn't have it all or he wouldn't be snooping around.*

Black leaned forward in his chair and said, "I'm here to facilitate; don't forget, we're on the same team. I have contacts in every agency. I'll snuff him for you."

"I'll do it, if the need arises," Sanderson said with clenched teeth, "Branford Industries and his mercenaries are backing my operations. I'm happy with their performance; the others don't have a stake; they have no need-to-know. We clear?"

"Of course, you understand the CIA, NSA and FBI are watching: everybody knows something is happening." Black said. "But let's stay focused, you're right. The U.N. and Galactic Trade Organization have terms. Time is running out. The NRO, perhaps soon, will be playing a different roll. I can't speak of details, of course, but I can use my men without them knowing about our joint venture."

"I see," Sanderson said quietly. "Keep your boys out of it. This is my problem. I'll let you know if I need anything."

"Remember, we can't trust the GTO. They're up to something, not even the U.N. has all the pieces." Black said forcing a little, tight Ken doll smile. "Are you sure you don't want me to find whoever saw the video. What if it's U.N. spies?"

"I said I'll handle it. Back off."

Sanderson stood. His chair fell over. Mr. Black got up slowly and showed himself out.

Sanderson retrieved the chair, sat and drummed his fingers on the polished teak. So that's how it is, the NRO is out of work. The Government never lets an unnecessary bureaucracy die. Another thought struck him. The NRO isn't supposed to know about the GTO negotiations. Does Black know about Dark Side Moon Base?

With his MAC pilots on ice, the Admiral decided it was time to dig clams and he'd pry someone's mouth open if it took a hammer blow.

He hit the intercom, "All clear?"

"Yes, Sir, Mr. Black has left the building."

He opened his secure email and read the latest security memo. Black was right, someone near the base, besides Colbert, saw the MAC on line. More importantly, it was someone Black didn't know about. The perpetrator tried to sign onto the Military Satellite Link, someone in Geiger Key. Was it his former Field Commander, Levine? No, Levine was retired and hated computers. Was it Branford's daughter who Levine was supposed to keep an eye on informally? It was possible. Something was going on. Black knew too much, but he didn't know everything—first things first.

He pressed the intercom, "Book me a moonlight flight. I'll go as soon as I have a few things lined up. Call the Chiefs: Tell them to keep Majestic and whoever else is looking over my shoulder out of my way. Our team's handling it."

"Sir, we don't have a team."

"We do now Yeoman, I'll use Colbert."

"Sir, he isn't qualified."

"That's exactly why I'll use him. He's off everyone's radar, he has security clearance. On paper he's not leaving the brig."

"Can he be trusted?"

"Doesn't matter, I'll wipe his memory after I have what I need."

"You'll lose a good pilot, Sir."

"A sacrifice I'm willing to make."

His wheels were turning now. He pressed the intercom to tell her another thing but let go of the switch. Something still wasn't right. How did this Yeoman know about mind-wipe side effects? He shook off the paranoia. She wouldn't be here if she wasn't cleared. He pressed the intercom.

"Secure this office until I get back. I want watertight hatches." He let go the button and said, "It's time I find out what Mr. Black and the GTO is really about."

He trusted no one. Black wasn't so much a trader as an opportunist. Everyone in black-ops was on the take somehow. 'Keep a poker in every fire' was the old operational standard and, 'get paid for the effort' was right behind it. Sanderson wasn't about to let the Security State crash down on his game. He just needed to find the connections in order to build defenses. *Step one; make the GTO slip.*

Black had to have a pipeline to the aliens. That would explain a lot. When it came to intelligence gathering, the GTO made the National Security Agency's technology look like kids playing with tin cans on strings. Maybe the GTO was planning an end-run. They tried it in 1952, had the balls to fly over Washington D.C. Whatever the case may be, he'd get his piece of the pie.

He'd arrange Black's visit to Branford's ship, alright. That was already in the works. With his man on board the research ship, whatever Black said or did would get back to him in due time.

EIGHTEEN

On ice, Friday 5 a.m.

Jon lay on a hard bunk in a gray-walled high security cell looking at the ceiling. The guard who locked the door said food came at 0700. He had no way of telling the time; no windows just one curly light bulb inside a recessed lamp that never went out. All he knew was his guts cried for chow; nothing but beer since yesterday.

Without warning, the cell door flung open. The florescent light flickered. Sanderson lumbered in. He was as crisp and dry as sagebrush and about as coiled up as an angry rattlesnake. Even his jarhead haircut stood ready to strike.

Jon jumped up and shot off a rifle fired salute.

"At ease sailor, why'd you go and fuck me like that?"

"Sir…I…I…I, oh hell."

"Goddamn it, I said at ease! That means relax. Sit, sit down, son."

Jon reluctantly eased himself down onto his bunk, his back straight and his mind alert. He waited as Sanderson's big shoulders slumped ever so slightly. The Admiral allowed his obedient round gut to protrude naturally. Sanderson didn't sit; rather he paced with his hands behind his back. Jon almost pulled a muscle trying to keep his leg from jumping. Sanderson's demeanor was thoughtful as he paced.

"Look son," Sanderson said kindly, "that was a pretty slick move you did, bouncing the MAC like that, smart thinking, I like quick thinking."

"But, Sir, there was this big old fish and…"

Sanderson put up his hand for silence. "Don't insult my intelligence, Sailor. The Flight Room is under observation, I saw and heard. Nothing gets by me, better get used to that right now."

"Yes, Sir!"

Jon couldn't understand why, if the Admiral saw it, why'd he'd wait so long to arrest them? The girl on the com must have let it slide a while. Sanderson couldn't have seen it in real time; he must have really gone out for a drink.

"I needn't say how you broke protocol and your actions were illegal. The question is what do I do with one of the best remote pilots in the Navy? Federal prison, ship you off to Cuba? No, that's a waste. I need creative pilots."

Sanderson stopped pacing and faced Jon.

"Ok, you've seen the MAC and nobody sees the MAC. In there lies my problem." Sanderson spoke as if he were working out the problem with Jon. "You already know that its nature is magnetic and that, Sailor, is a State Secret of the highest importance. All I can do now is bring you along or kill you. I decided to bring you in deeper, not very deep, this is a need-to-know situation, understand?"

"Yes, Sir, what exactly…"

"You're flying that bird so you have a need-to-know, I'll grant you that."

Sanderson paused to collect his thoughts and resumed his pacing. Jon had the feeling the Admiral already knew what he wanted.

"We're lucky no one was on that beach, Sir." Jon interjected.

"Or, I'd be obligated to pick them up and hold them…indefinitely. And, I'd have you keelhauled. You didn't get off scot-free. Someone was recording that webcam fly-by in real time besides you. I don't know exactly who, but I know the approximate location of the receiving computer, and you Sailor are going to ferret out the culprit."

"But, Sir, I ain't no spy. Hell, I ain't even a good liar. How am I going to do that? Can't you get the CIA—?"

"This is a need-to-know project and the CIA doesn't qualify. No Sailor, I don't trust them, this is a closed project. The FBI, the CIA and the NSA can all go take a flying fuck at the moon. This is my goddamn problem, my operation and my solution. What will it be Cuba, or some R and R at Mark's Marina?"

"Whatever you say, Sir," Jon said without much conviction. The idea of sneaking around like a thief made him squirm. It reminded him of how some of the good-old boys back home would sneak up on the Mexican sharecroppers' canteen at night and piss in their water cans.

"Good, come with me."

Sanderson led the way outside. It was earlier than Jon had thought, the sun was just rising. A salty mist was in the air, birds and other critters were chirping. Sanderson stopped at a black town car with tinted windows which was parked in an isolated spot and flipped open his cell phone. Sanderson signaled the driver to roll up his window. He put the phone on speaker and set it down on the roof of the car.

A stern but awake voice answered. "It's rude, calling me this early."

"Don't give me that crap Captain Levine; you're in the fishing business, you've been up for an hour. I need a favor."

"Sanderson, what in the hell…I don't work for you anymore."

"Nothing like that, Mark, listen, I got a sailor here that's gotten into a little trouble. He's a good kid, and I need him fit and ready. He needs a place to work off some piss and vinegar. I hear you got a gym over there?"

"Dojo, Admiral."

"That's fine. Look, Mark, I'm giving this seaman a week off. I'm sending him over to you. Keep an eye on him, will you? Take him fishing or something, the kid needs down time. Don't ask why, it's classified. Help me out … Mark … Mark?"

"Sanderson, you never do anything out of the kindness of your heart. What gives?"

"All right, you got me. I need this kid under wraps where I can get to him when I need him. Come on Mark, old times sake, do me this favor. I'll send some cash to cover him, whatever you need."

"That's not the point; I've got a business to run here. I'm busy. I don't have time for babysitting."

"That's fine, put him to work. I'll pay you to let him work." Sanderson said with a wink at Jon.

"I'm going to regret this, send him over." Levine hung up the phone.

"Free money works every time." Sanderson said. "Best damn Seal I ever commanded. He's not your target. I'll brief you on how to proceed and what you're looking for back in my office, get in the car Sailor."

Jon got into the back seat and sank low into plush leather. He was deeper in cow shit than any cowboy should ever be. For the second time in less than twenty-four hours Jon Colbert was given a chauffeur driven ride at Uncle Sam's expense. Only difference, this one was a limo that had donuts and coffee, but he didn't feel like eating.

Jon had the feeling this free ride was going to cost him.

NINETEEN

Day of the dance

They met twenty minutes before the warning bell. Homeroom was the safest place. Last night's conference call didn't convince Aggie's compatriots. "Dude, tell again, how we'll get past Billy," Mel asked.

Jimmy winched. "I don't want to get jumped. Love bears; hate silverback gorillas."

"This will work," Aggie said without much enthusiasm.

"We're scrapple," Jimmy said. "This'll never work."

"We'll go in from the north, just shoot between the bushes…" Aggie voice trailed off. She swallowed the guilty bile creeping up her throat. "It has to work."

"Dude, the plan's OK, what kills me is we can't track him." A dramatic contorted Shakespearian expression appeared on Mel's face. "Nobody brings a backpack to the Dance. Scooter, no way, he'll have his Dad's limo; nice ride, too. We don't have the technological high-ground."

Jimmy started thumbing his phone. "Bitch-in." Jimmy had Mel's My Page up. Mel had posted a shot of her Dad's town car. He waved dramatically. "Hello, your Dad's car is fucking fab, can't waste it. Let's bug out."

Mel shoved her I-know Ultra phone under Aggie's nose. Jimmy looked too. Billy's People Place webpage was on screen.

"See what he wrote about us?" Mel stabbed her finger at the touch-screen. "Not so well disguised bloody murder is what's on his mind. Let's take the limo to Miami. Jim's right. Parents will never know."

"Yeah," Jimmy said, "Let's do Hullabaloo. Mel's ready, black velvet dress and combat boots works in any upper crust social situation."

Mel pushed Jimmy, "Butt munch."

"He doesn't scare me." Aggie lied. Her heart rate was climbing; she felt flush on her cheeks. 'Fake it till you make it,' scrolled past her mind's eye. "Taking the car out of the Keys would get us in bigger trouble. We're rolling. We got to go. He's not going to terrorize us out of it. We have rights, OK. Principles, OK, OK?"

"Hippie Principles: whatever," Jimmy said with a hand flip. "Limo. Hello! It's Hullabaloo."

Aggie always wanted to do Hullabaloo. It was the best teen dance club in Florida. A place where nobody knows your name and geeks and freaks are welcome.

"We'll get past him; trust me." Aggie said, but didn't feel sure. "We can't miss."

"Gray matter over meat heads." Jimmy said. "I like the concept."

"He'll watch for the limo. He'll have to take us outside. We'll get out of the car behind school; send the driver around that circular driveway so everyone sees the car, and then, the car parks on Flagler out of cam range. How can they resist? Billy will think we're shitting our panties. The car will divert his attention."

"Once we're inside, he can't do shit, right?" Jimmy asked.

"I promise this will work or I'll take the hit." Aggie slumped a bit and tried not to push her hair into her face. "Come on guys, it's the Winter Dance. We can't miss this. Imagine how stupid everyone will be. This is the greatest anthropology study of our lives — a living comedy of errors."

"She has a point," Jimmy said.

"I hate when she's right." Mel said.

Mel got up, marched toward the door, swung her tiny black purse like a bola, sent it toward the doorway, and yanked it back with a snap. "Let's go." Mel stopped at the door for dramatic effect. "Science needs us." And she launched into the hallway. Aggie and Jimmy followed. Not even professional geeks would be caught dead hanging out in homeroom this early.

TWENTY
Dancing around trouble Friday night

They always meet at Aggie's house to get ready for events. Jimmy was late. He was always late. The girls took over the living room. Sky and Po-boy weren't around. *Thank the Goddess.* Mel's mother wasn't keen on having Jimmy and Aggie over together. Aggie could hear Mrs. Van Ness inside her head saying, 'Melissa, one friend over is quite more than I can tolerate! I simply can't have it.' The Van Ness matriarch wasn't exactly supportive but at least she lent Mel the 1929 Rolls and a driver. It was a totally old car, but a limo is a limo. They would arrive in style, sort of.

Aggie felt guilty about everything but bailing out of the car to sneak in really sucked. Mel and Jim-Jim could have made a grand entrance. It was too risky with her on board. Making her friends help wasn't fair either. They should have gone without her. Billy's People Place page alluded to a paint ball attack so the front door was off limits. She just had to talk to Mr. Osborn and that would be impossible covered in paint and more impossible without help. Jimmy and Mel insisted on the Geek Squad going together. Aggie's face felt like it was twisting into a prune. *Maybe I should cancel the whole thing.*

"What's that look: You stuffed your bra with dead fish again, right?" Mel said.

"I'm the daughter of hippies, hippies and limos don't mix." She said to cover the turmoil in her heart. "It's kind of distasteful, I guess. Weird, Mom didn't give me crap about riding in 'The Man's' symbol of oppression."

"Relax, Dude," Mel said while struggling to mold Aggie's hair into a 1940s style. "The car's perfect for this outfit. Where'd Sky get you such rad stuff?"

"Jo's Thrift, Mom takes recycling seriously."

"She'd like Dad's old car," Mel said. "It's recycled."

Aggie had checked the outfit in the mirror that hung on the living room side of the bathroom door before Mel started on her hair. She wore a long black pencil skirt with little lace flares at the knees and a lavender puff-sleeved silk blouse featuring an intricate lace trimmed high collar and V-neck panel. The clothes came from the 1940's and still looked fresh. Mom even got her this little, cute matching pillbox hat with eye netting and a glass beaded bag. She felt like Bonnie

Parker without the anchor known as Clyde. Sky had a knack for finding cool stuff although Aggie hated when the kids teased her about Sky's dumpster diving.

"You're right," Aggie said. "The recycled car matches. Mom would like it."

"Wish Jimmy would get here, he's good with hair," Mel said. "I suck!"

"Don't let that get around." Aggie retorted.

"Yeah, I might become popular or something. But really, I'll stick with chicks, thank you."

"Besides, we must protect your virginity for the human sacrifice." Aggie added.

Mel made a show of false shock. She wasn't pure at all. She tried boys and girls before. Aggie was the only virgin in school. Jimmy strode through the front door like an actress taking the stage at the Grammy Awards. He had a big bundle in his arms and exclaimed dramatically as he dropped it on the sofa.

"The power of three will set you free!"

Jimmy took any opportunity to make an entrance. Gays were as common as sand in Key West so Jimmy had raised flamboyance to an attention stealing art. *That's why he gets into so much trouble.* Jimmy the ham just had to rattle cages and that's why they got along so well. They were kindred spirits, Athenian Goddesses one and all. He was the only kid in school who was in as much hot water as she was.

"Gather and worship me, bitches."

"You're whacked," Aggie said with a laugh. "You want incense with that?"

Jimmy opened his bundle on the faded loveseat. The white wedding dress unrolled and a yellow wig popped out. He had a huge hoopskirt type wedding gown. It was no surprise that Jimmy would go in drag, but this was way over the top, even for him. Aggie loved it.

"How you bitches do-in?" Jimmy said as he pulled more stuff out of the pile including his prized stage makeup kit.

"I'm trying to fix her hair. What's it look like, brain surgery?" Mel said mumbling around the bobby pins in her mouth.

"Never let a Goth chick do the work of a sexy gay man, move over Sister."

Jimmy opened his magic box and took a couple of huge barrel-curlers and a spray bottle out. He stuffed a handful of hairpins into his mouth.

"What're we doing here?"

Mel pointed; she had a picture on her lap-top. It was an old still photo of Lois Lane from the original Superman TV show. Jimmy looked at it once and went to work.

In only a few minutes, Aggie's thick mane was pinned and piled with hidden rollers. Her long hair looked 1940 put-up short, better than Lois Lane's do. Jimmy topped off his creation with the pillbox hat. He placed it just so, adjusted it to tilt, and applied bobby pins. He stepped back appearing satisfied.

"Don't touch it, Aggie Piper, or I'll bust you open."

"Got it boss man!" Aggie saluted like the Rosie the Riveter poster girl except her tongue was hanging half out.

"Don't make me kick you bloody."

Jimmy then got dressed, did make up and wig, and it didn't take all that long. He had drag down to a science. By eight p.m. the Geek Squad was ready and the Van Ness's car was on the way.

Jimmy just had to prod Aggie. "Bitch, you clean up nice. You'd get any man in school, if you lost them damn sundresses. All the straight boys would be all over you. Girl, you got to go get you some."

"We lesbians like you just the way you are." Mel said batting her eyes. Aggie didn't even notice Mel had slipped into a black tux that had watch fob chains dangling from every pocket. Mel had changed while Jimmy worked on Aggie's hair. Mel's pant legs were rolled up mid-calf to show off her polished black Army boots.

Aggie checked the mirror and had to admit Jimmy was right, she was pretty. She even had makeup on; black eye liner, gray eye shadow, pink blush on the cheeks and killer red lipstick. She'd have to fend them off. But she reminded herself, the last thing she needed was a boyfriend, or girlfriend. She wouldn't let anyone stand in the way of college. Too many girls did too many dumb-ass things over a stupid boy and there was too much drama in girl-girl relationships. The car pulled up and blew its weird ah-ooo-ga horn.

"I don't have time for boys." She gave her standard answer. She wasn't about to add she liked girls too. Mel was her best friend and she wasn't going to mess that up.

"Give it up," Mel said, "She isn't a tart like you. I know I checked. Let's go."

The girls helped Jimmy with his train and they got into the beautiful car. The driver gave Jimmy a side-long glance—nothing new there. A man's voice coming out of a petite bride was jarring.

On the way, Jimmy promised that breakfast was on him after the dance. He showed them four rolls of quarters he had stashed in his little, white purse. *Yeah, he stole his Mom's laundry money again.* She'll beat his ass for that, what else was new?

They arrived at 8:45 p.m. Mel had the driver round the circular driveway, just to show everyone they were in the car, and drive off. The car dropped them behind the school gym, as planned. They watched from the shrubs as the driver made the circuit again and parked way down Flagler. A group of boys took off toward the car; the plan was working.

She couldn't tell if Billy was with the group or not. She and her friends milled around behind a hedge debating what to do. Aggie, still unsure made up her mind. *My plan, my timing.*

"It's now or never, let's do this." Aggie said with steel in her voice.

The girls took up Jimmy's train and he led them inside a row of bushes along a brick wall that ran along the gym. The doors were around the bend. They bustled through the hedge nearest the corner. Aggie's heart was racing, but nobody was there. They dashed to the gym door, took a breath and entered like favored guests of the King.

Jimmy and his wedding gown had the desired effect; a lot of kids stopped what they were doing and flocked to him. Even the band hesitated in the middle of a Green Day song. Before long, however, the novelty wore off; the straight kids went back to dancing, or making out, or whatever. A few of the gay kids stayed with Jimmy.

Aggie drifted away into a dark corner leaving Jimmy to his glory wondering why she even came. She was too chicken shit to approach stiff-necked Mr. Osborn. *What would I say? 'Hi, Mr. Osborn, if you don't give me that scholarship I'll cry?'* She had nothing but her desperation to bargain with.

At least she supported Jimmy and Mel. That was something. They were having a good time. Jimmy was busy socializing and Mel was dancing like a crack-head with a fem-girl. Aggie hated dancing. Whenever she tried dancing, she looked like a martial arts training video.

Alone as usual, she decided to check the tracking phone. The satellite said Billy's scooter was home. *Dumb-ass, nobody rides a scooter to the Winter Dance.* She closed the phone and scanned the room. The chaperones were spread around, Mrs. Preggey wasn't there and neither was Billy. *He's in the parking lot drinking beer.*

The band was pretty good and she was in the safe zone between chaperones, so she relaxed and kicked off her high heels. She hated heels. Laid back on the bleacher, she let the music wash over her. She had to figure out what to say to Osborn and forgot about Billy Barns.

After an hour the band took a break and a lot of dance-sweaty kids went outside to cool off. The air conditioning at the gym wasn't great. From her vantage point, she saw Jimmy heading out, and not far behind, Billy Barns and his Bandits followed. The chaperones stayed where they were. She picked up her pumps and ran barefoot for the door. Mel caught her there.

"Where're you going?"

"Billy is going after Jim-Jim," Aggie said. "I got to stop him."

"Dude, are you nuts? If you get into it with Meat-Head you're cooked."

"I won't touch him," Aggie said, "I'll just keep him off."

Aggie sprang away and left Mel standing at the door holding her pumps. It was a nice clear night with a cool salty Atlantic breeze. She stopped and searched. Groups of kids were standing on the grass or on the wide circular driveway; a few went across Flagler Avenue to smoke cigarettes. She coughed at the idea. It's hard to miss a big, white wedding gown, Jimmy was nowhere in sight.

A pair of kids walking fast caught her eye. They disappeared around the corner of the main building which was off-set from the gym. She bolted down the sidewalk with her bare, calloused feet slapping concrete.

She made the turn and ran right into Billy and his minions. Tom and Jay each had Jimmy by one arm. Jimmy's eyes flew open as she stopped short.

"They tricked me," Jimmy cried, "Jay said I was hot. He wanted me!"

Jimmy went limp like a deflating air bed and almost hit the ground.

"Let him go," Billy said. "It's Big Bird I want."

It's a trap!

Tom and Jay let go. Billy took a step forward and then the unexpected struck. Jimmy suddenly swung his purse full of quarters and smashed Billy square in the back of his head. Billy fell forward like bag of rocks and face-planted on the lawn. He raised his head slightly. Blood gushed. Tom screamed like a little girl. The posse scattered. Feet ran toward the scene.

"I showed that bastard," Jimmy said with his lips quivering. "Nobody tricks the trickster."

He had never hit anyone before.

"Jimmy, look what you've done," Aggie cried, "They'll kick you out! You need to graduate; it's your only hope."

Jimmy turned a horrid shade of gray. He also qualified for the scholarship and staying out of trouble really was his only chance of escaping his abusive mother. Jimmy collapsed on the lawn gasping for air. He looked down at himself and saw he was splattered with blood and wailed. "Look at me, I'm ruined."

Several kids and Mr. Albert the science teacher came running up. Billy rolled over on the grass; his face was a mass of blood. His nose was flattened and his lips were split. Billy raised his head, pointed at Aggie and laid back.

"Someone call 911." Mr. Albert yelled. Several cell phones dialed at once.

"Who did this?!" Mr. Albert demanded.

"I, I, I'm…" Jimmy stammered.

"I did it, Mr. Albert, Billy was going to hurt Jimmy." Aggie said calmly.

"No, it was Tom, I saw him do it!" Jimmy said in a squealing excited voice. He quickly hid the bloody purse behind his back. "They were fighting over who got to punch Aggie first."

"I did not!" Tom yelled. "Jay will back me up."

"You and Jay are kidnappers!" Jimmy screamed, "I'm telling what you did."

Mr. Albert was a kind old guy whom came from good nerd stock. He was in his last year of teaching. He rather liked the Geek Squad. He understood and sided with them more than the other teachers.

"I see that we don't have any reliable witnesses," Mr. Albert said, "Scientifically speaking, the data is flawed. All of you go home now before the police arrive and arrest you. We'll sort this out on Monday."

Mr. Albert stopped Jimmy and looked at the blood on Jimmy's gown. He then examined Aggie's feet and hands—no sign of a strike. Aggie wasn't the slightest bit wrinkled or soiled.

"Ms. Piper, come clean. You shouldn't lie for your friend."

"I did it, Mr. Albert, really. Jimmy had nothing to do with it."

"Well, if that's the case then, you both had better get going. Hear the sirens? The police won't be so easily fooled."

"Thank you, Mr. Albert. Come on Jimmy let's go."

Aggie pulled out her cell as they walked across the lawn toward a side street and away from the school. She hit Mel's hot key.

"Mel, we got to go. Where's the car, have him meet us on First Street. I'll explain later, Jimmy is in deep shit. We got to lose his dress."

A few minutes later, Jimmy in his boxer shorts, and Aggie shoeless, flagged the limo over. They had taken a bag out of an empty garbage can and stuffed the gown in it. Aggie and the bag squeezed in after Jimmy.

"Where to?" The driver said.

"Anywhere but here," Aggie said.

They drove off without a word. Jimmy's boy clothes were in the car so he got dressed while the limo did laps around the island; he had brought them just in case he got lucky. His pockets were tight stuffed with quarters which bulged impressively but Aggie didn't shoot any quips. He was dropped off first then she was taken home. She took Jimmy's dress over to Mark's place and tossed it a dumpster that smelled of rotten fish. *Nobody's diving in that dumpster.*

They couldn't pin the assault on him, too many conflicting stories. Aggie thought. Mr. Albert would see to that. Tom, Jay and the others committed a crime, too, so they won't talk. Billy didn't even know what hit him. Lack of facts, however, never stopped Mrs. Preggey before. *Nothing stops the Terminator.*

"I'm toast," Aggie said as she let herself in at home.

Mom and Dad were already in bed and it wasn't even ten o'clock. It sounded like their waterbed was making tidal waves. Sky and Po-boy were busy, sometimes the Goddess came through.

At least she had one less worry. Jimmy proved resourceful and brave. He'd be OK without her watching his back. She felt a little better knowing he could take care of himself. Once she was officially kicked out of school on Monday, he was on his own. She suddenly felt exhausted and stripped right in the living room, pulled the pins out of her hair and collapsed on the sofa and there she slept like dead meat.

TWENTY-ONE
Aggie and Jon Saturday

The birds started their pre-dawn chirping so Aggie got up and she never got up early, not on a Saturday. Thank Goddess her parents were still in bed. She crept into her room, grabbed some clothes, slipped them on in the living room and woke up the computer. It was running and Dad's icon was still in a UFO chat room. *Stupid conspiracy crap.* Disgusted, she shut down the computer; tracking didn't matter anymore. She slipped out the door and headed to Mark's place. Anything was better than hanging around waiting to tell her folks how she got kicked out of school. Even if Mark didn't have any work, she could hit the bag and maybe find someone to spar later.

She walked over to Mark's swatting a mosquito every second. Thankfully Mom wasn't a Buddhist, too. Aggie was free to kill bugs without hearing a bunch of crap about it. She didn't hate bugs but this morning, she hated everything. She slapped another mosquito a little too hard and it felt good.

"OK, Universe, this is why morning sucks!"

The sound of a boat motor gurgling and the smell of two-stroke engine smoke met her as she crossed the road onto Mark's property. He was always busy on the weekends. She found him at the dock casting off a fourteen-foot Starcraft rental boat stuffed with Yankees. Mark pushed the bow away with his foot; the renter gunned the boat and started down the lagoon way too fast.

"Slow! No wake," Mark yelled.

"That sucks," she said coming up, "Don't they know wave action hurts the eco system?"

"And, every boat moored along the lagoon," Mark said. "What brings you here so early? I thought you'd be out all night."

"I was wondering if you could use a hand today. I know I'm not supposed to come in until lunch, but…well I'm here."

Mark waved his hand around like a magician and said, "Pick a job, Jack's not coming in."

There were a dozen men milling around waiting at the boat launch, a few men were on the dock eyeing rental boats, others were at their own rented slips making ready to sail, some guys were in the parking lot getting gear out of their trunks and thankfully, not a squid in sight. The café wasn't open. Mark's hands were too full at this time of day and the morning guy didn't show.

"I could open the café," she suggested.

"Great idea: Make a big pot of coffee. Handle the grill, OK?"

"No problem."

That was all the answer Mark needed. Before she could turn around, he was off helping someone get their rental situated. She opened the café's storm shutters and went straight to work behind the counter. She got the coffee perking first, then fired the propane gill and set up the rest while the grill heated. She busied herself cleaning what the MIA guy failed to clean yesterday. A fisherman came over for coffee and an egg sandwich, then another. Aggie was suddenly busy. The breakfast shift wasn't half bad. Nobody was drinking beer or hitting on her. She liked it. Time passed quickly.

"I could get used to this," Aggie told the Universe between customers. But another thought struck her, "I better like it, this is my future."

She suddenly recalled her dilemma; kicked out of school and her parents didn't even know.

"I'm so doomed."

Her mood and stomach began to sour.

A stupid looking squid in long, black jeans, a black cowboy hat, cowboy boots, and a gray Navy t-shirt sashayed across the deck toward her. He had a big, stupid grin on his face. Not good for her mood. The dark-haired wiry boy sat on a bar stool, tipped his hat and grinned at her like a third grader anticipating candy. He wasn't dressed for fishing.

"What the hell you want?" Aggie snapped. The Navy guy retracted like a fiddler crab into its shell. "Why can't you Navy guys ever leave me alone? I'm a lesbow, all right." She immediately felt bad; she never disparaged lesbians. Her best friends were gay and maybe she herself was bisexual.

"Sorry Ma'am, I didn't think...well it's all the same to me. I like queer folks just fine...it's just that I'm here to see Captain Levine, is all."

"Captain who? Oh, you mean Mark. He's on the dock."

"Much obliged Ma'am," the cowboy tipped his hat and slid off the stool and started across the deck with boots clunking away. He was a little bow-legged. He stopped, turned and tipped his hat again. "Sorry Ma'am. I'll be working here a spell; I'm Colbert, Jon Colbert. Happy to make your acquaintance...Ma'am."

"Oh great, just what I need," Aggie said.

Colbert spun on his chunky heel, and strode away.

A little while later, things slowed down and Mark came over for coffee. Jon stood a few paces back roasting in the sun. Mark had his serious Yoda-is-going-to-fix-it look on his face.

"I hear you met my new employee," Mark said.

"Sorry, I didn't mean to be pissy, it's just..." Aggie felt tears welling up. She had to stop blabbering or she'd start crying. "I'm a little cranky."

"Don't worry, he's tough and he won't be here long. I'm helping out a friend of Jon's. I see you have problems on your mind."

"That's an understatement. I socked Billy last night. I'm getting kicked out Monday."

Mark didn't act surprised. He already knew she lived on a knife's edge. He had this weird way of knowing stuff before anyone else did. He always knew just what to say, too. Maybe the guy really was a Jedi Knight. His afro hair looked like a halo with the sun behind him.

Mark's forehead wrinkled in concern. His brown doe-eyes made her want to cry even more. If she said one more word about school, she'd bust open.

"Tell you what, Ags. "Work here full time, save money for college. I'll help anyway I can. My earlier offer stands; if you want to take my skiff out to see the Old Man you have my blessing."

"Thanks, I'll think about it." But she didn't need to think about it, the answer was no. She was in enough crap already; Sky would blow a gasket if Aggie took off to go see Grandpa Branford. And besides, open water scared the crap out of her.

"It is 01100 hours, the bar-stool warmers will be along soon, why don't you show Jon the kitchen; show him how we run the café, before it gets busy."

Mark waved Jon to come forward. Jon took his hat off and held it with two hands at his belt line. He could have just hung it on his big brass belt buckle. Mark grabbed his coffee and headed around back to the rental office. Technically, she wasn't allowed to serve beer but Mark didn't follow technicalities and she always worked the counter anyway. She should give Jon that job but she had a better idea.

"I'm not really a lesbian, you know," Aggie said. "But don't get any ideas. I'm saving myself for college."

Jon stiffened his back and replied. "Yes, Ma'am, read you loud and clear." He started to salute but stopped half-mast and put his arm down. His cheeks flushed red. She felt a little silly and embarrassed for him. He looked harmless enough and weirdly, kind of cute, too.

"Come on I'll show you the place."

She led him into the kitchen and started by showing him how to use the dish-washer—one job she didn't like at all. Maybe having a little help wasn't such a bad thing.

Mark was short on manpower and she was sick of scraping and painting rental boats anyway. Jon might come in handy. For once in her life she had seniority.

TWENTY-TWO

Karnack attack Saturday

Aloysius "Lud' Branford's stateroom on board the Contention was not only opulent by research vessel standards; it was opulent by any vessel's standards. Branford's stateroom was a juxtaposition of ultramodern furniture surrounded by and infused with rare, exceptive maritime artifacts. He had four Phoenician stone sounding weights, which were intricately carved serving as legs beneath his crystal map table. Two ceramic Greek amphorae were converted into lamps that were set on glass cube tables. Glass display cubes and glass shelves ringed the room and held remnants of treasure ships dating from three thousand B.C. until the last century. Branford's desk was a sixteenth century captain's map table brought up from a sunken British man-of-war. His paper weight was a barnacle encrusted matchlock pistol salvaged from one of Ho-Chi's fifteenth century junks that was lost in South American waters: it was a find no one was allowed to know about. *Too costly, rewriting history books upsets the public.*

Branford loved historic anomalies. Yet he didn't think much of the anomaly who stood before him now. Mr. Black and his tactics were years out of date.

"Our intelligence picked up your MAC on a webcam in Key West," Black said, "We traced it and know at least one viewer captured the imagine. Why are you flying near populated areas?"

"The NRO has no authority here. Talk to Sanderson, he's operations manager."

Black took a step nearer the desk. He picked up a limestone stalagmite that had formed around a piece of alien technology. It was twenty million years old.

"You aren't authorized to handle objects such as this," Black said. "You have enough off-limits material here to jail you for the rest of your life. Cooperate or I'll have you arrested."

Branford stood and knotted his thick fingers into two ham-fists. He placed these meat-hammers on the desk and leaned his fireplug body forward as if bracing for a gale. Black didn't react at all.

"You and whose army," Branford said hotly. "In case you didn't notice, international maritime law applies here. On this ship I am the law."

Branford stepped back and plowed a hand through his thick gray hair. He needed a breath before his temper got the better of him. He rounded his desk slowly. He didn't need to jeopardize his relationship with the Pentagon for this pissant. The NRO was switching gears of late, but they still had their insiders and influences. He took the object from Black's hand and gingerly put it back on its pedestal.

"Look, Black, I'm a team player, make no mistake. Tell me what you know and I'll tell you how I can help. Don't ask me to reveal classified information."

"We traced a transmission to a computer on your property."

"What property?" Branford said suspiciously.

"You have a facility on Geiger Key."

"That property's abandoned. I haven't seen it in years."

"You still pay taxes on it, sewer bill, and water bill. Someone's using it."

Branford had to think about it. He had properties, used and unused, all over the world. He had accountants and property managers taking care of them, keeping tabs. What did he do with that place? Then he remembered.

"My daughter and her husband live there. They aren't working for me. They don't work at all." He did not keep the bitterness out of his voice.

"Your daughter must be a spy."

"Sky Child, or whatever she calls herself these days, a spy?" Bradford had to laugh. Black didn't laugh with him.

"Mr. Black my hippie-dippy daughter is about as far away from spy-craft as anyone can get."

"That's not what my intel says." Black countered. "Apparently Mr. Piper is a UFO researcher. Did you toss him a bone, tip him off? Key West isn't part of the test flight parameters."

Branford didn't like being threatened or accused of treason. This was more insult than his Irish would stand. He knew about the accident; it wasn't his fault and it was none of Black's business anyway.

"Get in your goddamn helicopter and get the hell off my ship! Before I have security toss you over the side!"

Black didn't move. When Branford yells, people jump. Black didn't even flinch. Rather, he took a cell phone from his pants pocket, pointed it at Branford and pushed a button. A little orb of light shot out and hovered over Branford's head. There was a flash of yellow light and Bradford was instantly inside a nearly clear enclosure. It was like a giant soap bubble. Black touched his ear.

"Karnack, I have him and a bonus. His daughter, or his son-in-law, was the one…Yes Sir, handy for cooperation; I'll have them picked up."

Black took the intercom mic from Branford's desk, held it to his mouth and put his cell phone against his neck.

"Attention, this is Branford," Black said in a perfect rendition of Branford's voice. "Security, make ready for a live rendition pick up. We strike tomorrow when ready. Mr. Black is in charge. Communications blackout until I give orders. Secure decks. I don't want any disturbances up here."

Black folded his phone closed. Branford could see and hear, but he could not talk or move. From the corner of his eye he saw Black walk toward the front door. Branford heard the glass sliding door open and close. He heard the gears spin for the forward retractable storm shutters. Mahogany rattans rolled down inside their tracks. The gantry way's windows were still unshielded, but no one was authorized to use that catwalk. The room had light but his hope went dark. *How did Black get a force bubble?*

He couldn't see out, nor could anyone see in and there was nothing he could do about it.

It was going to be a long night.

TWENTY-THREE

Sunday morning

Aggie got up earlier than needed for her second day of full-time work. Wild roosters woke her, but this time, for once, she didn't mind. She didn't tell Mom and Dad about school last night. Dad was too pumped up about some stupid UFO crap and Mom was too distracted to listen. Any excuse was a good one not to talk about it anyway. She had no clue what they'd do after she told them, but it couldn't be good.

She dressed in twilight; a bikini, oversized Grateful Dead T-shirt and a pair of old cut-off jeans. She felt just as faded and twice as blue. She never knew what was in store for her at work so she grabbed her backpack: Extra clothes, her workout gear, and a few books were always loaded. She stuffed Mel's phone in her pocket, too. *I'll tell them when I get home tonight…if I get home.*

Her first day at Mark's started out fun but didn't stay that way. That dopey Navy guy, Jon, followed her around like a lost dog. She couldn't figure out whether he was a Navy brat or a squid or just someone the tide washed in. He looked about her age but he wasn't like school kids, and he wasn't like the Navy guys that hung around Mark's. He was quiet, alert, and respectful and kind of reminded her of Dad; lanky, dark haired, funny accent. Only, Jon spoke in a different style. Dad's accent was way slower, weirder and louder.

Jon only got pissy once all day when a half-drunk Navy guy started on her. The only other pushy thing the Cowboy did was insist on using Mark's computer. Dumb request; Mark didn't have internet but Jon wanted to mess with it anyway.

Aggie grabbed a hairbrush off her dresser and headed for the bathroom and crept through the kitchen without putting on the light. The front room was dark so she felt her way along the wall to the bathroom door. She heard Po-boy snoring in his bedroom. He never booked on Sundays. Kind of dumb, Sunday was the best charter day for tourists. She turned the bathroom doorknob and the lamp next to Sky's chair clicked on.

"Agatha, you're up early."

Aggie was afraid to look but she did anyway. Sky was sitting cross-legged on the floor naked in the lotus position.

"Sunday, duh…morning meditation," Aggie said slapping her forehead. "Work Mom, Mark is really busy this weekend."

"I know, Honey, you don't have to hide it. Haven't I taught you; honesty leads to the higher plane?"

"What are you talking about?" Aggie's voice was shrill, "Mark needs extra help, that's all, OK, OK." She smacked herself on the forehead a second time. Everyone knows that whenever her voice goes up in pitch, she wasn't straight. Aggie sucked at lying.

"No, Mark doesn't need additional help; Mark desires helping others. It's his way of making up for the atrocities he committed as a Seal. He's putting positive energy back into the Universe."

She ignored Sky's comment and cut to the facts. "So, you know…I got kicked out of school. Mark didn't rat me out, right?"

"Of course not, Honey. Mark has honor and honesty confused." Sky stood up like a graceful scissor drawing closed, took the dress off her chair, reached up and dropped the tie-dyed frock over her head. "Mrs. Preggey called me yesterday and I'm fine with it."

"What?!"

"Whatever happened at the dance is at issue. Mrs. Preggey said if you come to school on Monday, and tell the truth, she'll let you stay. If not, you'll be expelled."

"No way Mom, I can't."

The Terminator will milk me for info and spit me out, Mom is so dumb.

"I'm fine with that. You have enough credits to graduate. Why waste time in that mind-fuck institution? There is so much more to learn in life not found in propagandized schools. I'm sure this is a jump forward."

"Jesus Christ Mom!"

"That poor man has nothing to do with this."

"Yeah I know; it's the will of the Goddess." Aggie said with an intentional sarcasm laden voice.

Aggie clenched her hairbrush so hard she squeezed the blood out of her fingertips. What was the use of explaining the facts of life on Earth to a woman whose head was in the clouds? And, Po-boy; his head wasn't even in this Universe.

"I'm going to work, Sky. See you later, if you can manage not to float up into the ozone layer."

"Daughter, you have a fire in you, direct it positively before it burns you up."

"Yeah right, I guess you haven't noticed my life's a fire extinguisher."

She grabbed her backpack, stormed across the room, and kicked open the screen door. Aggie looked over her shoulder on the porch and Sky called, "Aren't you going to brush your teeth?" Aggie stopped in her tracks.

"No, the tooth-rot fairy is providing funding for my college education."

Aggie threw her backpack and startled the chickens that were pecking at the sand but they didn't run. She kicked at them as she marched toward the lane and they scurried under Sky's hemp plants. *Yeah, she even makes her own rope.* She wished Mom would stop feeding the damned wild chickens and start serving them for dinner. She was so sick of fish, home-grown veggies and everything else in her life.

She arrived at Mark's and he was already busy helping a renter get under-way. Mark was boarding a small party onto one of the fiberglass tri-hull boats, a very stable platform for amateurs. It had a new Bimini top, too. *Sun-fried tourists were bad for business.* Mark kept all his boats ship shape. *Maybe I will take one out to Grandpa. That would rattle Sky!* Of course, that wasn't happening.

She noticed that dopey guy Jon was already at work further down the dock washing out an aluminum flat bottom from yesterday's rental; proof positive the Universe really hated her.

"Just what I need," Aggie said staring at Jon with her hands set on boney hips, "another wild rooster but this one's got an annoying twang."

Mark came up onto the higher deck. "Look at the bright side, Ags, its Sunday."

He was right; Sundays brought serious fisherman, especially the boat owners that rented slips. They were self-sufficient. It would be an easy day and the locals were good tippers. The Navy guys were all hung over like everyone else on the Key. Sundays were mellow so she wouldn't need to handle drunks.

Best of all, Sunday afternoon Mark closed early and ran his dojo. It was sparing day. The Navy guys that trained here were lesser horn-dogs but they were still sailors, so at least when they hit on her, she got to hit back for real. She needed to kick someone's ass for sheer relief. Who better than a Navy guy?

"Open the café, Mark?"

"Yes please, Jon and I could use some coffee."

Aggie stood tall, thrust her little boobs out and stuck her tongue out of the side of her face, and made a silly, fake salute. "Aye, aye skipper. Should I swab the poop deck, or just poop on the deck?"

"Wise ass," Mark said with a smile. "Remind me later to tell you about my idea for your college fund. I have you covered."

"A-vast! Don't pull me peg-leg, pirate walkin's harrrrd enough. Ahoy!"

Aggie swung her leg weirdly and proceeded with a stiff-legged limp. She opened the storm shutters, put on the coffee and lit the propane grill. She was busy at first but things slowed down by nine a.m. Without much to do, she grabbed a book from her backpack and sat at an umbrella table.

Normally, she didn't pay much attention to helicopters but this one was close. Suddenly the air was charged with volcanic thumping. Before she could put down the book, her table blew over. Another sleek, black helicopter shot past very low like an angry storm god. Mark came running up as she found her feet. Three choppers were hovering over her house. Men in black uniforms were repelling down.

"Jesus Christ!" Aggie yelped. "DEA! Mom's pot plants. She grows more than her license allows!"

"No," Mark said, "They're black-ops."

Mark's office was on the back side of the café. He flung open the door, pushed the desk away and lifted off a floor hatch. Aggie stood in the door mesmerized. Mark pulled two nasty looking military rifles out of the floor. Jon crashed into her and spun her out of the doorway. Mark tossed Jon a rifle and both men bolted.

Mark yelled, "Don't shoot the Huey—civilians. Aggie stay here!"

She instantly realized the implications. She turned and followed. Jon and Mark were running but they were gun-heavy. She kicked off her flip-flops and ran flat out leaving them behind. They were a hundred yards back when she pulled up short next to the old van Dad used for storage. Gunfire chattered, the sand around her spiked up. Fear cemented her feet like the day of the stingray.

Frozen there, the memory she couldn't face flooded in.

She was a little girl again out boating with Mommy and Daddy. They had beached, she was playing in shallow water just off the edge of the sandbar. Daddy's boat was far away. A stingray barb had just skewered her foot. She saw her blood in the water. Mom was screaming. A bull shark was wiggling closer and closer over the reef, smaller black tip sharks where all around her. She could not move, or even scream. Daddy was on the boat looking at the sky, a big silver disk. I want Daddy, why won't you save me, she cried. The bull's jaws were inches away when Sky yanked her backward and onto the sandbar.

Someone was yelling, "Get down, get down, move, move," But she could not. Aggie was a statue.

Mark ran up and stopped short. Fire strafed the ground between them. Mark stiff armed Aggie and knocked her backwards, she twisted away and fell behind the old rusted van. Mark had snapped her out of it. Recovering, she crawled over to the corner of the van to see.

Mark and Jon were crouched on the edge of the house plot's clearing near the garden. The big chopper with a 'B' painted on its side took off low and fast. The others followed. Mark was shooting, Jon too. The report of gunfire made her ears ring.

"No," she screamed, "my parents, you'll hit them."

Mark kept firing. He flipped the magazine and continued firing until all three choppers were far off shore. She ran forward toward the little beach and peered through a hole in the foliage at the water. Three machines skimmed the surface until they became dragonflies over a distant pound. Then, like magic, the dots just disappeared while heading southwest. It all happened too fast. Aggie's head was spinning.

Jon secured his weapon with a muffled clack. Mark did the same.

Aggie's hair and emotions were a sea of tangles. The smell of gunpowder was smelling salts, ignoring the fact that Mark had just knocked her down; she shouted to him, "Who were they?"

Mark gritted his teeth. He wasn't going to tell.

"Branford Industries," Jon said. "Huey was, anyway. Never seen Cobras like them."

"NO WAY!" Aggie was screaming; she never did that. "WHERE'S MOM?"

She charged to the house; the front door was busted off the hinges. She ran all around inside. Sky and Po-boy were gone. Sky's favorite glass bong was smashed on the floor, her homegrown stash was still inside its ceramic box. *If this wasn't a drug bust, what the hell was it?* She stood in her ruined living room blinking until Mark came up and put his hand on her shoulder.

"Why'd Grandpa do that?" She said.

"It wasn't Branford, Ags, Branford doesn't have cloaking, if it was government, they would have done it different, taken the computer for sure."

"I don't get it."

"Come on Ags let's go, I got calls to make. Best you stay away from here until we figure this out."

She moved to the yard like a zombie. She stopped, turned 180 and stared out into the soft, blue-green Gulf with nothing but revenge in her heart. The helicopters were long gone. The van was full of bullet holes. A dead chicken lay near the garden. She should have been scared, or upset, or something girly, but all she was, was mad, really, really mad.

"Dad's right, never trust The Man," she exclaimed. She picked up a conch shell and whipped it into the mangroves.

Mark pulled her close, his fishy smelling finger pressed against her lips. He whispered, "Quiet Ags, they might have ears on us. Let's go back to my place and figure this out."

Mark popped another clip into his gun and signaled Jon to alert. The two spread out and started toward the marina, with their heads swinging back and forth like lighthouse beacons.

She walked in between them and slightly behind with thoughts bouncing around. Her brain felt like a ping-pong ball on crack. Whoever did this, she'd kill them with her bare hands.

She didn't know what to do, call the cops? *Yeah, right, maybe after I tear out all Sky's pot plants, she's only allowed to grow a few.* What good is reporting it if they rescued Mom just to put her in jail? And look at Mark, he's a real killer. Po-boy would be appalled. And Jon, what is he some kind of secret spy guy? He's the same kind of guy that snatched Mom and Dad. Just when she starts warming up to the Cowboy, he turns out to be a dick. *Just my crappy luck!*

"I'm calling the cops," Aggie said, "Before I do something stupid."

"No, no cops," Mark said evenly.

Mark lowered his gun once back on his property and led them straight to a private room next to his office behind the café. He spun the combination lock. She had never seen the inside before. She thought it was a storage area.

The place was hot and dusty. Mark clicked on the air conditioning and lights, on one switch, before pulling an old bed sheet off a wall. There were half a dozen security camera monitors there and a laptop on a small, cheap desk. He opened the computer's lid, quickly clicked through some software she didn't recognize.

"We're good. No ears on us. We can talk freely." Mark said.

"Sanderson tells it, you're retired," Jon said.

"I am. However, my former line of work requires I watch my back...and everything else."

Jon held up a small Wi-fi detector. "I'm not reading a dog-gone thing."

"Hardwire," Mark said, "They never check for old-style technology. Let's see what we have."

Mark rolled back the camera views and they watched the choppers all over again. Aggie put her brain into study mode. She wasn't going to miss anything. Mark had cameras everywhere. She had never noticed them before. She mentally kicked herself in the ass.

Po-boy always ranted about the Police State and now she wished she had listened. But who listens to their dopy parents? *Geeks like Mel, that's who.*

Mark zoomed in. Apparently, one of his cameras was motion-decisive and it followed the choppers.

Mark said, "Not regular military or police, the operation is too sophisticated. I doubt they're Seal, likely private mercenaries. Their procedures weren't The Company kind. Such Cobras are defiantly Special-Ops quality hardware. Sorry, Aggie, that Huey was Branford Industries', no doubt."

The details felt like swallowing a live crab; her inside wanted to crawl outside. Her mind wanted to flee from the evidence, but she wasn't wired that way. She lowered herself slowly into a dirty, orange fiberglass chair pushing hair into her eyes.

"Grandpa's responsible. How could he do this to me?"

"It's not necessarily him. Contract mercenaries are compartmentalized. One unit doesn't know what the other does. Branford can't know how his clients use rented killers. My guess, the Old Man has nothing to do with this. Going to him is your safest bet; they might come back, go after you, pros don't leave loose ends."

"Why'd they take my parents!?" She said springing out of the chair with a puff of dust.

"Somebody's squeezing Branford, it's leverage. Branford doesn't know who's subverting his hardware, but I'll bet he's about to find out. Chances are he doesn't know they were kidnapped...yet. Mark took Aggie's hands in his, "It's time you talk to him. I'll work on it from this end. Forget the cops, it's too dangerous. Sailing out is your best option."

"I don't know...I can't, I just can't."

Jon suddenly blew out a lung full of air and slumped. His eyes turned downcast. His boots scuffed the sand speckled wood plank floor.

There was more to Jon than he said, Aggie realized. The way he ran down her road firing that high-tech gun like an expert. But, now, guilt seemed to wash over him. He wasn't like a professional.

She looked square at Jon with a pissed-off expression. "You know something, don't you?"

"Careful, Sailor," Mark said sternly, "Loose lips sink ships. Don't get us hung for treason."

"Goddess save me, I don't give a crap, Jon, tell me what's going on!" Aggie cried.

"Oh, hell," Jon started, "All my fault…I…I…" He bet lower and took his hat in hand.

"Report Sailor," Mark barked.

She had never seen Mark act so military, so tight-assed. It was really weird.

"Hell, I pilot this here remote aircraft prototype for Sanderson. It's secret; I can't tell you'll nothing about it. But I flew it past this here webcam, up yonder, accidental like. Security pinged someone over this way recording it. Sanderson sent me over to find out who saw. He says it wasn't Mark, the only other computer round here is yours, Ma'am."

"I don't fish webcams," Aggie said. "I don't use it like that." A thought crossed her mind. "Wait, Dad uses the computer. He's all up into UFOs and junk…it was him. He was way excited about something. Oh crap!"

"Branford develops drones, among other things," Mark mused, rubbing his chin. "Scuttlebutt has it that the Admiral and Old Man Branford are involved. Did Sanderson order this strike, Colbert?"

"Naw, I don't reckon so, Sir. The Admiral's away. He called me last night: Sounded scratchy like a sat-phone. He must be halfway around the world."

"Let me guess," Mark said, "Your drone was built by Branford?"

Jon's shoulders dropped even lower; his easy cowboy stance was a tortured statute. "Can't tell you, hell, I'm not supposed to know, ah, bullshit."

"There's only one way to solve this," Mark said. You need to go to Branford's ship. They'll have me on face recognition so extreme prejudice is required. I need time to plan. I can't get near classified operations any more. Ags, you can help, he'll talk to you. You're blood. Go to him, warn him while I move. He'll protect you. But, first…I can't say anymore."

Mark kept brainstorming in whispers with Jon but Aggie wasn't listening. She slunk back into the dusty pizza parlor chair. She knew the real answer. She had to go but she was afraid. It wasn't Mark's problem, it was hers. No way would she drag her friends into this; the dance disaster was still fresh and she wasn't making that mistake again, but she had to talk to someone.

Thinking about the sea made her stomach hurt. Going out on the water totally freaked her out, she just couldn't do it. She hadn't been out since the stingray. She just couldn't move then, not even to save her life and she felt exactly that way now and for the second time in one day. If Dad hadn't run his boat up on that sandbar…that bull almost shredded her like chum. Daddy moved like a slug, that thing in the sky. Boats, open water, sharks, guns, government, all of it filled her with dread.

I can't let it beat me, who am I kidding, I'm toast.

She determined not to let fear glue her down again. She had to move, somewhere, anywhere, before the glue took hold. *Move Aggie, just do something.*

"I need to chill. I can't go home. I won't stay here. I'm going to Mel's."

She got up. Jon moved to stop her, but Mark got between them. "Let her go Jon. She'll work it out, she always does. Let's get to work. Aggie, don't let the cops see you, avoid SUVs and any blacked-out car."

She pushed past Jon and went to the tool shed. Ignoring the fact that her moped license was in her backpack behind the counter, she proceeded anyway. The Vespa was still where she had left it days ago. She kicked it to life and drove off. As she passed the Navy base entrance, she flipped the guards at the gate the bird. She had had her fill of all things Navy.

TWENTY-FOUR
Karnack on the move

Branford counted time in his head. Black's energy field had suspended him facing an antique ship's clock that didn't work. Overnight, he redirected a boiling temper, which was the trick that made him rich, and channeled his focus on thoughts of action and revenge.

The sound of his helicopter brought with it a realization; he would see his estranged daughter. The last time he saw Charlotte they had fought bitterly. Anger for his nut-job daughter and son-in-law was long forgotten, but he was too proud to reach out. This failure gave way to the other mistake; he had not seen Agatha in fourteen years. And now, his only granddaughter was in serious peril and she did not even know why. *My fault!* He had another starling idea which sank his heart further. He loved Charlotte, Agatha and even Charlotte's no-account husband. *If anything happens to them...*Bloody revenge redoubled in his mind. He was a warrior long before he was a businessman.

Mr. Black entered the stateroom. The two security men with Black, *my men,* were dragging Charlotte and her Creole husband by the armpits. Charlotte and Sonny appeared drugged; they flopped like dead fish.

Charlotte suddenly pulled her arm away from the Spec. She wasn't drugged. Branford had seen her non-violet resistance before. It once seemed like a regular feature on the Six O'clock News. 'Famous industrialist's daughter arrested again.'

"Father!" Charlotte cried, "Why didn't you just ask us to come? Why so rough!"

Branford couldn't answer. His eyes opened wider, he rolled them toward Mr. Black. That was all he could do.

"I see you are angry," Mr. Black said. "In this suspension field, the more you resist, especially with anger, the greater it holds. Relax, will you? We need to talk."

Relax was the last thing Branford wanted to do. He wished looks could kill. Charlotte and Sonny took notice of his predicament with dumbfounded fascination. Black nodded and a soldier of fortune placed the Pipers at the center of the stateroom. Black did something with his phone and the Pipers became encased in another force shield. It twinkled like a backlit glass box. The captives moved around, tried the clear walls like mimes playing invisible box. Sonny shouted. The sound was muffled.

Black walked over to Branford and lowered his dark glasses. They met eye to eye. Black's eyes were that of a machine, like the alien androids.

"Mr. Branford I will release you. But first, the conditions. I need your cooperation. To ensure it, I'll hold your daughter's life in the balance. You see a person's Life Force is a commodity of galactic trade. Without it, interstellar travel would not be possible. Your relatives are in an extraction chamber. I've set it for slow, safe extraction. If I don't stop the process in time, well, her soul will be no more. Her physical life will be forfeit. Think about it for a moment."

Black put his hands behind his back and paced the room between Branford's soap bubble and Charlotte's magic crystal box.

So that's what instigates the quantum drive! My hunch was right. Years of research in the wrong direction! Magnetic drive is a toy next to this. My God, the profit potential of interstellar travel is unlimited. The wheels of fortune turned in Branford's head; the clockworks of the Universe were exposed. He would find the inroad. More important problems were at hand, how to save himself and his family? He had to play along until opportunity struck. He got his anger under control and found he could move his hand; he tested his mouth opening and closing it.

"You see," Mr. Black continued. "My…er…partner…and I need to procure materials, a small Soul Harvest if you will. Cooperate and you'll be well paid, your daughter, nobody, comes to harm."

"Is…this…a trick…what about the…GTO," Branford said against the force field.

"I work for an independent contractor. The GTO is not the only game in this part of the galaxy. It's simple, help us and get rich, save your family; refuse and I'll use control bracelets on you and the ship's crew, as I've already done with your mercenaries."

This isn't adding up. Nothing's that simple.

"Why don't you … do … that … why use me?"

"Control bracelets limit free will. Really, you know that. Your bio team examined the MAC pilots that my recon teams supplied. Intelligent biological machines require controls. I need you to think on your feet, better to protect this operation. My … partner … needs a local entrepreneur for future business."

Doesn't matter what he says, it's all a lie.

Branford was able to turn his head now; he looked fully at his daughter, who looked back at him with a horrified expression. She shook her head no. Sonny's eyes were attentive. She and Sonny heard everything.

Branford remembered that when Charlotte was little, they played team board games against the neighbors. He had told her that when he was bluffing, he'd let her know with a wink of an eye. It was a secret between them. He hoped she remembered his tell. He winked. Branford needed freedom to work the angles. She winked back.

Turning to face Black, he examined the trader in detail. Black had an ear-phone in one ear and a thin wrist bracelet on his left wrist. *Control, ha.* Black wasn't acting on his own accord.

"It's a deal," Branford said. His body was almost completely free. "What do you need from me?"

"Move this ship, a new base of operations. We'll make for a small island; I have the coordinates. Once underway, we must go carefully. Karnack will cloak this ship, but we'll be exposed at sea level. We don't want the Navy or anyone else spotting our movements."

"Takes time to make ready to sail," Branford said.

"Have non-essential crew take the launch before Karnack arrives. The fewer people see his shuttle, the better. Time is short."

"Fine, whatever you want." *This is my opportunity.*

Black pulled the phone out of his pocket and pushed a key.

Suddenly, Branford was completely free. He'd take theses bastards out if it's the last thing he did on Earth. First things first; he cobbled a hasty plan together. With Black's phone he'd free Charlotte. But he had to wait, security was on alert. *I can't take them alone.* Branford went out on deck to make arrangements. He quietly instructed his First Mate to take the launch and run wide, call the mainland, and then follow the ship. Black didn't know the launch was loaded for bear; full galley, small arms and a handheld rocket launcher. *Illegal as hell, even for me.* His men would board the Contention late night; the man who shot Black dead was in for a monster bonus.

Twenty minutes later the launch was steaming away. At three hundred yards off the port side a blue ray of light beamed from the only cloud in the sky and struck the boat. The launch was instantly a blaze — flaming men were jumping overboard. Within minutes the launch was listing badly.

Branford was on the bow watching. He ran down the flight deck and yanked a com-phone off the bulkhead below the pilot house.

"Turn to port one quarter, the launch is burning, prepare to pick up survivors!" His words boomed over the entire com system. But the ship didn't heel. "Turn to port, goddamn you!"

"Can't Sir, the guards won't let me." The pilot reported with a trembling voice.

Black came up behind Branford and put a hand on his shoulder. The Captain spun about. The com-phone was on a wire, not a good weapon. He balled his meaty fists ready to kill.

Black raised one hand and said, "We have it under control, watch."

The dark cloud descended lower as if under intelligent control. The cloud's bottom was metallic! A thin red beam of light shot out and jumped from one survivor to another. Each man was vaporized in turn. Branford staggered like a drunken man. He leaned on the bulkhead for support with fear replacing fury.

"Why, why did you do that, goddamn you?"

"Waste of Life Force, I know," Black said without moving his lips, "There will be plenty more once the chain reaction starts."

It was not Black's voice; someone or something spoke through him. Black was not a partner; he was a puppet.

"Ah, Captain, you see we can't have any deterrents to our purpose. The GTO, or perhaps your government, will be on our tail soon and we don't want them to know our business, do we? Time is not our friend. Move the ship. Mr. Black, please explain our destination to the Captain."

Black shivered and put one hand to the microphone hidden in his ear as if he were in pain. The moment passed and Black spoke in his own voice.

"There's an island southeast of our position, isolated with a small population, a mix of scientists and their families. It meets our requirements. It's close, but to avoid detection, we must circumvent the shipping lanes. I have the coordinates."

"We'll cross the lanes, it's unavoidable."

"Proceed carefully, or she will die."

The cloud moved directly over the ship. It settled seventy-five feet above the fight deck. Bumping the coning tower's antenna array, it smashed the tallest protrusions, and the radar dish was destroyed. Navigation would be difficult. Branford cursed himself; he had an antique astrolabe and other vintage navigation equipment on board and he knew how to use them.

Branford squinted at the aircraft above, he had no doubts; it was a spaceship, cigar class about half as long as his eight-hundred-foot vessel. It sure as hell wasn't an Earth craft. With it sitting over the communications tower there wouldn't be any radio signals getting out, no GPS getting in, nothing for the Feds to track him with.

"Mr. Black." The voice came over the com this time. "I will protect us from an air...what is the word...aerial view; stay clear of any small craft. Don't forget, we are visible at sea level."

One consolation, the radar tower won't help. Small vessels can approach undetected. No radar slows progress. Gives me time to plan and act. Stupid bastards.

"Understand Mr. Black?" Karnack's voice filled the ship.

"Yes Master," Black replied as he touched a thin silver belt on his waist. Two guards came running and stopped before him. The guard's eyes were pools of deep, sunless water. Branford's hopes of escape sank into those dark, hopeless pools. *I'll find a way, I must.* Each man grabbed one of Branford's arms and together they led him to the bridge.

TWENTY-FIVE

Aggie on the run

Aggie pulled up to Mel's side gate and phoned. The last thing Aggie wanted to hear was Mrs. Van Ness bitching. Of course, by now, it was out. She's kicked out of school. In Key West secrets were strawberries on a sun-beat sidewalk fruit stand: No shelf life at all.

Mel opened the wrought iron gate remotely. Aggie crept to the pool house and found Mel at the door still in her black footie pajamas that were covered in white skulls and spider webs. Despite trauma, Aggie couldn't resist a wisecrack.

"Only you can find Goth PJs. Where'd you get them, We-Be-Dead?"

Mel was more pale than usual. She stepped out, looked to the right and left, stepped back inside and said, "Shut up; get in here." Mel grabbed her by the arm and jerked her thought the door. "You got to see this."

Mel slammed the door and locked it. She went straight to her computer and motioned Aggie to look.

"I tapped into your computer; I wanted to see if you were up. Naturally I activated the webcam…look at this," Mel said.

She played the recording. The computer was situated on the front wall so it captured the back of several men wearing black uniforms, helmets, and black Kevlar vests right after they busted down the door and rushed in. They had assault rifles on point. The video didn't show Mom and Dad, someone had knocked over the computer seconds after entry. Aggie felt sick and totally freaked out all over again.

"Fricking DEA," Mel said. "Good you weren't home when the Nazis arrived."

"It's not DEA," Aggie whispered. "It's Grandpa."

"Dude, no frickin way!"

"Way." Aggie said.

She told Mel the whole thing—everything she knew—even Jon's story about some mystery aircraft. Before the end of her tale, Mel had turned a whiter shade of gray. Aggie worried she'd faint. But then Mel's wheels started turning and her cheeks flushed pink; a familiar sign. Mel still had enough blood inside her skinny-ass body to keep her brain running. Mel started clicking away and hammering on the keyboard.

Mel brought up an image on one of her screens; she had three of six monitors going. An image of a flying disk appeared. It had a weird wobble. It hung there a split second, flipped half up and took off. The background was wide open, just empty beach, water and sky.

"Where'd you get that!?" Aggie choked; fears were exploding in her throat.

"Off your computer," Mel said. "I back up your files on my server, duh. I upload your system every fifteen minutes."

"Holy crap, they'll find you, they'll come and—."

"No way, Dude. They can't. I'm on my Dad's secure link, can't be hacked. Dad sells his stuff to the government. He doesn't tell them everything. Let's take a closer look."

Mel played back the recording, slowed it down and blew it up. When the craft flipped, 'Branford Industries' was written in the margin between the shiny top and black-blue bottom.

"That explains all his weirdness," Aggie said, "Dad didn't want me to know about Grandpa. What's he up too? Bring up Earth-Watch. This confirms it. I know where the choppers went."

Aggie knew Grandpa's research ship was off the Federal Reserve. It took no time to find it. The ship was moving. There were two black helicopters on the fantail. The big one was in the drink and sinking fast.

They must have pushed it over the side. The ship was like a small aircraft carrier but it only had room for two copters. Suddenly, the image pixilated and the ship vanished.

Mel tried the public satellites. The ship didn't show up at all. "Of course, it's secret, they'd edit it out." Aggie said. Mel switched back to military's Earth-Watch and zoomed in. Google and the others didn't have nearly as good a resolution.

"Weird. Something is masking it. It's not internal on Earth-Watch. Dad's company built it. I'm relaying through Dad's computer now; he has direct access."

"You hacked your Dad's computer?" Aggie was incredulous. The guy was un-hackable. Mr. Van Ness's telecommunications company created the world's tightest security systems.

"Of course, I didn't hack his PC. I'm good, not that good. Dude, I stole his password."

"Daddy's little girl strikes again. Low-tech solution, I like it."

"No visual on that boat, for sure." Mel said.

"I'll never find them now." Aggie's heart sunk. Even if she had the guts to sail out, there was no way to find them. She wished to the Goddess that she had taken Mark's boat when she had the chance. "She who hesitates gets messed-over. It's moving. I'll never find them now."

Mel looked at Aggie perplexed and said, "Oh ye of little geekery, I'll just track it."

"How?"

Mel rolled her eyes. "Dude, I thought you got 'A's' in science. It's a boat, not a ghost. It makes a wake, heat, gas exhaust, and other signatures."

Aggie slapped herself in the forehead. She also jarred an idea loose.

"Mel, can you set up a tracking program and bounce the location into my cell's GPS?"

"Do drunken tourists piss on the beach?"

Mel went to work. It didn't take long to set it up. Aggie checked her phone. It worked fine. The ship was only making a few knots, moving really slow, heading southeast and closer to shore.

She could run out to Grandpa's ship after all. But she had a lot of doubts, a lot of questions. Would Grandpa even let her board? Did he even know what his guys were up too? Did he have anything to do with it? Would he help? Mark didn't even know.

Whatever the answers, she had to figure it out on her own. Aggie suddenly realized she wasn't getting into any boat; not blind, too sketchy. Fears reared up like the mystical hydra. Cut one down, another popped out. She hated herself. She knew how to handle watercraft, no excuse. Before the accident, she was a confident sailfish racer. That was then, what about now? What was stopping her? She knew how to do it; she just couldn't bring herself to do it. Her heart felt like lead.

"I should take Mark's boat," Aggie said miserably.

"Dude, you hate boats."

"I know. I, I, I can't. Need to think, clear my head."

"You'll need to borrow Jimmy's balls," Mel said, not joking.

Aggie slunk over to the daybed and flopped down on it. Her phone rang, it was Mark. Why did she give him her number—oh yeah, work. She ignored it. She pushed tangled hair into her face and closed her eyes. Her hair was a royal mess so her bangs hung in clumps. She sat up, crossed her legs Indian style and started doing Sky's breathing technique.

"I need focus." Aggie whispered.

"I'm plotting its trajectory. They'll pass right off Geiger if they keep their heading." Melissa said. "Plenty of time to catch up at their rate of speed it...What am I saying, let's call the cops."

"No, no cops," Aggie said.

"Why?"

Aggie didn't respond. She was busy beating back the debate raging inside her head.

Think Aggie, Think! But nothing came. Sky's words fell in, 'when the left brain fails release the right side.' There were storms on every horizon and her boat was sinking fast. The last thing she needed was an emotional flood sweeping her downriver. Nothing left to do but start bailing.

'Fear and panic are the mind killers,' washed in from the either. One by one she faced and put away concerns. What she would do with the rest of her life melted into nothingness. Mom and Dad were in danger, that's what mattered.

'Fear and panic are the mind killers,' she chanted in her mind. The torrent of emotion that assaulted her must be cast off, so she drifted it away like so much flotsam as she chanted the mantra Mom taught her to combat the terror memory of the shark. The Universe opened its arms and she fell into its embrace.

"I have to save them, I'll go."

"Dude, call the cops, shit this is not a joke. You can't go. Bad decision."

Mel was right about most things but this wasn't one of them.

TWENTY-SIX

Sanderson and the GTO

S anderson was being observed, always the case on alien property. He put on a hard-nosed face and entered the M-Class MAC. Flying remotes was one thing but riding in an unmanned version of the MAC was quite another, especially since it wasn't his and the pilot wasn't human. Sanderson had seen all kinds of conflicts. He watched his best men die, saw their blood and guts up close, felt no fear, never unnerved. But this… this was different.

Snow White's dwarf with an over-sized head showed him to a seat. This android was supposed to look more human for human contacts. They weren't even close. Its skin wasn't bright white like the early models. It wore a NASA jumpsuit, not convincing.

The creature put a three-fingered hand on Sanderson's elbow and he shook it off. Sanderson didn't need or want the robot's help: All the passenger seats were situated around a central hub and only two were designed for Earth humans. The little gray abomination motioned him to sit and then it departed without a word.

"Thank you," Sanderson said then mentally kicked himself in the ass for speaking to it. Extraterrestrial Biological Units didn't care. Communication was pointless, EBUs never answered. It bugged him. Most disconcerting; the pilot was a machine, yes, but alive. It was just a wired-up soulless pile of cow parts. The very idea caused his skin to crawl. His own emotional reaction angered him.

"Goddamn it, can't you people fly me up with a real pilot?"

"Sorry Admiral," said a nebulas voice. "It's against GTO's policy. We don't allow sentient beings to fly populated atmospheres. At least not until we have open trade."

Nice dig at me, asshole. He didn't know if it was an advanced EBU, or a GTO air-traffic controller from Moon Base, or the ship's artificial intelligence speaking. One thing he did know. *They're full of shit, we've got more UFO activity than ever before. Black is on to something.*

"Jesus Christ, just get going. Give me a monitor."

He ignored the flight harness. Rules were for peons, not him. A 3-D hologram appeared before him. The M-MAC was already outside the deep underwater

Earth base and accelerating for the surface. No Earth sub could ever go this fast. It broke the water without a splash and raced skyward. Within two minutes he was in space. His monitor split into two of equal size. One was a real-time outside view and the other was a whole Earth graphic showing every GTO and Earth craft or satellite in orbit. The EBU steered a wide birth around the International Space Station and headed for Dark Side. The monitor's graphic display showed his M-MAC's flight path. Sanderson was halfway to the moon in fifteen minutes.

The flight went the same as all the others, from takeoff to landing thirty-one minutes. It took longer to get to the Earth Launch site than to fly the trip. When the craft rounded the dark side of the moon all monitors went dead, 'for security,' so they sold it.

That pissed him off. The goddamn ETs saw everything on Earth but he wasn't allowed to see Dark Side base. *How the hell were we ever going to make terms? Where's the trust?*

But, of course, human leadership wasn't trustworthy and Sanderson himself the least trustworthy of all. He once suggested to the Joint Chiefs that the U.S. should launch nukes and wipe out Dark Side. *Who would know?* But that wasn't the answer. The Chiefs then let him in on a secret; the ETs had long ago shut down the world's nukes. He doubted any nukes anywhere on Earth were still active. *The cold war was a giant money-sucking scam. If the people knew, good-bye defense industry.*

Sanderson felt a bump. There was never any sound. He checked his watch, right on time. A section of wall split horizontally up and down like gaping jaws; the lower half became stairs. He descended into Moon Base's massive hanger bay.

There were hundreds of craft in all shapes and sizes. The nearest cigar class vessel was as long as two aircraft carriers end to end. He was told it was over three thousand years old. There were dozens of 'sport model' type craft near his launch tunnel. The ETs said their smallest ships belonged to students. He didn't believe it; they looked like fighters. Why let him see the invasion fleet? It was for show, intimidation, a scare tactic pointed at the U.S. Armed Forces. *Peaceful trade, my ass.* He didn't trust the ETs any more than he trusted Majestic.

His escort was heading toward his position from a service door about a hundred yards out. There was time to eyeball everything and look for weaknesses. But his approaching escort was a big distraction. It was human; the GTO insisted only humanoids could interact with Earthlings. 'The Earth human race is not yet ready to engage nonhumans.' They said humans were the most common species in the Milky Way. But they sure picked a bad example for an escort to demonstrate the claim.

Praytis was insectoid, still human, but very insect like. This creature's lower body resembled a praying mantis; in that vein he had an extended lower abdomen with elongated hips and four legs. His ass stuck out like a torpedo. He was a bug without an exoskeleton. His waist was too narrow and reminded Sanderson of a nineteenth century corset wearer. Praytis's waist was thorax-like. His chest, head, neck and arms were Earthling-like. Long face, pointed chin, and blue eyes passed for Earth-normal. From behind a table, Praytis seemed to be an average American right down to his thinning hair and beard shadow. However, Praytis scurrying across the plastic-metal deck always gave Sanderson the willies.

"How nice to see you, Admiral Sanderson," Praytis said. His voice was high-pitched but passable. "I trust our gift, the MAC drone control systems interface, is satisfactory?"

"Yes, yes, of course," Sanderson said military curt. "I'm not here about that. We have another problem. One of our departments has info they shouldn't have. You people are leaking."

"Oh, my, this calls for a meeting. I'll walk you to the conference room. The contact team is on its way."

"How the hell do you people do that?"

"Do what?" Praytis shrugged his shoulders. His blue unit-suit crinkled like a second skin. Praytis was dressed like an EBU except for the loose open trench coat falling off his shoulders.

"Never mind, lead the way," Sanderson said with a stiff wave.

He followed Praytis, fascinated by the way the Alien's four bare feet curled up when raised and flipped out onto the deck with a slap. Two cattycorner feet were always on the ground. Sanderson wondered how he walked in zero–G. But what he really wanted to know was how these people generated Earth-normal gravity in space. They weren't telling him shit. Some Galactic Trade Organization; seventy years of negotiations only resulted in the U.S. possessing technology they recovered from downed craft. In recent years visitors helped the U.S. understand this technology better, made it human-control capable, but Branford's laboratories would have figured it out eventually.

"This is going nowhere," Sanderson muttered, discussed.

"Certainly, we are," said Praytis, "We are going to the conference room."

Sanderson grumbled. Fifty thousand years of observing Earth and the aliens still didn't understand Earth-human nuances. *Thank God I have that advantage.* Two naked gray EBUs walked past at an intersection. He resisted the urge to kick the nearest one in the ass.

The conference room was Earth-normal, wood-paneled walls, florescent lights and a long mahogany table with fourteen matching chairs. The set was a gift from the Eisenhower Administration.

The team was already seated: A bone thin seven footer balancing an over-large bald head, a five-footer with light green skin and an extremely recessed forehead covered in Earth-normal hair, a frail woman almost normal, except she was seven foot tall and had white wings, and a guy that could pass for a gray EBU only he was taller, responsive, his eyes weren't dead and he made facial expressions.

The gray smiled at Sanderson as he took his seat. It didn't work, the mouth was too small and his teeth were too even. He inwardly cringed but maintained composure. Praytis found a spot without a chair—he didn't have the ability to sit. Each alien had a name, but Sanderson was damned if he could remember them. The team changed every time he came up. Praytis and the winged woman were the only constants, had to be a reason for that.

"My fellow beings," the Gray started, "I'm honored with your presence. What brings you to us Admiral, the next regular meeting of the GTO has not yet scheduled?"

There was no point beating around the bush. The aliens always spoke directly so Sanderson got right to it. That's why the Chiefs hired him. He wasn't a bullshitter just an expert liar.

"See here, I've got...the NRO boys know about my MAC program. Mr. Black has been snooping around. He knows far more than he should." Sanderson took a deep breath. "Have you people communicated with other American agencies, other than the Joint Chiefs Task Force on Alien Relations?"

The five aliens looked at each other one after the other; they were no doubt passing a sub-vocal hot potato. They had telepathy, Sanderson thought, and he was sure they used it now so he couldn't hear.

"No Admiral," the gray said with a tip of his big head. "As per our agreement; none of our GTO craft have gone Earthward. Our only communication is with those who come to us here."

"What about the other ships?" Sanderson asked.

It was the same question he had asked before. He hoped to catch them off guard. The GTO wasn't the only game in town and he would love to pit them against the competition. He'd get a better deal. The UFO **reconnaissance** boys had to be working the odds with the others, or maybe Black was acting alone with a third party like he said.

"We can assure you, Admiral," said the angel-winged woman," We haven't communicated with Majestic's NRO employees, they still hunt us. However, I must be honest; we are tracking Mr. Black's aircraft. He visited the Branford research vessel. It may not have been him personally, but helicopters under his direction are there now."

How does she know Mr. Black or that I'm thinking about him? He wanted to launch a tirade. They claim, out of respect they say, that they won't read his mind. Maybe they weren't reading his mind. Could it be logic? Even so, his so-called alien partners were holding back. He felt it in his guts.

Sanderson's satellite phone rang. There was no point in excusing himself, all communications were monitored. Sanderson flipped open the phone.

"This better be good."

It was that shit-head Colbert. A Branford Huey and two Cobras had just picked up the Pipers. Colbert had tracked the recording to Branford's daughter's place. Their teen girl wasn't picked up. No doubt the GTO heard as well. Sanderson had to get back pronto.

"Colbert, don't move a muscle. Stay put, I'll have my Yeoman handle it. Call in your report, tell her everything."

Sanderson hung up and hit the office hot-key. "Take Colbert's info. Have the cops pick up the Piper girl and any witnesses. Do it quiet. Use the local cops,

FBI, MPs get everyone on it and arrest Colbert too after you get his dope. Stay away from Levine...Leave the NRO and CIA out. I don't need a blood bath. Keep it quiet."

"Should I call the President?" His office girl asked.

He said, "Hell no," and flipped the phone shut.

The flight to Earth was short, but traveling underground tubes from Deep Ocean Landing to New Mexico and then an air flight to Key West would take a day. Black wasn't supposed to touch his operation. Sanderson smelled a double cross and couldn't do shit about it without his secure communications.

"I got to get back fast. Shuttle me to Groom Lake?"

"I am sorry," Praytis said, "Admiral, you know the GTO never breaks its protocol agreements. How else may we two develop mutual trust?"

"Trust, what trust, don't answer that."

"If you wish to propose an exception to protocol, please submit it at the next GTO gathering. Our arrival and return methods have been long established for security reasons, I'm sure you understand."

"Jesus Christ! Fine, let's go."

Black went rogue, had to be, there was no time to lose. He stormed out. Praytis followed immediately. Dogged by the suction-slapping of Praytis's weird feet, Sanderson's blood pressure elevated, he felt his temples pulsating. Calm down, keep your cool. Praytis caught up at the hangar door. The bug-man offered to accompany him down. Sanderson accepted. He would use the time to milk intelligence. Praytis was a regular chatterbox he'd get something useful. This trip wasn't a total loss; he learned something nobody knew. There was another Power playing at the game.

TWENTY-SEVEN

Aggie jumps the wall

"Aggie, Aggie, snap out of it," Melissa said, shaking Aggie's arm.

She rolled off the daybed and glanced at a mirrored wall; her hair looked like an explosion in a mattress factory.

"What's going on? What time is it?"

"You've been meditating like an hour. The cops are here looking for you."

She came fully awake, her mind clicked into hyper-sharp. She felt exhilarated and yet strangely calm, like on the eve of final exams. Whatever came next, she was ready.

"Show me," she said, knowing Mel had access to the home's security system. Mel brought up the front gate and the two side door cameras each view on its own massive monitor. There were cop cars near each entrance. A car was across the street from Aggie's scooter.

"Dude, you should turn yourself in before you get into mad-ass trouble."

"How do you know they're looking for me?"

Mel backed out of the gate screen and went to the front door and rolled the recording back from real-time to five minutes ago. Mrs. Van Ness was chatting with a cop at the front door. Mel cranked the volume.

"I'm sorry officer," Mrs. Van Ness said, "We haven't seen Aggie Piper since last week. My daughter says she has a job somewhere. What's this all about? Is she in trouble?"

The cop pushed back his cap and scratched his forehead. "The Navy asked us to pick her up; there was an incident that she may have witnessed. Tell me this, Mrs. Van Ness; why is Miss Piper's moped parked on your property?"

"Oh, that. It's not the first time she left that ugly thing here, she's done it before. She and my daughter are off somewhere with their friends."

"You don't mind us keeping an eye out for her, do you?"

"Of course not, we always support the police."

The cop didn't look convinced. But he wasn't about to challenge a major PBA contributor's word. He shuffled his feet and pushed his hat brim up before saying, "If you hear from Miss Piper, let us know." The cop started to turn but stopped. "Tell her if she comes in, the scholarship is hers."

Mel stopped the video. "Dude, you hear that? Man, you got to do it, this is your break."

"No way, never trust The Man, let the tape roll." Aggie said, thinking of what Mark said.

Mel brought back real-time video and toured the perimeter cameras. The cops were planted like palm trees on the two sides of the estate property facing the streets. There were four cop cars within camera range on the block.

"Time to get out of here," Aggie said, feeling filled with determination.

"But how, why?" Mel said, her eyes were wide, she was scared for sure.

"Over the back wall, what else is there? That place behind you is private property, they can't hang out there. I'm more worried about that big dog."

"My buddy Skipper?" Mel said and laughed. "I've been tossing hamburgers over that wall for two years. He loves me; he'll love you, too, but…"

"Sometimes low-tech solutions kick ass." Aggie said. "I'm doing it."

Mel raised her hands and shrugged her shoulders, her sign for 'I give up,' and went to the refrigerator and pulled out a package of hamburgers. "You're sure about this?" She handed Aggie the meat bag and said. "I can't believe Mom lets me eat this stuff. What's next?"

"How'd you do in Domestic Skills class?" Aggie asked. The meat felt like a bag of cold poop.

"Fine, why?"

Aggie rummaged thought Mel's office supplies basket and took out the biggest pair of scissors. She grabbed a hand full of her own hair and snipped off a chunk.

"No way, Dude, not your hair!"

"I need a disguise," Aggie said handing Mel the scissors, "Here's another low-tech solution for you, cut it all off. Go nuts."

"Radical, Dude."

Melissa hacked away until she produced a fair representation of a punk haircut. In Key West weird hair was the norm. Aggie's long, thick, straight blonde hair stood out like a fuck-me beacon. Mel used some food dye and painted bright red and blue streaks into the do, then applied gel and made it spike all over.

"It'll wash out soon as you get it wet," Mel said.

"Now for part two."

Aggie searched the room for clothes. Mel spent more time in here than in the house. The place was littered with stuff Mel didn't want her parents to see. Aggie slipped a pair of big, black baggy pants over her cut-offs. She pulled on a ratty oversized forest green T-shirt that Mel pilfered from the gardener. A pair of orange Converse sneakers topped off the bottom.

"Dude, freaky,"

"Thanks, you look really nice, too."

They proceeded around the security camera's view field, through the back yard and into a place between the pool's equipment fence and the back wall. The wall was only five feet high there. Mel called Skipper over. Together the girls fed the happy rottweiler two pounds of raw meat. Aggie and Skipper became fast friends. He really was a sweet dog, but you'd never know it by his deep bark.

When Aggie jumped over the wall Skipper wagged his stub-tail so wildly she had to quip, "Slow down Skipper, you'll screw yourself into the ground." The dog danced around in a happy-circle-dance, lost his balance, and crashed into a bush. She couldn't help but laugh. The dog nuzzled up to her. "Such a big dog shouldn't have such a little tail," she cooed while scratching his massive jowls.

She gave Mel the thumbs up and was off. Skipper showed her the way thought the thick vegetation of the lot's natural garden. Aggie never got near the house; the owners had to be home. She went straight to the garden's street gate. Leaving, she tried to act like she belonged there.

She gave Skipper one last scratch behind his ears before venturing out. There was a cop car half way up the block, he looked over at her but didn't react. She put her hands in her pockets, leaned way back and pushed her shoulders down. She slunk up the block like Mr. Natural from the underground comics. The cops were looking for a tall blonde, not a slow-motion punk slinky.

She walked right past the guy sitting in his patrol car. He was reading a titty magazine. *What a perv.* She checked her own boobs, *I'll never qualify*, and headed toward the beach to catch a bus.

When she got there, things weren't good. The cops were doing a homeless sweep. The town often picked up vagabonds for health reasons, or so they said. It was more about tourist dollars, really. Sky totally hated it. Aggie saw why. The beach patrol acted super obnoxious with them. *Homeless didn't bother anything.* There was also a cop stationed at the bus stop. *Boy they are really serious, that's not good.*

She crossed the boulevard and slapped herself against the side of the public restroom. She couldn't take the ocean-side path in this outfit. The sun was way too hot for her clothes. She couldn't stay incognito wearing a heat-sink for long. She couldn't go around in her regular clothes; they must know what she was wearing.

She hung there thinking with the gravity of it all pressing down. Mom and Dad were toast if she didn't act fast. No matter how scared she was, she had to do whatever it took. The big wide Atlantic glistened. It was standing between her and her parents: The ocean wasn't as scary as life without Sky and Po-boy.

She checked the beach and followed a set of bicycle tracks in the sand. Some drunken guy had ridden his bike, which was hooked to a kayak caddy, out onto the beach, fell over and passed out. The guy was frying in the sun. He smelled like grilling fish but the boat was OK.

She tried to wake him. Nothing but an alcohol infused snort came out of his mouth. *Out cold.* She stripped off her disguise and covered him with it and liberated the kayak from its caddy and dragged the little boat to the water.

She wadded in up to her ankles, although the water was warm, and the sand inviting, she shivered. *What am I doing, I can't do this?* She turned to leave but a beach patrol woman had found the passed-out guy. Aggie had no choice; it was the water or jail.

She paddled out a few yards and took off north as fast as she could while praying to the Goddess that the cops wouldn't see her. The water was shallow for fifty yards off the beach in most places. The ocean kayak drafted very shallow; she didn't need deep water. It was a blessing; she wasn't yet ready for a deep-water adventure.

At first, she followed close to shore. As she traveled along the Atlantic side off Key West, she steered further out. By the time she had gone a mile distant she was a hundred yards off shore. Still only three feet of water, she could walk back if necessary. It was muddy there, no stingrays, rays like sand. That gave her confidence.

The further out she went the better she liked it and that was weird. She felt remarkably good. *It's nice to be on the water again.* The juvenile barracuda and needlefish that darted around didn't faze her at all. She loved kayaking when she was little.

At the north end of Key West, she either had to cross open, deep water, or land and start walking up Route One. No bus stops. She paddled toward the bridge. At few hundred yards off she spotted a blacked-out sedan parked on the median at the bridge ramp intersection—it was the only road out of Key West.

"Unmarked cop car; crap."

She instinctively reached to push bangs down over her face, but she couldn't hide that way anymore and she decided she didn't want to either. Aggie held her head high, turned the kayak for open water, and started across the deep, dark channel.

TWENTY-EIGHT

Muddy waters

The Naval Air Station was a really big obstacle. She paddled way out into deep water to avoid the security cameras. Po-boy's mantra, 'never trust The Man,' rang inside her head like a hippie alarm clock. She knew about the cameras. Po-boy got chased out of there regularly, he even got arrested once. She paddled like a machine until rounding the airfield. Once clear, she headed inshore.

Aggie had to cross many small, natural channels, pass thought mangrove stands, and dodge the little islands that dotted the waterscape. She powered the kayak quickly across the last big channel that led to Mark's place and the other lagoon's marinas. Fast felt good. She hadn't worked out in days.

The weird part was after years of avoiding live waters it felt amazing. She was a dumb-ass water-rat kid all over again having no fear. But this was not a pleasure cruise. *It's past time I act, but, don't act stupid.* This felt different: She was thinking like a grownup for real.

A Coast Guard pursuit boat held station at the mouth of the channel outside of Mark's deep lagoon. She cut through a mangrove stand, crossed the main lagoon out of sight of the channel, and slipped up into a drainage cut.

She rowed as far as she could until running out of water. Getting out of the little boat, she had no choice but to walk the muddy, bug-infested ditch inland until she finally found a way onto dry, higher land that didn't require hacking through thick brush. Once out of the drainage ditch, she checked herself—she was all scratched up. Mel's orange Converse sneakers were muck-black. She smelled of sweat, rotting vegetation, and salt spray. Her skin was encrusted with crud. *Glad I cut my hair. This place is a dreadlock factory.*

With a burst, she jumped the fence of Bobby's RV Resort, dived into the pool, swam across, popped out, and sprinted to the further fence. She scrambled over the tall slat-on-slat wooden barrier and landed in Mark's boat storage lot.

She ran from one blocked-up boat to another, hiding as she went. She hoped Dad's boat had gas. Mark's offer was cool, but she was on her own now. She wouldn't get him in trouble, too, no way. Besides, he was military and could not be trusted, he's got guns and everything. Before she got very far, someone tapped her on the shoulder from behind. She spun fists posed to strike.

"Aggie?"

"How'd you know I was here!" she said. "Crap, I almost socked you."

"Cameras, remember?"

"Oh, yeah I forgot you're not really a Jedi. I'm taking Dad's boat. I'm going to Grandpa."

"That's not wise, the authorities are looking for you; they know Po-boy's boat."

"I don't give a crap, I'm going, I got this far...I'll...I'm going that's all."

"Quiet, Ags," Mark put a finger to his lips and lowered his voice to a whisper. "The Feds might have ears on this place. I'm not stopping you. There's a better way. They can track any transponder or radio. That boat is marked. I'll use it against them and take the Uniflight out. I'll distract them, give you cover."

"Great, distract them while I do what? Sit here and rot. I'll blow up a tire tube and float out." She said with iced sarcasm.

Mark's rare full-faced grin made a sudden appearance. He wasn't one to take offence at her barbs but it wasn't the joke. She knew that look; the one reserved for marina poker games after winning a big pot with bluffs: Mark's triumph look. She bit off and swallowed the next insult.

"What?"

"Take my sailboat. It's all wood, no transponder, hand crank radio. The only hard tech is a wind generator and sealed batteries for lights. The kicker-motor is magneto and points, no computer. My boat is hard to track or detect. Wide beam, drop keel, foam filled, she'll go anywhere. I keep her ready...just in case."

"You have a sailboat?"

She had never seen it and she knew every boat on Geiger Key. There weren't many places to dock. She painted the bottoms of most of them herself. Mark was the only guy doing repairs on this Key.

"Follow me."

Mark went back the way she had come only he moved further down the fence line. He jumped the fence, crossed Bobby's parking lot, went around the drainage ditch, crossed an overgrown abandoned parking lot and climbed over a high, slatted chain-link fence. He moved quickly like a sudden storm.

She cleared the last fence as he entered a lone three-sided boathouse straddling the end of a narrow, overgrown dead-end lagoon. Nobody used this waterway; it was supposedly silted up. Mark stuck his head out of a side door and waved her over. The place was wood and painted camouflage, it blended like it grew there. The shed was obviously ship-shape despite the paint job. Mark was anal like that.

It was a forgotten place. A construction company had cleared and filled the land with lagoon dregs before she was born. It was a condo project gone bust. The lagoon head was seventy-five feet from the road and behind a ragged cyclone fence. The lot was covered in thick foliage. She never paid attention to it, nor did anyone else.

The first thing she saw when she slipped through the door was that hick, Jon Colbert.

"Oh, no, not him again."

"He's here to help."

"I hate spy crap."

Jon was lowering a box of supplies into the sailboat from a suspended dock hung below the bulkhead but well above the water.

"Me too Ma'am, hate it like a rattle snake in a sleeping bag."

He pulled himself up onto the upper deck, wiped his hands on his jeans and sat on the top of a piling. He looked up at her with doe-eyes and his leg started jumping. *Jeans, who wears jeans and boots in the Keys?* Then a thought slapped her.

"He came down here to spy on Dad!" She shot a deadly look at Mark. "He's the enemy. He called the cops. He's the rat."

"He had to cover his ass." Mark said with a calm voice.

"Pardon, Ma'am," Jon said standing up, "It's not like that. I ain't no dog-gone spy, just following orders." He tipped his cowboy hat and ducked like he was dodging a bullet.

"Why're the cops after me if you didn't call them?"

"The Admiral," Jon said, "had to call in, orders Ma'am."

"Tell her Jon," Mark said evenly. "You two are shipping out together, be straight. Team members keep no secretes."

"Well, dog-gone it, I'm not a good liar…I told him about the choppers. Oh hell, I'm sorry Ma'am. Sanderson's office must've called the sheriff."

"That's it!" Aggie said, "He's not going with me. Fuck that! I can't trust him." She wanted to storm off but there was no place to go. She turned her back to Jon and crossed her arms defiantly.

Mark grabbed her by the upper arms and spun her toward him.

"Look, Ags, you can't do this alone. You'll need fire power. I know you; you won't touch a gun. Jon's an expert marksman. He has inside information. He knows how to shoot, you don't."

"How do I know he won't rat me out?"

Jon took his hat off and held it with two hands by the brim at his waist. He lowered his eyes.

"Well Ma'am, I'm AWOL. I had to report. Deputies showed right quick after I called and they were lookin fer me. I ran the other way. My boss's in transit. I reckon we'll be long gone a-fore he gets back. When he finds what I'd done, spilling the beans, hell, I don't much cotton to the brig."

Jon looked pathetic. She doubted he'd be useful. But Mark was right: She didn't know what she was sailing into, and if it came to blows, she had no idea how to use a gun and wouldn't anyway. *I'm a hippie love child. I'm for the Goddess. I won't kill, no way.*

"I'm staying here," Mark said, "you'll need cover. I can do much more for you from here."

"Fine, whatever."

She pushed past Jon and looked over the boat. It was a sleek twenty-six-foot Bermuda Sloop with a tall forward mast that ran through a cuddy cabin. She noted the drop keel aft of the cabin. The boat felt strong, capable; it energized her confidence.

She'd have to hang over the gunwales. A deckhand to rig, counterbalance, and bail would make it easier. With someone on the hand pump she wouldn't need to drop sail to bail. It took focus to run a spinnaker. With extra sail this boat would fly like a greyhound. She'd make better time with help.

"OK, he's in, if he follows orders. If I wasn't in a hurry I'd go alone. Wish I had my backpack."

"On board," Mark said, "It was in the café."

That settled it. She jumped in. It didn't take long to situate the boat. She was impressed with this little craft. It was in top condition, typical Mark. Trick rigging too. Fitted with foam glued inside the hull, it was unsinkable. Mark had it ready for war. Inside the cuddy was an AK-47 and lots of waterproof ammunition boxes mounted in the overhead and cabin sidewalls.

Aggie looked up at Mark on the dock. "Expecting trouble?"

Mark explained his plan. He'd take Po-boy's Uniflight and run the blockade, draw the Coast Guard off. Dad's boat had twin jet drives. It was a converted Vietnam era military riverboat designed to draft shallow, take fire, and go fast. Once he was underway, she'd sneak out. Mark left and it didn't take long.

She knew the sound of Dad's powerful engines a mile away. When she heard the Uniflight idling down the main lagoon, she started the outboard motor with a quick jerk on its recoil rope.

"Jon, cast off."

"Sorry Ma'am what's that?"

Some Navy guy, is he for real?

"Untie the rope and jump on…don't call me Ma'am. Got it!"

"Yes Ma'a…right."

She steered Moon Dodger down the narrow lagoon overhung with foliage wondering if Jon knew his stern from his asshole.

Rounding the bend of the side lagoon and into the channel, they were treated with an entertaining sight: Mark was racing Dad's boat across the sand flats with the Coast Guard in hot pursuit.

Aggie had to motor slowly like any other boater in a no-wake zone as to not arouse attention, so she had a good view of Mark's show. Mark let the jet drive churn up sand and mud so the larger craft in his wake got confused. The Guard had to know they were in shallow water. Mark let them get close, gunned it and jetted far ahead several times leading them deeper into the flats. The flats were crisscrossed with narrow channels, channels the Uniflight didn't really need.

Mark took off across the shallows again. The Coast Guard followed. The last thing she saw was the anti-drug runner boat pitching rooster tales of muck.

"How the hell he'd do that," Jon asked? "He's slipping them like a greased pig."

"It was designed for rivers; it doesn't have props, it's jet drive." She said with pride. It may have looked funky but it was a sleeper like her Vespa; ugly but kick-ass.

"Glory be," Jon said shaking his head.

She could have gone into all the clever nautical details. She knew a lot about Dad's boat. Remembering working on it with him made her heart sing. But the thought also made her ache for her parents. This was no time for memory lane. If the Coast Guard saw them, they'd be toast. Radio is faster than any boat.

Free of the no-wake zone, she twisted the hand throttle and maxed out the ten-horse motor. She needed deep water to drop keel and sail. The wind was onshore and that required room to tack. She made for open water driven by the winds of determination.

TWENTY-NINE

Mark goes rogue

"No regrets," Mark said as he raced across a mud flat. Evading the Coast Guard's chase boat was easy and illegal as hell. The Coast Guard's high technology pursuit skiff was fast. It was a forty-foot modified V-hull, armed to the teeth and designed to intercept smugglers in all waters; but it wasn't equipped to catch him. He hated to see such a nice piece of equipment run aground. *After all, we're all on the same side.* That programmed thought automatically came to mind but he knew it wasn't true. While the CG was running down empty cigar boats the CIA docked freighters stuffed with dope.

Mark was on his own side and right now that meant the Pipers' side.

He didn't hate 'The Man,' as Po-boy would say; the Coast Guard played its compartmentalized role just like the other rubes. If that Captain knew what Mark knew about the Coast Guard's real mission, he'd help Mark escape. Nobody liked acting as cover for black-ops.

Mark ran off the channel. The pursuit boat balked and twisted hard away; they caught on to Mark's drift. *Time for another ploy.*

He spun the wheel of his jet-drives and cut across their bow. This tub didn't look fast, but he had installed two modified 350 Chevy motors. It was the perfect sleeper; his alternate escape launch. Po-boy couldn't fathom why Mark did so much work on this beat-up looking riverboat just to give it away. Nobody gave away boat slips, either. Mark needed a fast boat at hand not registered to him.

He slid back into a channel and let the CG close.

Sure, he liked the Pipers. Good neighbors. Training Aggie is what drew him close, something he swore he'd never do. It wasn't smart. They became the family he never had and that was bad for business — the Government's business.

Branford paid him to watch them, not love them. *Too late now.*

He came about hard and charged the chase boat, cutting off a collision at the last second. *That should piss them off, perfect.* He shot toward the shoreline. The big speed skiff rooster tailed mud as it came about.

He got a quick look at his stealthy sloop. Aggie was clear. He turned north into the sand flat where there were channels the CG boat couldn't navigate. *The Cap must know these waters.* It was time to crank up the confusion.

When the CG boat came up on his tail, he gunned the engines and ripped up the bottom clouding the water. Bullets started flying. He repeated the tactic twice more. *The Cap had to be losing it.* They tried sinking him; rounds hit his deck and transom. *No problem.* They didn't know his motors and cockpit were shielded. The hull was foam filled. They could Swiss cheese it and it wouldn't sink or slow down.

Mark, far ahead, picked up the radio. "Attention Coast Guard, I don't know who you're looking for, but I'm Mark Levine, Navy Seal, retired. Back off, copy?"

"Levine, I know you, what are you doing in Piper's boat?"

"Making you look stupid." Mark hit a hidden switch and started the oil smoker. "Shit, engine's on fire."

He slowed as if the boat was in trouble. They moved in to pick him up. They were far inside the flats. They didn't notice him skipping out of the channel. They closed. He spun the wheel and gunned it. The CG pilot reacted and grounded into a mud-bar.

Game one over.

He killed the engines and let her drift inside a cloud of homemade smoke. *Time to borrow Po-boy's snorkeling gear.* The CG boat had problems. It was revving its docking jet-motors trying to free itself. Once she wiggled out and into deeper water, deckhands lowered two rubber launches. Mark watched from the blind side of his craft. He rolled over the side when the dinghies were underway.

The rubber boats circled his position several times before someone boarded. Mark was submerged under his boat between hull spines. He ducked under or behind each of the three boats as needed. He heard clearly.

"Where'd he go? I'll kill that bastard."

"He must have gone overboard when he turned out."

"The Skipper says he's an Alpha Team Seal. Could be anywhere by now."

"Those guys are good."

How did they know his Alpha Team status? Only Sanderson knew that. The chase boat Cap must have his service record. *The crew shouldn't know classified information.* There are Seals on base; that's no secret, none with Alpha Team clearance. Sanderson screwed up, he told the Coast Guard too much, and the Cap ran his mouth. *Bush operators.*

The dingy nearest him cast away from the Uniflight. Mark latched onto its prowl and flatted himself to lessen drag. The ride gave him time to think.

Sanderson had to know Mark's connection to Branford. All Branford wanted was someone keeping an eye on his estranged family. The Old Man hadn't called to check up in years although the money kept showing up in Mark's Swiss bank account, which was also in Aggie's name but she didn't know it yet. The Old Man was big on her earning her way in life and Mark agreed. Struggle builds character.

The last thing the Old Man said was, 'Guard my granddaughter above all. I won't force love. She'll come to me, maybe my daughter and son in-law, too, when they're ready. Help them when you can.'

Mark didn't care about the cash. He'd protect the Pipers any way he could. Maybe that's why the Old Man backed off.

Mark had stashed all of Branford's money and never touched it. The Old Man had to know Mark saved it for Ags. Mark didn't get the chance to tell her. *Kidnapping's one a hell of a way to pull a family together. That's not the answer.* This wasn't the Old Man's doing. What about Sanderson?

As the crew hauled up the first dingy, Mark floated near the stern deciding his next move.

Branford was a hard ass, strict self-imposed rules. Sanderson, on the other hand, was a three-timing back-stabbing psycho spook that would kill his own mother for mission success; especially if there was a buck in it. Those Cobras weren't Branford's. Sanderson had to be involved. *How does Branford's Huey play? Why go after Sky? Was Sanderson blackmailing Branford?* Anything was possible.

Sending Aggie off was the right move. Branford would pull all stops once he heard Sky and Po-boy were casualties. *The Old Man will keep Ags safe.* He had to go after Sanderson. Sanderson was the key.

Mark would eat bullets for the Pipers. Family took care of family. Sanderson's ass was grass.

Mark climbed over the stern while the crew lashed the second dingy on the foredeck. The dive room was aft. Mark didn't waste time. He found dive gear, checked it, and suited up in the dark as the pursuit skiff backed into wider water and turned to.

A sailor opened the darkened dive room's door. Mark put out his lights and accepted the donation of the Seaman's water-proofed forty-five caliber handgun. The signal horn sounded. They were getting underway. Mark jumped clear of the propellers as the CG boat accelerated.

The Navy Air Station was a five-mile swim. Mark did it underwater. He knew his way around the channels. He had studied his surroundings just in case.

There's no such thing as an ex-special ops officer. He stayed close to the Navy for good reasons. They paid less attention to him. His retired guys, living in the mountains or Mexico, were under orbital microscopes. He confirmed he wasn't watched. Even so, he was ready to bug-out at all times.

The Navy's secondary runway ended at water's edge. There wasn't much cover around it. The water just off the strip was muddy and knee deep running into the Atlantic two hundred yards off shore. He never figured on sneaking onto base, just how to escape it if he had such need. *Same thing in reverse.* Mark removed his dive gear while in the water and sank it by blowing the air out of the tank and attaching the weight belt. Head just above the surface, he spotted what he needed; a four-foot round ground water drainage pipe sticking out from a line of low, thick foliage.

Jon had mentioned the location of his quarters. Milking Jon for intel was too easy. Mark rolled in the mud, making certain his orange trimmed wet suit was well covered. He squirmed through the mud shallows up to the drain like a slow-motion eel. Checking for hidden cameras, he noted their positions and located blind spots. Once at the drain, the water was deep at the pipe's spill-out. Mark striped off the wet gear, washed the mud off his face and proceeded along the pipe until he arrived at a security fence. He squeezed under it. Two minutes later, he located Jon's bungalow complex.

He checked out the area from the brush, no obvious cameras. He examined every possible avenue for hidden wires and confirmed signs. Jon's room was bugged. The kid worked for Sanderson; standard procedure. The other quarters were not—no need. Sanderson was too cheap to spend money on perimeters. Mark slipped into the end unit: The officer that lived there wasn't home. He took a shower, put on a uniform, shaved off his afro hair. *Time to pay Sanderson a visit.*

He washed the forty-five, checked the action and found it in good order and walked into the parking lot a crisp Navy resident. The ignition keys were in Jon's Yamaha. Security would think it was Jon; the motorcycle helmet was natural cover. In the two days Jon had spent with him, Mark learned a lot. *That kid is no spy.* Mark knew exactly where to find Sanderson.

The brick office on the flight line was nondescript and good cover. The cams were easy to locate, as were blind spots.

He parked the bike close to the building's front, away from the door's camera view and out of range of the sweeper-cam mounted on the roof. Just in case, he kept Jon's motorcycle helmet. He slipped behind the junipers that stood between the building and the walkway, slinking between the plants and the wall until he made the front door. He moved inside. No alarms. Nobody was in the front waiting area. Hopefully the inner reception desk was quiet, too.

He took the helmet off, sat down, picked up a magazine, and hid the forty-five in his lap. A sailor came out of the bathroom from the right.

"Oh, sorry Sir didn't know anyone was here," the low rank Seaman stiffened to attention.

"At ease Sailor, I'm here for Sanderson. Where is he?"

"Down the hall, take the first hallway on the right, Sir. Shall I buzz his receptionist?"

"No, no, he's expecting me." Mark said. Standing, he slipped the gun into the helmet and placed the magazine over it. "Mind if I take this, like to finished the article."

"No, Sir, I mean yes Sir, please enjoy it."

Mark marched down the hall like he owned the place, turned down the side passage and switched to silent running. Sanderson's unmarked door would be on the back wall of an open waiting area. Mark drew his gun and slipped inside.

A dark-haired Yeoman sat behind a metal desk with a phone glued to her face. She looked familiar, but different hair color. He noted the oak door behind her to the right. Mark put a finger to his lips indicating quiet.

"Put down the phone."

She didn't comply.

"We've been looking for you Captain Levine," She said. "Nice job getting here unseen."

"I trusted you in Barcelona," Mark said, "That was a mistake. Phone down or I'll blow your head off."

Mark cocked the hammer of the forty-five. He drew a bead. She smiled and covered the phone.

"Sanderson's not home, bugs are off. You know his routine." She said. The lady had lost her previous Euro accent. Mark wondered if the sex was fake too. She pulled her hand from phone.

"Madam President the man I spoke of just arrived, care to speak with him?"

He pressed the gun barrel against the Yeomen's temple and took the phone. She smiled at him knowingly, same damn way she used too. *Odd reaction with a gun at your head.* She wasn't the needy women he made love to in Spain. And, this wasn't the first time he spoke to a President. The protocol would ensure authenticity.

"Alfa contract five zero five," Mark said.

"Oh yes, I know that one. Give me a second…Here it is, stand by."

The voice sounded like her. She had to match the code to an index book only Q-clearance had. A special tone rang into the receiver. Every President is issued the list. They punch it in and a tonal signal tells the story. It only works on the Presidential private line. Every operative that works with a President is required to memorize the tones. This was real.

"What can I do for you, Madam President," Mark said. He stiffened and lowered the gun. The lady laughed. This fake Navy officer found his changed attitude humorous. *She's a pro.*

"Call me Jane," President Albright said. "Look Mark, I know why you are there. Sanderson is out of control, I'll admit. I saw the kidnapping just now. Sanderson is forever using government equipment for unauthorized…adventures. But, he's not responsible, not directly involved in this one. Something else is happening. It's big. All hell is breaking loose. Every alphabet agency in Washington is in a tizzy and pointing a finger at the others."

The President rustled papers in the back ground and continued.

"When he gets back from the Moon…wait you didn't hear that. I'm not even sure. Look, work with my special…er…agent here. You'll have my protection. Will you do that?"

"I'll sign on…Jane. But, for only one reason, the Pipers are my friends. I'm in it for them with or without your cooperation. I'm with you only until the Pipers are safe, copy?"

"I can live with that."

"Leave me out of your internal wars. I'm done with that. I help the Pipers then I'm out. No limits, full action. I get immunity. Deal?"

"Deal," the President hung up.

"Welcome aboard," The Yeoman said. "Jane is absolutely trustworthy, you know."

"You're with that scum-sack Sanderson. Should I trust you, you screwed me before?"

"Not really," she said. "I had orders in Spain. I was CIA then. Now…I don't work for anyone but my sister."

Mark immediately saw the resemblance and knew why Nostrum wasn't in the public eye. Her professionalism obviously came from years of service. She was a Company asset—maybe she'd gone rogue like she says. The Lady was placed years before the election. Trusted operatives were hard to come by for presidents. This president had a built-in family ace. Presidents were traditionally kept out of the loop. This one could crack the bubble. Mark liked the possibilities.

He placed the phone gently in its base and jammed the gun into his waist band. The Yeoman's disposition didn't change at all during the exchange. *Defiantly a deep cover pro.* Mark liked her better this way. Before she was weak, that former persona was an act, of course. Her real nature was steel. He respected that.

"What's the game?" He asked.

"Branford has materials and information vital to national security."

"Don't give me that line, whose security, your sister's?"

"We need him. Jane needs him, what he knows, his hardware; she wants to blow the lid off UFO secrecy."

"If that's the real deal, I'm fine with it." Mark said.

"If anything happens to his daughter…Branford is stubborn, he'll blame us. He won't get on board. America can't afford to lose him. If the Powers can't make a deal with, I can't say who, the long-term public good suffers."

He looked at her name tag, "OK Yeoman Nostrum, let us start by you briefing me. Don't give me any need-to-know bullshit. Sanderson is on the moon, so what. Branford is reverse engineering alien technology. The aliens have a base on the moon; it's been there thousands of years."

Nostrum took a quick breath, her eyes shot wide and quickly returned to business face. Her cool took heat and her cheeks flushed pink. She was genuinely surprised. Mark had cracked the façade.

"I know more than you think. Spill it all or I do this alone."

"OK, let's go to the basement: Seeing is understanding. Call me Jennifer."

She didn't look like a Jennifer, why did spies always choose names that didn't fit?

She led him into Sanderson's office. The Admiral never spared any expense while accessing the public's dime. They went directly into Sanderson's bathroom shower. The elevator ride was long.

Mark had time to think about Nostrum. She was an almost too-good-to-be-true pro, such coolness. But in Barcelona she was a needy wreck. She has serious acting skills so he'd have to watch out for that.

She strongly resembled the President, a younger version. It was a wonder nobody figured it out. Good timing or good luck for Madam President, he didn't know or care. He had questions. Could this lady be a surgical double? He wondered how real she was. Was she human, alien or what? Alien androids existed, that was true enough.

Mark looked her over carefully and decided she wasn't enhanced other than dyed hair, no plastic surgery scars. Eyebrows weren't plucked high and fine, like in Spain.

He inhaled deeply. She was human. Aliens couldn't possibly smell that good. There was that time in a Spanish elevator…she was passionate…but he wasn't here for that. No doubt, she's human.

The President was going for an end run around the Military Industrial Complex, the same sort of thing that got JFK and Bobby Kennedy killed. Mark wasn't the only one going rogue here. President Albright wanted to topple a mountain of secrets that had been piling up for eighty years. It would take an unexpected earth-shattering event to really change things. He didn't know how they planned to do it, if they could do anything at all, but this off-the-books mission was going to be very interesting.

THIRTY

Shark tails

Aggie had kept half an eye on Mark while she motored into the clear. "Thanks Mark." The Coast Guard was not her problem. Did he get away? The scene was too distant to tell, but she had the feeling he did.

"Mark rocks," Aggie said. "See how he zipped north? Stupid shore patrol."

"Yes, Ma'am," Jon said hanging on to the port gunwale with an iron grip.

She ran six hundred yards south east on the motor until she hit the local shipping lane that was wide and deep. *Time to set sail.* She ordered the First Mate into action.

"Jon, set the jib. I'll drop keel." She said as she pulled the motor up and tied it off with rope.

"What's a job?" Jon said not moving. He had both hands on the gunwale now. He was as pale as Edward Scissor Hands.

"Job? It's a jib. I thought you were a Navy guy. Don't you know anything about sailing?"

"No Ma'am. We got us a lake in Grainger Texas, but, I ain't ever been on it. Hell, never been in it; I can't swim."

"Crap."

She gave him a life jacket and seated him at the rudder, told him how to steer. She showed him some of the basics as she worked on setting sails.

"Watch what I do, Cowboy, it's important."

Mark's sloop was freshly maintained. She had a hinged-locked mast so it could be quickly removed or dropped flat to batten down for storms, the boom folded onto the mast and locked as well. All the hardware and pulleys were polished brass, the sails and ropes were new hemp. Every part of the sloop could take massive punishment. Even if it wasn't foam-filled bullet proofed it would be hard to sink her.

"This little boat will go anywhere, survive the worst beating." She said. "Cool, right?"

Jon was too freaked out to respond. The only thing she didn't like, she hated it in fact, was that rifle mounted on the cabin's wall and right under two fishing poles, fishing stuff they might actually need.

Lots of other boats were around but spread out. It was no place to teach Jon how to sail. Having set the sails, she took the helm and changed heading tacking dead south. A big Coast Guard cutter raced toward Mark's channel from the northeast. It wasn't aimed at her. She got up and adjusted the rigging.

"When Mark makes a diversion, he doesn't mess around," she said flopping down next to Jon at the helm. He held the rudder like it was a live snake.

"I've got to call Mel. Steer like this." she said and pulled the rudder.

"I wouldn't do that, Ma'am," Jon said. "They'll ping and locate the caller. They know about you, they'll be looking."

She doubted they'd get caught. This was Mel's phone, on Mr. Van Ness's protected network. *If the Feds could trace a random webcam to her house, who knew what they could do — Jon was right.* Mr. Van Ness made spy stuff for the government, but he didn't make everything they had. She just learned spies never trusted anyone, not even the guys they buy stuff from, for sure. She needed a semi low-tech solution. She yelled "duck" and swung the boom, yanked the tiller and changed tack heading.

"I know a party spot south of Key West."

"How's that Ma'am?"

"Dozens of boats moor around this set of tiny islands short of Fort Zackary. There are always flotillas off the tip of Key West. Lots of islands, sand bars and party boat spots inside the Wildlife Preserve." She said. "I have an idea."

"Lost in the herd I reckon."

The place she had in mind was close and populated with out-of-towners. No cell towers, just a huge population of pleasure boats, fishing charters and dive boats, most with satellite capabilities. If they traced her there, they'd have to search every boat within ten miles of Jefferson's Ranger Station.

"Lots of sat-phone signals bouncing around."

The wind shifted south and they made good time. She spotted a big tie-up, slacked sails and drifted toward the makeshift flotilla. She flipped open the phone, switched to sat-phone, hit Mel's hot- key and put it on speaker.

"It's me. We're underway."

"Triangulating, I have you," Mel said. "You're logged in. He's moving, but slow. If they stay on course, you could meet him in like three to six hours depending on speed. He's not that far."

The coordinates and mapping information appeared on Aggie's phone screen. She had to cross the main shipping lanes to get there. He was currently sailing between island channels. *Grandpa's laying low.* She had to cross wide water to get there and she never sailed out of sight of land before.

"Crap."

"Ma'am, best tell your friend about them tracing us. Ought not to talk long."

"Who's that?" Mel asked.

"Just some sea cow I netted at the dolphin rodeo," Aggie said, deadpan. "He's right, they'll find me. I better go."

"Wait," Mel said. "Dude, I bought you time. Hacked the NSA, put their satellites on delay. If they come, they'll be two hours late. Keep the phone off. Only link-up randomly to get position, then shut it down. Turn off the phone's battery. They'll figure it out before it gets dark. It's time for you to get really lost."

"Lost, that's what I'm afraid of," Aggie said with full realization. Without the phone zeroed in, outside of shipping lane markers, she'll be sailing blind.

"Just stay away from Cuba; they have a thing for white chicks. Got to go, Mom's here." Mel hung up.

"She hacked the NSA?" Jon asked incredulous. His seasick face had regained a little color.

"Don't ask, I'll have to kill you," She dead-panned.

"If that don't beat the mule."

Aggie turned the boat according to Mel's map. With the boom lashed secure, Jon moved from stern to the built-in live bait box amidships. Mark had thought of everything. The bait box's lid was padded, a good place to sit while managing the bilge hand-pump. He gripped the keel frame like his life depended on it and started feverishly tapping his boot heel. The deck vibrated like an ore master's drum skin. This was going to be a very long trip.

They had sailed well past the Key's tip before heading east into deep, blue water. The teal green of the shallows faded and became deep gray. Between Jon's tapping and no line-of-sight markings she was getting nervous. With nothing but the sun, her cell phone clock and a magnetic compass she managed to stay on an intercept course, or at least she hoped so.

Mark had sea charts, astrological charts, and other old-fashioned crap on board, even a sexton, but she never used one before. Reading about astronavigation was one thing, making it work was something else. She could figure it out, if they had time but the clock was ticking. *Time to rig big sails.*

"Hey, look at that," Jon said pointing aft, "There's a dolphin, always wanted to see one."

She was at the rudder and turned aft. She couldn't quite see with the sun sparkling on the water. Shading her eyes, she stood up. A very large dorsal fin was in their wake, a smaller one ten feet behind it—only it wasn't a dorsal, it was a tail fin.

"That's not a dolphin you lug-head, that's a shark, a big one. Oh crap!"

Sitting on the live bait box gave a low water view. Jon stood and took an unsteady step toward Aggie. The full body of the shark loomed large as a giant shadow.

"It's a dog-gone cow. Damn if it ain't big as this here boat." Jon staggered back plopped onto a seat. Sweat started pouring off his face. He was freaking out.

"I hate sharks," she said. "I almost got eaten once."

She tried to relax, told herself it would eventually leave. She tried an internal mantra and felt a little better. She pressed on. After an hour she checked; it still trailed them. The longer it followed the more Jon tapped his boot heel and the more agitated she became. The theme song from the movie Jaws played over and over in her head with Jon's foot leading the beat. *Why won't it just leave?* She squeezed the tiller handle so hard her knuckles turned white. That's when it hit her; Jon's tapping had gotten its attention.

"Jon, knock it off! You're a Morse code shark attracting machine!"

Jon stopped tapping and looked back at her with an ashen, contrite face. He wasn't doing well. She felt bad for being a bitch. He was obviously scared, like she would have been only yesterday. *Poor guy.* He was such a nerd-fest. Cowboy outfit with an undersized orange life-preserver vest made Mel's clothes look cheerful.

She felt bad about disparaging him and said of herself, "What an asshole." And, of course, Jon took it the wrong way. He looked crushed.

"Well Ma'am one thing my Daddy liked to say was, 'when things get tough, just don't sit there like a steaming cow pie.'"

Jon disappeared into the cuddy cabin. *Oh great, I wonder if I'll treat Grandpa like shit, too.* She turned away and looked back. *Where'd it go?* She read sharks are attracted by sound, especially drumming. The tapdancing cowboy must have drawn the shark. She looked port side. They still had company.

The wind had slacked. Progress slowed which gave the primitive monster time to circle. It came up broadside and bumped the boat with its snout — its tail slapped the sidewall as it departed. She didn't freak, rather she studied the beast. Her scientific minded brain engaged and she became fascinated. She had this weird ability to remember almost everything she ever read. Shark facts came rushing to mind.

Sharks bump things to test them, especially a meal, just before the big bite. This one was a sixteen to eighteen-foot hammerhead. It wasn't looking for a meal, just confused by Jon's drumming. The boat must have a scent trail, another thing it was curious about. She looked around and found a nylon line trailing. *Must have been knocked overboard.* She reeled it in and hosted up a small near empty chum pot. She sniffed it and let it drop. More than enough stink left to keep the hammerhead interested. Sharks didn't like motor exhaust, she read once, so she slacked the sails, lowered the kicker-motor and fired it up.

"That'll scare it off…I hope." On impulse she yelled, "GO AWAY SHARK!"

Jon didn't know why she started the motor, she didn't say. Maybe he thought she was frightened. He bolted up out of the cabin with the AK-47 in one hand and a big black clip in the other. Just then, the hammerhead butted the boat's side, but harder this time. Jon almost lost his feet.

"Don't worry, Ma'am, I'll take care of it." Jon jammed the long clip into the rifle.

He didn't have balance even slightly resembling sea-legs. The gun wavered all over the place. Aggie ducked for cover. Before she could say stop, he leaned way over the side, gun first, and promptly fell in.

"Crap!"

The splash got the great fish's attention. It was only ten yards out and started to turn. Aggie quickly turned the motor hard to the transom and lashed it so the boat would circle. She ripped the life vest off, grabbed the flare gun off the gunwale and wrapped its tether around her wrist. It was made to float. She dove in. Jon was floundering badly. *His stupid gun's too heavy.* She got to him a split second before the shark closed in.

"Drop the gun! It's pulling you down," She yelled as the big fish bumped him and swam past spinning them in its wake. It began a slow turn. Monster-size fish need room to maneuver. The boat arched far away; it won't be back soon enough. *Next pass, the shark feeds.*

"Waterproof, it'll fire," Jon said spitting water.

"Drop it, idiot!"

Aggie kicked him. He let go. The gun sank. He bobbed up spiting and choking.

"Save your own self," he screamed.

She had fresh cuts on her legs and arms from crawling through bushes earlier, was oozing blood smell into the water. *I'll draw it off.* She swam out from Jon.

It worked. The monster came at her. She dove. It passed overhead. She reached and grabbed a fin. Getting pulled along, she stroked its belly with the plastic flare gun that was tethered to her wrist. The shark slowed, stopped and rolled over. She had seen it on the internet, making sharks sleep, she rubbed his belly and it might have worked. But she ran out of air, had to let go. She surfaced. *It won't sleep long.* The beast was still too close to Jon and the boat was closing in. Aggie swam to him, grabbed his collar, and started stroking them toward the boat's path.

Jon's frantic splashing woke it. It started toward them again, this time with jaws agape. She had to choose the boat or the shark. She kicked and dove under Jon and came up facing the adversary. She brought up the flare gun as its jaws opened wider.

The monster closed in. She smelled rotting fish on its teeth, inches away she fired. The flare rocketed down its' gullet. It rolled and thrashed widely. She kicked away. Then it hit her, what she had just done. *I killed it, I killed it.* She hung there fighting tears. The shark's blood drifting surrounded them. She wanted to heave her guts but there was no time. The boat was almost in reach.

She grabbed Jon's vest, kicked her feet, stroked with one arm and propelled them away from bloody water. The sea was churned red with guts and gore. Pink foam floated on the waves. New shark fins appeared. She closed in on the boat just in time. But she was spent. She couldn't swim another stroke dragging dead weight.

That noble fish sank as Moon Dodger motored through their position and out of her reach.

"Rope, get the rope!" she yelled.

Jon thrust out a long, muscled arm grabbing the chum-pot line. Her adrenalin was toast, her emotions drained energy. *I can't believe I killed it.* Jon hung on to her and the boat. He pushed her over the side with a big, rough hand cupping her butt. The last guy that did that got kicked in the face. She landed onto the deck like a waterlogged sack. *Way strong for a wiry guy.* He hauled himself up and over the gunwale.

As she lay on the deck panting, Jon plopped down in the pilot's seat and untied the motor; he checked the compass and brought Moon Dodger back on course.

"I need a break," she muttered. "Shut down, we'll drift a while."

"You sure Ma'am," Jon said. "I reckon a sailboat ain't any different than a Cessna in one way; the wind sure as hell will blow you off course if you let it. We ought to keep going, find someplace to land."

"This is mutiny," she said halfhearted. "We aren't landing anywhere." But he was right; they would lose time and the further away from the feeding frenzy the better. Her stomach hurt. There was nothing in it but raw nerves.

"Think you can handle her, I'm hungry."

"I was watching you, Ma'am, I know the course. I'll get those sails up, take her awhile."

"OK but let's make it official, I hereby appoint you Cowboy of the sea. It's like chicken of the sea without mayo. Mr. Spock you have the com."

"Yes Ma'am," Jon said. He took off his hat and peeled off his wet T-shirt, "As acting Captain, I reckon you ought to take a siesta. Said you didn't get much sleep last night this morning."

Aggie really did need it, she hardly slept over the last few days since the dance, and dragging Jon through the water and all that kayaking took a toll. She was totally wiped out.

"OK fine, no spinnaker, too dangerous." She'd take the cowboy's advice. "Let's eat first."

She went below grabbed a sleeve of crackers, some peanut butter and jelly and a bottle of water. She made cracker sandwiches and placed them in a plastic container before coming topside with the eats.

He had the sails out and Moon Dodger was underway making good time. She squeezed in next to him on the pilot's bench. They ate and passed the water back and forth. PJ crackers never tasted so good. The company was kind of nice, too.

The sun was warm. Her clothes were wet. She took off the shorts and T-shirt thankful she always wore a bikini underneath her work clothes. He stretched out on the cabin's roof and leaned back against the mast. Without turning, she watched the rigging and sail adjust. He did it from the pilot's seat. He was doing OK. When he came forward to secure a loose knot, he didn't look sick anymore, or nerdy, in fact, he looked pretty 'durn' good with his shirt off. Maybe I'm not as bisexual as I thought?

As she lay back on the deck, she noticed this little flutter inside her stomach, it was something PJ crackers couldn't cause or cure. It was a feeling she never let herself feel. She thought, as she dozed off, I kind of like that feeling.

THIRTY-ONE

The GTO

Pharaoh was at table nervously flexing her wings waiting for the twelfth to arrive. Things were changing radically and the GTO wasn't ready nor had they anticipated such events. If the AI saw this coming, it surely didn't share that information.

Pharaoh mused on the number while she waited. Twelve was an auspicious number. Her estranged brother Karnack had taught it to Earth seven thousand years ago, before he himself was infected. Earth had long forgotten their visits. Earth had lost the gifts of great knowledge. After millennia of gentle interventions since, and Earth's archeology, they were yet to understand. And time was short.

The key to free energy had fallen from haven into Earth's hands and they did not see. She had written the formula in crops, in sacred books, in the Zodiac and they still did not see prime twelve. Earth humans were dense and as the sociopath genes spread since Karnack's failure, many of the GTO thought it good that Earth humans were thick minded.

No, not true, they are not stupid. It is the affliction that suffers their judgments.

At first Earth understood. They raised great monuments, they stopped starvation, they diverted the Nile, and they inhabited mountaintops and stopped war for a time...*for a short time.* Matriarchs ruled with love and preached peace but men's imaginary war gods built from greed had won. She missed the gardens of Babylon. No garden would ever match Eden.

Certain Earth humans, with an unforeseen genetic weakness, became mentally ill, craving narcissistic satisfaction, blood lust and worse. That insanity controls the powerful, they rape their own world, devastate their brothers.

Sadly, this bio-spiritual ailment was designed to inhabit the ruling class but the malady's foremost outworking evolved unselected and became uncontainable power lust. Karnack himself and his forbidden love of Earth's women, many thousands of years past, introduced it to the ruling elites. It spread over the generations.

Sanderson and the bulk of his ilk, industrialists and all manner of leadership whores had it. As such sickened minds seek grand heights, they often achieved power by ruthless means.

In that lay the Galactic Trade Organization's problem.

The nature of the disease compels some to lord over others. The affliction took Karnack before the immunization was discovered; he had said it was love that twisted his mind; he said his anger was because Earth's women rejected him, so he in turn rejected humanity. It wasn't true. Sociopaths, no matter their planet of origin, were delusional. *Even my brother lost his way.* She should not have allowed him to become infected.

Praytis arrived and took his place. Pharaoh stood.

"This meeting of the Galactic Trade Organization is now in session. Ladies and gentlemen, we have a problem. Karnack is moving: he is more active than ever before. Several dozen Earth humans have been abducted recently. His incursions are all over the internet. He is near the end of his resources. He is desperate. His insanity is escalating."

Pharaoh paused to allow them thought. No corrections came.

"Life Force traders, private, corporate and otherwise long ago backed away knowing the legal market would soon open. What they don't know is we are no closer to a contract. If Karnack continues the others will learn of it; illegal raiders will certainly move in and the secret of star drive will not hold."

"We should tell the U.S.A. about pirates," The marsupial from planet Moby said.

"Yes, we need their help; we can't do harm, not to our own kind," Said the tall gray. "Let Earth fight the raiders. Isn't that why we made genetic manipulations so long ago? Did we allow them mag-drive for nothing?

"We're out of time," Praytis said. "Once privateers learn of Karnack's actions, they will descend as a plague of locusts. We can't stop them. Karnack emboldens them."

"The larger problem still exists," Pharaoh said, "Sociopaths control Earth. If we break our agreement and disclose ourselves to the populations, they will attack Moon Base as indicated previously. There are far too many students here. Asteroid Belt Station can't hold us all. We cannot give Earth the weapons necessary to disable Karnack and his ilk either. Earth may well turn on us."

"They cannot penetrate our defenses with primitive missiles." The Nordic said and several species agreed telepathically.

"Perhaps," Pharaoh said, "Let us not forget they have a dozen MACs. They can reach us. They may not cause us an abundance of harm, but they will succeed in self-destruction. The population will suffer the aftermath."

She paused to gather her words. The implications of a nuclear attack from Earth were well understood by council. Earth can only succeed in destroying its stratosphere. Their attack will only unleash a slow, miserable, complete death upon themselves. All that LF wasted. Such a thing only sick minds could do, and such minds rule Earth. A dead planet did not serve the GTO's ambitions.

"We can't take warheads in space. We must take their missiles before launch. Fallout will kill billions. They will suffer for generations, but some may survive."

"...and we wait another eon to reap our harvest seeds," Someone vocalized.

Telepathic debates went around until one idea emerged prominent.

"We can't use Earth's military, that's given," Praytis said, to encapsulate the agreed facts, "If we don't remove Karnack the consequences are sure to be dire. Earth's people must unseat the monsters who rule them, first, of course. We must tell them. Then, with a trade contract, we can communicate openly, honestly and introduce the cure."

"We cannot interfere," Pharaoh said, "Else we break galactic law and invite sanctions on the GTO. We've tried informing the people subversively. It can't work. Government controls media. They will squelch us. We need another way."

"Seed the Earth with medication, eliminate the sociopaths," Demeter the Tuchman said. Her race was indistinguishable from Earth humans. She, a launch station specialist, was eager to begin operations planet side.

"The present generation will not heal. It breaks our U.N. agreement." Pharaoh said.

Not for the first time Pharaoh regretted sharing MAC control technology with the U.S. Government. Demeter's idea was good, but it requires the entire fleet and massive exposures. Earth would give chase. They have atmosphere operable MAC killer rockets. The idea was bold, illegal and too risky. There was not time enough.

Praytis shot up on all four legs. He moved back from his place at the table as was his usual reaction when he had an idea. Everyone waited for him to speak while he kneaded the floor with his feet, building confidence.

"Our long-term solution is still viable. Earth's people can continue waiting. The infusion will run its course down in a few hundred years more. But Karnack, he must be stopped and now. With the Board's consent, I will take an armed shuttle and go after him myself. I will program it for total destruction. If I am attacked, Earth will not recover the quantum cannon, LF drive or my body. Karnack must be stopped. They say on Earth, 'one step at a time.' I will take this step."

Pharaoh balked inside her heart. No member race of the GTO was war-like. The capacity for it had long ago evolved out of advanced people. Praytis was practical but he wasn't a policeman. Pharaoh desired capturing her brother. She would heal him. But his sociopath ways made him cunning. His capture proved impossible thus far. *His death is necessary.*

Earth people's primitive state, less the ailment, made them good candidates for the Galactic Police. They had the ability to act aggressively at need while retaining love and good will generally. It was a strange but ideal mix. *Something for the future.* Such a race could remove the likes of Karnack throughout the civilized universe if they could be tamed and that was unlikely.

There was another factor the Board did not yet know: They were obligated, by law, to leave now. Her delaying tactics were being questioned. *What a waste to fail so close to success.* Earthlings recovered quickly from Life Force donations — a boon to Earth and the universe, but no good to anyone should the planet die.

Leaving Earth to the raiders was heartbreaking. Pharaoh had great hopes but two obstacles remained immutable, one really, Karnack's and Earth leadership's mutual insanity.

Praytis is right. It is time to break the stalemate.

Pharaoh raised her hand in approval; sadly, the rest of the Board did as well. As Praytis left to make ready his flight Pharaoh wondered if she would ever see her old friend again. Karnack was no pretender at war-craft. Praytis was a gentle soul. *Could he actually kill another?* Should Praytis succeed, he would forever lament.

The team separated and each went to his or her duty station. Pharaoh went to Space Traffic Control and personally tracked Praytis's progress. He was away within the half hour. Her instruments showed two MACs approaching his craft a short time after entering the atmosphere. True to her fears, Praytis's ship went off line and less than an hour after he departed. Karnack had to be waiting for such a move. *An ambush, I killed him.*

Pharaoh activated the com. "This is the Commander. Our permit has not been renewed. Please begin withdrawal procedures. We will evacuate as soon as the fleet is ready. Leave no controlled technology behind. That is all."

Hope failed, her servant gone, with bitterness overflowing she hung her beautiful head and wept.

THIRTY-TWO
Karnack meets Branford

Branford stood at the end of the launch deck, balancing against the wind. He walked the very edge of The Contention. He wanted out from under that goddamn space-launch which hovered above. He needed sunlight, a clear view. A gust of tailwind buffeted him: he was unmoved. The sea winds always tasted like history, but lately its flavor had soured. History was about to change and not for the better.

He had bits and pieces. Building the MAC provided them. He learned of the aliens by drips and drabs. He was a key defense contractor reverse engineering 'Chinese technology.' Obviously, what he had wasn't from Earth and he wasn't allowed to say that. A trusted contractor of the righthand puppet master wasn't supposed to register what the left hand was doing. But someone had access to all the strings and he had a pretty good idea who that was. The Pentagon wasn't forthright. He found his own answers. The torpedo shaped MAC hovering above him was a suspicion personified, Karnack wasn't a big surprise, either, but nothing prepared him for what he saw now.

Another spacecraft descended through massive artificial black clouds. The craft was beyond his wildest extrapolations. It was the size of two aircraft carriers set end to end. He was too fascinated to be afraid. Whoever or whatever this Karnack was, it had some damn interesting hardware. *If this ever got out, the energy industry would collapse.*

No wonder the Chiefs kept the public in the dark.

He took the portable com-phone off his belt, "All stop; let's see what this sucker wants."

The Contention was in deep water, and out of the shipping lanes, but not so far out of the lane that they wouldn't be spotted. Karnack didn't seem to care.

Whatever this Alien was up to, his security was too loose. *America's security apparatus is tighter than a buzzard's ass in a power dive.* Maybe the Alien operated sloppy like a cheapskate subcontractor. Branford knew well how to use that to his advantage.

The pitted and scorched steel tube-like craft settled along the starboard side three hundred feet above water without a sound. The sea below flatted still as a duck pond. A side hatch appeared. A yellow light beam shot out and hit The Contention's flight deck. The light blinked out and two figures appeared who defied Branford's senses. He rubbed his eyes. They didn't change.

A winged man, tall and angelic stood with his legs wide, hands on narrow hips. He wore a white pleaded Greek tunic draped to his knees; he could have been a Babylonian God. He even had the wide golden belt. His long white hair flowed around him as if riding an electrical current. His face was long, pointed and handsome; the impression of onboard ego was palatable. *Has to be Karnack.*

But the other—did the devil walk with Gabriel?

The other was a cross between a man and a praying mantis, save his four legs didn't touch the deck. Branford squinted; the creature was inside a force bubble. *He's a prisoner.* Black came out of the wheelhouse and waved. Karnack moved toward Black. The force bubble followed. Branford did too; a few minutes later he entered his stateroom with curious trepidation.

Branford stopped cold in the doorway.

"Ah there you are, Mr. Branford, my newest and dearest partner." Karnack said from behind Branford's desk. "I see Mr. Black has things well in hand." Karnack gestured with a sweeping arm, "This is my former friend…made adversary, meet Praytis, the GTO's best effort against me." Karnack chuckled bird-like. His folded wings vibrated.

Praytis' jail rested near his daughter's cell. Branford looked past to Charlotte and Sonny. They were haggard, sick. Both pressed gaunt, wide-eyed faces against their crystal box. Branford balled his fists and stepped toward the angel man.

"Look, you bastard, this partnership is over," Branford said between clenched teeth. He'd try a bluff to gain information. He needed something, anything he could use.

"You can't run this ship without me and I'll go no further. I've noticed you don't have any men except mine. You control them with that wrist device. Humans made into robots can't think and you can't think for each one."

"Very good" Karnack said in a singsong voice. He stood and walked away from the desk. "Very observant, you have discovered a weakness of mine. However, my ship's computers have basic control; I don't need to think for them all the time, just the details." Karnack touched his belt. "Isn't that so…Mr. Black?"

Black hesitated. But his hand brought up a gun and pointed it at Branford. Black was struggling to disobey. Sweat burst out and ran down Black's face, his hand shook. He looked sicklier than yesterday and had lost more weight.

"I need only think the order and my human robots, as you say, start shooting: First your crew and then each other. I could tow this vessel to my destination but that would be too…observable and slow. I have no desire to play hawk and sparrow with your Air Force. Your cooperation will be well rewarded."

Karnack smiled with gleaming white teeth. His face lit with sincerity but his eyes were dead. Bradford knew that look, a man without a conscience like the self-serving slick generals and politicians he dealt with. Karnack could not be trusted.

Branford needed time to discover and exploit this Alien's weaknesses.

"A show of good faith is in order," Branford said. "Release my daughter and son-in-law and I'll steam ahead."

"I've noticed your progress getting underway is quite slow, Captain, I'm not so sure you have my...our, I should say...best interests in mind."

"You need stealth and that takes time. I must avoid shipping and stay in deep water. I'm doing my part. Stop screwing with me. You're the one that fucked up my radar, not me."

"All right, Captain." Karnack touched his belt and the shield around the captive condensed above them into a small glowing orb. The orb slowly floated to Karnack's belt and disappeared. Sonny staggered but stayed on his feet. Charlotte slid down her husband to the floor.

"They're injured, deal's off."

"They will recover," Karnack said. Here is something your government would love to know: LF regenerates after a donation. Pick up the pace, Captain, or they go back into the chamber and this time I will bleed them until they are dead."

Karnack turned to leave but stopped at the door. He touched his belt and the insect-man was released. A small orb of light formed over the creature as it hit the deck. The light-ball flew to Karnack's belt.

"I need all my force shields for the...project. Praytis is a sailor, he'll assist with navigation. His home is much like yours, that is, very wet. If we aren't on location within six hours, I will kill your crew, one for every hour of delay. Come Mr. Black, walk with me."

Karnack ducked and moved through the door. He walked buoyantly across the metal exterior deck and seemed to float down the stairs. *Tall but doesn't weigh much.* Black followed slowly, one leg dragging. Bradford could take Black given a chance. The man was getting weaker by the hour. *How much longer will the guards remain strong?*

"I know what you are thinking," the strange creature said. Branford jumped. "Sentient humans aren't tolerant of android controls. Mr. Black is dying. However, he will fight with whatever power he has left, and once expended, he will die. Mr. Black isn't the enemy. He cannot help himself."

"Whose side are you on?" Branford snapped.

"I am on the side of life, Mr. Branford; Karnack is not." Praytis moved to Branford's side, took his elbow, leaned close and whispered. "Karnack intends to take Earth's Life Force, all of it. He wishes nothing less than a total Soul Harvest."

Branford twisted away. "How do we stop him!?"

"Nonviolently," squeaked Charlotte.

"I knew they were real," Sonny said, awe in his voice. "We aren't alone."

"No, you are not, Sir." Praytis said. "I am with you."

"We can't just stand here picking our asses," Branford said.

"My cohorts will inform your government that I've gone missing. It is protocol. Let us hope your government reacts in good time. Our best course is delay. We must do what we can to disrupt Karnack until your military intervenes."

"What about your people?"

"We cannot interfere. If Moon Base knew what Karnack has in mind, they would have just cause to break protocol. We have waited seven thousand years to act directly again, but without legal cause, we will continue to wait."

Waiting wasn't in Branford's vocabulary. By the time the military got off their ass they'd be dead, death was in the cards either way. *The Feds will blow his ship to hell.* That Alien is a murderer. *Pull out the stops.*

Ideas flashed through his mind; flood the bilges, release fuel; run aground, any of which would slow the ship. But missing port would kill his daughter. *Better to spring a trap once we arrive.*

"Come on, help me," Branford said to the Bug-man, taking his daughter by the arm. "They need fresh air, food. Let's get them outside."

Branford and the alien led his daughter onto the observation deck and helped her into a chaise. Sonny was in better shape and didn't need a hand. Armed guards stood at each corner of the bridges' overlook deck one flight above. The mercenaries looked down on the strange party unfazed by Praytis' appearance. His hired SWAT men were still too fit. Fighting them was foolhardy. They were in top condition and wouldn't fail, like Mr. Black, before the deadline.

For the first time since his wife took ill and died, Branford felt overwhelmed and helpless.

THIRTY-THREE

Elbow Cay

They sat together at the stern with a sea chart between them. *No help.* She had lost track of their position. Aggie shoved the plastic-coated chart at Jon in frustration.

"You're a Navy guy, why can't you read this crap?"

After all that spy junk she heard about over the last few days, she knew starting Mel's magic phone was a bad idea. Jon broke down and told her the details, the magnetic aircraft, flying it remotely from Grandpa's research vessel, the secret underground control center and how they knew Daddy had downloaded the webcam imagine. What freaked her out most was that the government would even do this stuff. Obviously, Jon didn't like any of it, either. She realized he was a decent guy stuck working for a bunch of butt-holes.

There wasn't much choice; she had to use the phone: they were lost. She flipped it open and activated the sat feature. She went to the relative position application. Grandpa's ship was close—only ten miles out and drifting. She shaded her eyes and scanned the southeast horizon. All she saw was an odd, low, black cloud. She had no idea where exactly they were. Something solid should be in sight. She pressed Mel's number and put it on speaker.

"Dude, you shouldn't call. The FBI and Navy were here. Dad's way pissed."

"Shut up Mel, I need a fix. I don't know where I am."

Mel's keyboard clacked in the background like a runaway subway car, "You're approaching the North side of Cay Sal Banks. It's the Bahamas. There should be a little island to your South East, Elbow Cay. Dude, I'm getting pinged, I'm out."

"Great, she's gone." Aggie scanned the southeast. There was an island there. "Why can't I see that ship?"

Jon was staring at the chart. A crooked smile spread across his face and his skin stretched over his bony jaw. He laid the chart on her lap and pointed.

"See it? There's Elbow Cay. This here's Cay Sal Bank, I confirmed it." Jon pointed to each location. "It's dog-gone shallow. They can't go in there. They got to go over top or around south way. We stay north of it and east a spell and we'll pick up the trail. They must-a gone that way."

She looked closely at the chart. The ocean depths were marked. Above the Banks the chart was marked 'Major shipping lane.' Grandpa's ship had crossed the lanes, he avoided them. Why would he make for the Bank when he could have gone down the shipping lanes and into the Atlantic? She checked the upload from Mel. *No, he sailed zigzags. He was avoiding sea traffic.*

She grabbed the chart. The Bank is way west of populated islands. The south end is remote but only twenty miles from Cuba. If Grandpa wanted to hide, this must be his destination. Grabbing Mom was weird. If Gramps was bailing, he'd take his family with him. It almost made sense.

"Best we head north." Jon said. "Besides, we get in trouble there'll be ships along, help us out."

"North, I don't think so. Grandpa's going south," She said swallowing hard. "Definitely can't be trusted. We'll cut across the Banks, head him off, he has to go wide. He's going around south."

"We have a chance to get out of here, we should go find us a rescue, call the military."

"Military, are you kidding, you're military."

"I'm a flyer, not a fighting man, unless I got no choice."

"I'm not giving you a choice."

Aggie took the rudder and steered for the Banks. The chart showed a nice channel above Elbow Cay, there was a network of small channels throughout the inner Banks. *We'll pull the drop-keel and do the straight shot, it's worth the risk.*

She hoped that cloud wouldn't open up. Getting soaked once on this trip was enough. They could beach to wait out the storm if it got bad. She handed Jon the rudder and pulled the binoculars to scope out the little island.

"That looks good. Take us over there."

Curiosity turned her attention toward that weird cloud, and as she watched, the storm rose straight up, slow at first rolling and curling. "Jon," she said poking him in the ribs, "Check that out."

It boiled as it climbed and then suddenly something huge shot up stupid fast and quickly went out of sight. The cloud funneled up after it like a cosmic vacuum cleaner sucking up terra forma.

"I'll be dogged. Looks like a little aircraft carrier yonder." Jon said.

"That's what I thought, some kind of mother ship. That thing was monster big," Aggie said with her eyes still in the sky. "Military, I bet; another stupid state's secret."

"No Ma'am, not that one, that one." Jon pointed south.

There was a flat-topped ship with an object hovering above it. She scrutinized it—a flatted cigar shaped metal tube inside another dark cloud. This remaining smog was bigger than the ship but much smaller than the departed storm. She handed the binoculars to Jon. All the while they were sailing fast on the spinnaker, right toward the edge of the Banks with less than two miles to go.

"Jon, how long has the Navy been making clouds?" She slacked the spinnaker and let it deflate. She pulled the jib tight.

"Far as I can tell, never," Jon said training the binoculars on the scene. "That there ain't our MAC. Ours got markings. But, that's Branford's ship all right. No deck guns. Research vessels don't carry arms."

"You're saying Grandpa's hanging with aliens?"

"Appears so."

"Don't just sit there, help me drop sails, they'll see us."

They quickly stowed the sails. She dropped the mast, too, and tied down the boom. She didn't dare fire the motor; instead she snapped the oars off their gunwale mounts. Jon lifted the keel while she set oarlocks. They rowed with the wind and passed behind the ship. Two black Cobras sat on its fantail. The Contention was actually anchored facing south in deeper water but not that deep. It was only a hundred yards out of the shallows. *Big ships near shallow water is nuts.*

They rowed Moon Dodger toward the Bank. *Jason's Argonauts on espresso.* They didn't slow until the water was blue-green and a few feet deep. They kept going until reaching a mangrove stand and put covering plants between them and the ship. There they tied up.

They lay side by side atop the fore of the cabin passing the binoculars back and forth. The ship's crew moved sluggishly, like walking in molasses. Men with guns followed deck hands around. A man in black stood on a balcony beneath the wheelhouse pointing and with him was some kind of alien man with four legs. She felt weak all over. *Daddy's right, they're real, only they aren't friendly.*

Aggie handed Jon the binoculars. He watched and mumbled under his breath.

"You better see this," Jon said handing them back.

She wasn't sure she really wanted to look. A short, thick-bodied man, with full gray hair appeared waving his hands. He was pissed. Was that Grandpa? She hadn't seen him since she was little and had no clear memory of him.

Then she caught a glimpse of Mom and Dad behind the old guy. Two guys in black fatigues, the kidnappers, ran up the stairs rifles ready. They pointed one right at the old guy's face.

"I don't get it," she said, "Who're the bad guys?"

"That man in black, I seen him before, he was in Sanderson's office. The Admiral didn't much cotton to him."

Jon didn't quite sort it out for her. She couldn't just sail over and ask. The guards were the shoot-first kind of guys. There was thick rope hanging over the side at the stern; a service catwalk was about fifty feet off the water and ran along the port side below the wheelhouse complex. She had climbed the rope in gym class like a mountaineer running from a Yeti. *I'll make that climb.* Aggie moved up onto her knees and peeled off her shirt. She still had her swimsuit on underneath.

"Where're you going?"

"I'm finding out what's going on over there."

"Dog-gone wish I could swim. That ain't right."

She slipped into the water and started toward the ship. It was only a few hundred yards from their position. *No big deal.* She does two hundred yards of laps in the school's pool just for fun. Swimming against the wind toward the ship couldn't be that hard, salt water is more buoyant than chlorine soup.

She took to the water and swam against the wind. She was tired after fifty yards and slowed her pace. I'll make it, I have to. Jon can't get home without me.

Panic started, her chest hurt, that wouldn't get her anywhere. She couldn't meditate, so she used Mark's Jedi techniques and slowed her breathing. She calmed, became one with the ocean. Relaxing into a steady rhythm, she made steady headway against the wind by diving and swimming underwater every few yards.

THIRTY-FOUR
Sanderson scrambles

S anderson had to ride the tube-car through hundreds of miles of deep tunnels and would be out of communication range. Before his transport hit the water, he called Nostrum. There was a security leak, he was sure if it.

She said Seaman Colbert was missing; she didn't have details on the kidnapping. More alarm bells. He had ordered the Yeoman to, 'Call the FBI, CIA, get the cops after Colbert, find the Piper girl, no MPs, and keep it quiet. Most important; find the leak,' before submerging.

He traveled harboring new suspicions. He had time to think, no communications along the way to distract him. The Sherriff's Department was on the Galaxy Project's payroll; they'd get on board, the others? He wasn't so sure. With Black rogue, the CIA would cooperate, they had to.

His car silently slowed to a stop. The metal pocket door retracted. He exited into an empty rock-cut chamber three hundred yards square. It was hot as hell. Tubes with magnetic rails led out in six directions and every time he went to Moon Base, he returned by a different tunnel. *How in the hell do they do that?* He entered the only elevator and sat down with the feeling that his Yeoman didn't spill it all.

He hated leaving his office. He trusted no one, not even his secretary. Time in transit was lost time. He wasn't sure of Yeoman Nostrum whom he had left alone minding the store. *Who is that woman, really? Her folder says she's clean as a new bosun's whistle and just as brass-shiny. Nobody's that clean.* Her security checks were too good.

Did the Chiefs have her watching him? He didn't tell them everything and they knew it. Why did they give him such a pretty girl? He didn't need the distraction. The fools, no amount of Viagra would get him hard enough to spill his guts and never to a lover. *The Chiefs have to know that, too.*

Fifteen minutes passed as the elevator ascended and its pressure system worked to regulate his body's systems. The GTO had an unexplained method that cut decompression time down from hours to minutes, and like almost everything else they had, they didn't share how it worked. It was just one more carrot on the stick. The door chimed; Sanderson got off his duff. The shiny door slid open inside his private bathroom's mirrored shower wall. Nostrum was waiting at the bathroom door.

"Sir, the situation has changed. The Pipers were apparently picked up by an unnamed black-ops team. They were pros. Colbert was on site. He may have been picked up as well."

"How!"

"Cobra-jets, possibly NRO, and a Branford Huey."

"Jesus H. Christ! Yeoman, where'd you get this?" He said exiting the bathroom.

"Navy local monitoring," she said. "Choppers came in under radar but one flight control tower saw it and recorded. I hacked Navy security after we spoke. The Coast Guard chased Mark Levine in the Pipers' fishing boat. We don't know exactly what took place. There were other witnesses on the ground but nobody had anything of value. I believe the Coast Guard handed Levine off to Homeland Security. He's MIA. Homeland won't cooperate. They're holding the Coast Guard crew incognito."

"What in the hell is this; a goddamn party? Why don't we send up a fucking flare," He was livid. Too many people knew too much. "Thank God the NSA didn't get this, that's all I need."

He was ranting, but the Yeoman always took it well, Sanderson liked that about her. Now, she cast her eyes downward, something she rarely did.

"What else Yeoman?" He asked, lowering his voice. He took his chair. He was less intimidating seated.

"Branford's ship, The Contention, disappeared from National Security Agency satellite observation. The feeds were looped like Google Earth and before real-time was restored, the ship had gone. No sign of her. Sorry Sir, I had to get intel directly from the NSA. Only alien tech hacks the NSA, but they think it's the Chinese. Someone, not us, corrupted the military sat-network's onboard computers."

"Goddamn it! It's The NRO. The tail's wagging Majestic's dog. They have tech we don't have; the Chiefs must crush them." He said it but knew that would never happen.

"Sir, the NRO claims no involvement. They say Mr. Black is missing."

"Where's Branford's ship now?"

"I can't find it, Sir. It's not on any of our off-network satellites. They were disabled as well. It's completely gone. Maybe she sank."

He wasn't about to tell her Black's alien co-conspirators might have smoked everyone's network. He drummed his pudgy fingers on the desk blotter. *Black must have made his move with his alien, that's a given.* Could it be another GTO trick? They have cloaking; another carrot on the stick. He wished, and not for the first time, he could beat the GTO in the head with America's bully club. Whatever was really happening, it was big and he had to contain it. In doing so, with a little luck, he'd cut out bottom feeders like Branford while doing it. *Opportunity for a bigger slice of the pie.*

Sanderson's top orders came first or the Chiefs would fire him. Preventing disclosure was top priority. The public can't know about aliens, no matter what. Extraterrestrial events called for extraordinary action. He hated to do it, but cooperation was necessary. He'd use it and pit them against each other later.

"Alert the CIA, code phrases 'disclosure is imminent.' Get Majestic on the horn. Tell them what we have. They need to scramble MAC hunters."

"They'll deny they have them. They aren't supposed to splash UFO's anymore."

"That's bullshit. MAC killers are on standby. It's not a Moon Base ship. We're hunting Branford's research ship and the alien that high-jacked it. I don't know who's behind it, but tell them it's Karnack, that'll get them moving."

"Should I alert the President?"

"Hell no, none of her goddamn business."

"Sir, splash Branford's ship?"

"Damn right. Get Majestic on the phone, if they refuse, I'll tell them myself."

Sanderson picked up the phone receiver. He had an active 1944 olive drab rotary phone. Nobody had the equipment in place to hack dial phones anymore, especially an antique. A trick he got from Levine; low tech gets ignored.

Nostrum stood by and watched keenly. *Who is she working for?* He stopped mid-dial and reprimanded her with a look. Nostrum backed out of the room. He dialed a special number only he knew. It was time to alert the Chiefs—unless, of course, Yeoman Nostrum had done it already. *That girl knows too much.*

With over sixty security agencies in operation, the failure to communicate between them was standard procedure. But they had one thing in common; they all kept the same secret. Over the last seventy years nothing glued spooks together like hiding the existence of aliens. Majestic would give him the National Recovery Office's fire power. They had no choice.

It wasn't the first time the U.S. Government sacrificed a primary contractor for secrecy. Sanderson just hoped that Black was onboard the Contention when it got blown out of the water. It would be ideal if Branford wasn't there, he could use the man, but Sanderson will do whatever it takes. *No witnesses.*

THIRTY-FIVE
Elbow Cay water ride

She swam toward the Contention wishing her swimsuit wasn't day-glow orange. If someone looked over the side while on top, she was toast. From the water, she saw no deck hands. The guys with guns had their backs to the rails. *They're not guarding the ship. They're keeping people onboard from leaving.* The helicopters on the fantail weren't even tied down like nobody cared if they fell over the side. *That's really weird.* Twenty-five yards out she dove and swam the rest underwater.

She surfaced at the hull and pushed along its micro fauna coated side until reaching the rope. The first few feet of the hull were slimy and she had cut her hands on the barnacles below the water line. Climbing, the rope grated her cuts raw. Her right hand was bloody by the time she hit a maintenance catwalk. Finally, safe, she needed to catch some air, but the ship's engines revved up. A cloud of French fry bio-diesel blew down the broadside and coated her with oily smoke.

"I hate fast food!"

The whine of an electric anchor winch started. The clank of an anchor chain followed. She had only a little time. *Thank the Goddess they have to raise one anchor at a time.* The ship's maneuvering jets below kicked on. *They're slacking an anchor.*

She climbed a metal service ladder up to a deck hatch. It was locked. She pulled herself up and over the rail to the wider deck above like a greased rock climber. She was seventy feet above the water. The highest she ever dove was forty feet. The school's high diving board made her head spin and this was way worse. Still, she looked down. There were black tipped reef sharks below. *They don't swim deep water.* Blue sharks were milling around, too. *Did my cuts attract them that fast?*

"Ok Universe, fine, just screw me, what else you got?"

She followed the cantilevered broadside deck toward the bow. Finding a row of huge windows, she stopped and peeked. *Nobody's home.* She slid one open and crawled through. The place was weird. It was a floating museum, not like any ship's cabin she read about. Swords, small brass cannon, old tackle and lots of shipwreck stuff ringed the place. She moved forward to an open sliding glass door to check outside. Beyond that, there was a shallow foyer and the exterior's expanded catwalk. She heard the first anchor banged against its topside cradle. Time was running out.

She'd have to bail soon. She backed into the room. Thinking about the sharks, she grabbed a short, sheathed dagger off a big wooden desk. Its hilt was covered in multicolored gemstones, leather sheath trimmed in gold. *This is really old.* She didn't care. Testing it, it was sharp enough to slice sharkskin. She tied it to her bikini bottom's side string while tiptoeing to the window. The forward room's glass door slid open. She dipped low and plastered herself against a wall behind a display case.

"No more delays." said a singsong voice over a radio. "…out of time. Move this ship or another man goes over the side. Karnack out."

A calm voice said. "Need I remind you Karnack has no qualms about killing Earthmen?"

"Shoot another of my men and we aren't going anywhere." A gruff voice said.

That accounts for the sharks!

"You can't sail without a crew. I don't have enough men as it is. This isn't a goddamn pleasure yacht! We must spot the anchors; you want the hull bashed in? That won't get you far."

"I'll see … Karnack, this is Black again. We need more androids…But we're shorthanded … No … Affirmative. You are on your own Branford…says you better … by sundown … "

The wind kicked up. She couldn't hear them anymore. *Branford, that must be Grandpa.* She had to chance a peek. *Who was who?* She slowly rose up and moved to the side of the pedestal with a glass display square on top of it. She peered through a glass cube and past the barnacle encrusted gizmo inside.

A gray-haired fireplug guy stood facing that black suit guy. The old guy's fists were knotted. The muscles in his Popeye forearms pulsed. He was winding up too hit somebody. *That guy's pissed.* She leaned into the case, it tilted. The glass display cube fell and crashed on the floor.

"Crap!"

The guy in black stumbled through the door. She charged. He fumbled with a pistol at his waist. Before he could level it, she kicked him in the face. Black suit tumbled backwards landing on the metal grate outside. He fell like a boxer out-cold on his feet.

"Grandpa, its Aggie!" She cried.

"Aggie! Jesus, how the hell?"

"I've got a sailboat."

"Never mind, get out of here, fast. Call the Navy, they'll kill you."

Black suit guy rolled to his hands and knees and used the walkie-talkie, "Stowaway, get up here." She heard boot steps racing down the flight deck toward them. Black suit guy started crawling toward his gun like he was fighting with glue.

Grandpa could have kicked the revolver away, but he just stood there. He rolled his eye at Aggie and motioned her toward the broadside. *If Grandpa helps, he's toast.* He was a prisoner, highjacked.

She backed up and used the toppled display case base to climb out the window. On the deck, she ran aft. She couldn't find the deck hatch! *How am I going to get off this tub?* Steel-toed boots were stomping up the stairs. She had to act.

She looked over the side: Sharks were too busy eating the dead guy to bother her. She climbed the rail, took a deep breath and dove. She hit the water perfectly. The momentum pushed her thirty-five yards out underwater. She came up took a quick breath and dove again. She repeated the process until reaching shallows.

Small onshore Black Tip sharks parted as she neared Moon Dodger. Jon reached over the gunwale, took her arm and hoisted her onboard.

"They're shooting," she said breathlessly. "We're in deep crap."

"I heard them. They stopped. We're in range, I can't figure it."

She grabbed the binoculars. The man in black was leaning over the rail with one of Grandpa's antique brass telescopes. Black waved his gunmen away and turned from the rail. The ship started to move.

"Why don't they come after us?" Jon asked.

"Tight schedule, they're in a big hurry." She said as she went below. She snapped up her sat-phone and came back outside flipping it open.

"Grandpa said to call the Navy. You got the number?"

He didn't answer. He pushed his hat back and shaded his eyes with a hand; the sun was low, right in his face. He pointed at the spaceship. She followed. A hatch had opened at its front bottom and a sliver disk floated out. The MAC hovered wobbly fashion twenty feet off the Contention's flight deck. It suddenly shot south, made a one hundred and forty degree turn and came right at them.

"That's not one of our dog-gone MACs. What the hell's it doing?"

The saucer swooped in so low they had to duck below the gunwales. Just in time, too. The craft swung high like on a pendulum and came at them again. This time it grazed the cabin's forward roof and tore off the mast's tie-down. As the craft swung high, she grabbed a rope and threaded it thought the top rail leaving two ten-foot rope loops. She stood up on the opposite gunwale with one rope and leaned out over the water.

"Jon, take that rope!"

Together they bounced up and down on the sidewall rocking the boat until it flipped up on edge. Water rushed over the side. The MAC swooped in low over the mangrove stand cutting foliage like deli-sliced broccoli. It was chopping everything down for a clean shot.

"Pull, Pull!" She cried.

The MAC caught the cabin's side and ripped a porthole away as they flipped the boat. She was thrust under. Touching bottom, she pushed off toward the surface meeting Jon on his way down. He didn't have a life jacket on. She pulled him up to the surface. The MAC arching high started another pass.

"You're loco," Jon said spitting water.

"Better crazy than dead, take a big breath and follow me."

She dove holding his hand and maneuvered them under the overturned boat. They surfaced inside the cockpit. She found what she was looking for, an air pocket. Water and snot spewed from Jon's nose. He gulped air. The MAC passed rocking the boat but it missed. Moon Dodger's hull was very low in the water. She remembered Dad talking about how UFO's went underwater, too.

"That thing can't get us here, can it?" She asked breathlessly.

"I don't think so...too shallow...he'll hit bottom. Quiet, might have audio sensors."

The MAC made two more passes causing the little channel's water to churn each time. Finally, the attack was over when The Contention's motors revved full throttle. *Grandpa's underway.* She listened until the motors faded. They continued treading water until the air pocket smelled like Jon's breakfast burrito and she couldn't take it anymore.

"Let's get out of here."

Jon managed to swim to the surface without help. He dog paddled through the damaged foliage that littered the waterway, and crawled onto a sandbar. She swam over, got out, and flopped next to him. The MAC and Grandpa's ship were nowhere in sight. That low, black cloud was far south and barely visible.

"That's a hell of a way to teach a man to swim."

"Everybody's got to learn somehow." She couldn't help laughing. He still had that goofy cowboy hat on.

"What're you funning over?"

"I've never seen a cross between a drowned rat and Yosemite Sam before."

"Funny, what'll we do now Captain?"

She reached for the phone, but all she had was the dagger. She thought she had the phone clipped on her side. It was gone and would be too wet to use even if she still had it. "Phone went overboard" Her humor abandoned ship. Mom, Dad, and Grandpa were all in serious trouble and there wasn't any help coming. They were on their own. *One step at a time.*

"We'll drag the boat over here, right it, and sail after them, that's what."

"You lost the phone, we ought-a high-tail-it out of here, get some help. No way to track them."

Jon was right, but she wasn't about to give up, not after all that. A fix popped into her head.

"Sharks—Grandpa's ship runs on bio-diesel. It leaves a slick, and sharks follow oil slicks. Eighteenth century whalers reported that oil processing attracted them. We'll follow the sharks."

But first, she had to swim with the sharks, find the sat-phone and whatever else sank. She read that black tip reef sharks were mostly harmless. If a big predator swam in, they'd scatter. *Early warning system.* Black tips were all around them now. *Besides, big sharks will go after the dead guy first, I hope.* She dove into the water and swam toward where the boat had flipped. There wasn't much sunlight left.

"Where're you going?"

"Straight to the bottom if you ask Mrs. Preggey. I'll tie on, bring you the rope, you haul the boat over while I recover stuff."

She never thought she'd make friends of sharks, or a Navy guy, especially a cowboy. At this point, she'd take any friend she could get.

THIRTY-SIX
Karnack moves on Anguilla Cay

Karnack eased deeper into Base Ship's command chair. His attention darted between holographic screens. Branford's ship was steaming toward Anguilla Cay, that little boat neutralized. The Americans had yet to launch pursuit. Mr. Black had done well but he would not live long enough to experience Karnack's triumph.

"A pity, really."

Operations would be in position soon after nightfall. In the morning, Karnack himself will deliver his last Life Catalyst generator. By noon, he will have enough Life Force to buy a fleet, a modern fleet with AI fighting droids. And best of all, the Earth's nasty, heartless, little women would be no more. Never again will Earth cause such harm as he suffered.

His wings fluttered on the thought. *Back to business.* He touched his belt.

"Mr. Black, push those helicopters into the sea. We won't need them. I will place a rather large machine on that landing pad in the morning. Tonight, we sequester captives. Have everything in place by morning."

He hailed Moby to the bridge: He could be anywhere. Karnack had Base Ship locate him on camera so he could watch Moby run. Moby ran like a gorilla; extralong arms swinging in time was ridiculous. *And that awkward stride!* Karnack never tired of it.

Karnack's race was graceful. Moby's was brutish. The First Mate was amidships and had a long trek. Karnack decided when he acquires a new ship, he would not include transport tubes. *My next crew will be all Moby's species.* However much the latest biological units made natural sentient crew obsolete, watching crews struggle, even human marsupial types, was far too much fun to relinquish.

Moby arrived with his chest heaving and his skin tinted greener. Oxygen was spotty along the gangways.

"Ah, so glad you could join me. Let us converse."

"Look, Karnack, I've got a lot of work yet. It's not easy. Half the androids are age-damaged. We should put them in regeneration chambers on low LF feed."

Karnack stopped Moby's chatter with a grand wave of his hand. His cackle-laugh always deflated Moby's building diatribes. The poor state of the equipment mattered not. Karnack's luck was superior, infallible in fact, the past proved it. He had no serious impediments before him, only less than ample resources. But it was enough to complete this operation. Nothing else mattered.

"How many class-A units do we have?"

"Not enough," Moby said, "I've only got twenty class-B grays; works for ground operations but they can't pilot. What good are they if we can't fly them to ground? We can't recall shuttle one and sacrifice cloaking. Satellites will see us."

"Enough! How many class-A pilots?"

"Two for Base Ship, two on Number One shuttle and two for MACs. I have one class-A for launch bay. We don't have any for Number Two shuttle."

"Load Shuttle Two with the LF generator. Give me two class-B units I'll fly it myself," Karnack said.

"You can't fly and still control all the androids, it's impossible. That Mr. Black isn't capable...It's going to take every bit of Base Ship's AI to keep everything running."

Karnack silenced Moby with a look. He opened the side compartment of his command chair and took out a belt like Moby's former facilities control belt. This one allowed Karnack override. He tossed it to Moby.

"Moby, Moby, have you no faith? You'll run the ground force units—in person. I'll do the rest. After nightfall, take an escape pod, and as many B units as will fit. You'll set up the vortex-ring by morning."

"But the pod is one way, I'll be stranded!"

"I'll be down in the morning with the generator and any B-units you can't take."

Moby didn't like it, by the look on his contorted face. Karnack understood his concern. They were dangerously low on androids and it was risky to use them all at once. Moby hedged at the door and opened his mouth. Another protest was forthcoming but Karnack wouldn't hear it. He jumped from his chair; wings spread wide. It was a serious threat. Moby's mouth snapped shut with a clack.

"Don't disappoint me. I retain command of Base Ships' computers. I'll have you sliced into pieces if you falter. Do your job. Now, get to work."

Moby knew of Karnack's trick. The tractor beam system that had taught Moby respect over Lake Michigan can tune narrow and thus make a lovely beam weapon. Such beams used excessive LF energy, and normally he would not waste power that way. Moreover, killing personally was far more amusing. Karnack would wait for an opportune time to remove Moby.

Games were at end. The time was right to act. Spend energy with abandon. If this operation cost Karnack his First Mate, so be it. In fact, it was past time he acquired a new crew.

THIRTY-SEVEN
Righting Moon Dodger

An hour passed before they righted Moon Dodger and ordered the gear. The sun was below the horizon and it was getting darker, but the sky was still lit pink. No ship's light appeared in the distance, no lights to follow. The sailboat wasn't badly damaged—luck was with them. Jon patched the porthole with a driftwood plank he found within the flotsam that had washed up on the sandbar. The wind generator was toast and that sucked. Hopefully, the phone didn't need juice. No way to tell, it was totally drenched, she'd boot it up later when and if it dried out.

She considered the damage. They'd have to sail without spinnaker; the pole was gone and its rigging scrambled. *Winds wrong for it anyway.* The jib's hardware was damaged too, but Jon used the remaining spinnaker hardware and fixed it.

Mark's little sloop proved tough. And Jon proved handy.

"How'd you learn that, you never sailed before?" Aggie said.

Jon explained as he finished, "A ranchers got to fix anything and everything fer himself. Ain't no other way out on the prairies."

"No wagon train Sears and Roebucks a-calling, I guess."

"No Ma'am. And Tractor Supply ain't just around the corner, neither. Gringo city folks." He rolled his eyes to the sky.

Aggie pitched a clump of seaweed at him. He ducked. She missed. Her Cowboy was resourceful, quick minded, not the typical Key West guy, for sure. *Maybe rednecks aren't so dumb after all.* He had even set up a laundry line to hang their wet clothes. The warm Caribbean winds had dried them fast.

She didn't have many wisecracks to shoot at Jon as she watched and listened. He had worked in nothing but his gray Navy boxer shorts. His deep tanned arms and face contrasted starkly with a glaring white body. That little tuft of hair at the center of his chest would pass for a wayward goatee. Jokes popped in and out of her head but she wouldn't spit them out. She was too busy admiring his ropey muscles and washboard abs. She stared as he dressed. Without that goofy cowboy hat, he was actually hot.

"What-cha gawking at?" Jon said. His cheeks flushed red, matching the sunburn on the top of his shoulders.

Thinking fast she said, "That nasty scar on your back, how'd you get it?"

"Ah, that. Some good old boys back home at the feed store was messing with this Mexican fellow my Daddy had hired. Pedro's just a little guy. I had to step in. One thing led to another and I got stabbed but good. Weren't nothing. I felt bad for the cow-poke what stabbed me, going off to jail with a broken nose and no front teeth and all."

A crooked smile broke across Jon's face. His teeth showed pink in the sunset's light. She always had a comeback but the only thing that came out of her mouth was a gasp. *Earth to Aggie, back to reality!* She shook off the spell.

"I hate when the big guy picks on the little guy," She said. "Speaking of the big guy, we have to figure out where Grandpa went. We can't follow the oil slick. It's washed out by now."

She sat at the tiller bench and set her mind on the problem. She knew they went south. They had to follow Cay Sal Bank. Too far south and they'd breach sea lanes and enter Cuban waters. West of the Bank was another shipping lane. She was certain Cuba wasn't the destination. Where could they go in two hours? She got the chart out of the cockpit's cubbyhole, turned her back to the sunset, and held it up for better light. The plastic sheet glowed pink and purple.

"They must be heading for Anguilla Cay," She said pointing to a spot on the chart as she handed it to Jon. "The space guys want to stay hidden, that's what they said."

"How do you reckon it's this here Cay?"

"Black suit guy said they had to make their destination by nightfall. It's the only place near without hitting Cuba. They didn't steam away very fast."

She examined the fine print. "This island has a research station or something like one on it. It's too far out from Bermuda's main island for tourists."

"Makes sense," he said. "Branford does research; he'd know this spot, the best place to hole-up is no-man's-land. Might be a no-fly zone I expect."

"OK, set sail Cowboy." Jon didn't move. "What's up?" She asked.

"Hell, how we going to sail at night? Fine, the batteries are good and the lights work, but we can't use no lights, they'll see us miles off."

"Good point; give me a minute. I'll figure it out, chart it in my head."

She never imagined that high school math would apply to real life. Trig formulas danced behind her eyes. She had wind speed; hadn't changed all day. She had compass direction. She had already figured out average speed without spinnaker. She calculated their rate of travel according to wind direction. The mechanical wind speed gizmo still worked. Mark had stored a sounding rope, just a weight tied on the end of a long rope with incremental knots. It was low tech, but a good way to figure speed and depth. It would work. She had relative position to start with. The chart gave destination. All the necessary facts were at hand. The math added up.

"Take us three or four hours. Got it under control," She said, "Weigh anchor Cowboy."

"Sailing right up to them?"

"No way, we'll take the channel behind Anguilla, come up from behind. The ship can't get close. They got to anchor south of the island which puts them one or two hundred yards off shore. The west is shallow a mile out, they can't park there. We'll go in from the north shallows."

Jon seemed less doubtful than she expected. She guarded her own doubts. She'd get them there, no problem, but how do they spring everyone? She didn't have a clue.

She used a piece of rope as a belt for her cut-off shorts and threaded the knife's sheath on her side. She fingered Grandpa's dagger thinking. *Low-tech solutions for high-tech problems.* The idea of using the knife the way someone had used one on Jon made her skin crawl. Kicking Billy Barns' ass was one thing; sticking a pike into some pirate's gut was a thing she could not do.

Maybe the Goddess would disapprove, but she wished Jon hadn't donated his rifle to Davey Jones' gun locker.

THIRTY-EIGHT
Midnight sailing

Aggie expected an easy, maybe even a little bit romantic sail southward to Anguilla Cay; the ride wasn't fun at all. A strong west wind blew in from the gulf. The sea churned up soon after they set sail. The blow relentlessly threatened to smash them on the reefs. All night she tacked into the wind only to be driven back. For every three miles she tacked outbound, they made a mile south. The only saving grace; wind forced waves to break in the shallows giving advanced warning of running aground. Jon became a fixture on the bow. He spent the night casting the sounding weight forward, calling depth and speed.

She had completely lost track of their position. She wondered if Anguilla Cay even existed. *We should be there.* Finally, exhausted, she dropped the mainsail and allowed the boat to go inbound on the jib. Despite strong wind, the smaller sail didn't push Moon Dodger hard.

"I need a break!" She called out.

Jon was drenched. His face was covered with salt and sweat as he joined her in the cockpit. He smelled like salted onion rings. Their stomachs grumbled a chorus of 'feed me'.

"Six hours. Dog-gone Aggie, you said three tops." Jon held his watch aloft and caught a sliver of light cascading thought a break in the cloudy sky. "Midnight, hell of a long day." His tone was pissy.

"I thought ranchers were hard assed." She snapped feeling hungry, tired and scared. She pushed the hand pump at Jon. "Here do something useful, do the bilge, pretend you're watering cows or something."

He ignored the pump and shot dagger-eyes at her.

Aggie slapped her forehead. She immediately regretted her words. Jon was OK, no need to treat him like crap.

"I'm sorry, just tired I guess." She said.

Jon slowly pealed back a crooked smile. He did have nice teeth. They brightened a dark sea. The only other things that stood out were the onshore breakers and the white-caped waves that drove them toward ruin.

"Jon, your watch illuminated?" She asked.

"No, it was my Daddy's, old-fashioned windup. It's waterproof."

"How'd you see it?"

"Moonlight," Jon said thrusting a thumb over his shoulder.

"Moon's over there," She said pointing in the other direction.

The moon was a dull crescent that night mostly hidden by clouds. She had kept track of its position. Together they turned and looked. Southeast orbs of light flashed off and on, there was a distant light on the water, like a ship lit for night diving.

She mounted the binoculars and spied a large, bright object hovering above a ship. A spaceship was descending very slowly thought the clouds. *That's what he thought was the moon.* They had been so focused on fighting the ocean they hadn't noticed lights on the southern horizon. Squinting into the field glasses, she barely made out a strip of white beach in the left foreground ten miles downrange and dim shore lights twinkled further east through a silhouetted jungle.

"See I told you," She said with a relieved laugh, "Only six hours, and right on schedule."

"Mama warned; never argue timing with a woman. I'm not poking that fire."

"Did she warn you about this?" Aggie grabbed both his ears, drew him in and kissed him hard on the mouth. "Come on, let's make landfall."

As they closed in, Jon resumed sounding while she steered for the shallows.

It didn't take long for her to find one of the many natural channels that spider webbed through the coral reefs. Guided by Jon, she steered to a place where waves didn't rage. White surf framed an inlet between coral heads. She pulled the keel and let the wind push them into a natural cove. Once inside, she gathered the sails. Jon set oars, and together, they rowed in and away from the breakers.

At a hundred yards, they turned south into a wide channel and calmer water. They beached on a palm-studded sandbar. Jon tossed the anchor ashore and jumped out. She followed. There was a sand dune, and below it, the wind wasn't so vicious. Jon flopped down on the sand, wiggled into it and locked his hands behind his head falling asleep immediately.

She sat back next to him watching the palm tree sway hypnotically against the black of night. His chest rose and fell in time. The universe seemed to breathe with that same rhythm. The sand was warm but thoughts of Mom and Dad as prisoners caused a chill to surface from within. With a sleepless storm inside her head, she fell back next to him. The heat of his body felt good. She felt safe and let the Sandman cast his spell.

That night she dreamed of space-cowboys, salted beef steak onions and sailing between the stars. Her dream was all so real as if the universe bespoke her future.

THIRTY-NINE

A long, dark night

He couldn't sleep so Bradford stood on the forward observation deck all night watching the aliens, trying to figure out how to stop them.

Branford had anchored off Anguilla by eight p.m. last night. He had done as told and was released from duty. He was surprised Karnack didn't have him shot. The aliens were too busy to bother with him. They locked up all of his non-mercenary crew in the hold along with Charlotte and Sonny before they started landside operations.

Limited number of force fields. They need them all on the island. They could have killed the prisoners. *Saving them for something, hostages?* The aliens need them for what? The obvious: Karnack's greed. The more donators, the greater the soul harvests. Branford suspected it was technical not emotional; more living victims must enhance extraction somehow.

Three MACs had danced over the island shooting beams of blue light at the ground half the night. The lights were tractor beams. They transported people dangling in mid-air to individual locations. From what he pieced together; the aliens had to position living people in a precise pattern. They formed a human circle.

There was mayhem ashore. *Had to be terrifying for them.* Night vision binoculars showed him people running and grays hunting them down. The gray's heat signature was low while the alien First Mate's signature was twice as hot as Earth people.

Aloysius Branford wasn't anything if he wasn't tough, but tough wasn't the answer—he had to work smart—he had to stay focused. *Play the game.* He had to remain free and watch for an opportunity to act.

It was dawn when Karnack returned in a launch. He floated down to the Contention's fight deck in a beam of yellow light. Mr. Black limped to Karnack and Branford decided to join them and see what he could learn although he didn't have much hope.

"Mr. Branford; how nice of you to join us. Perhaps you can help us with a quandary," Karnack said. "There aren't enough adult bodies to complete our little project."

"Take one of the guards," Branford said thinking that one less guard is one less problem he'd need to deal with.

"That won't do, not at all. No, control bracelets taint the quality of Life Force. I need good quality donations," Karnack said with a flutter of his wings.

Branford wished he knew how to read the Alien's expressions better.

"What about the other crew, the men in the hold?" Branford offered pretending to cooperate. His life and freedom hung on a thin thread.

"I've had them on bracelets," Black said, "None are unaffected. We could use him." Black pointed at Branford with his thumb.

"Mr. Black, I'm surprised at you. Mr. Branford is our partner," Karnack said. That singsong voice cut Branford like an ice blade. "I have it. The Branford children will do. They have been out of chamber long enough. They must have regenerated."

Karnack's chin jerked forward and back several times like a pigeon pecking a seed ball. *Careful Old Man, don't show your hand.* It took all his effort to keep from exploding. Surely the aliens would kill him once the project was done, or if he got out of line.

He could do no good dead. Sacrificing himself solved nothing. If it came to that, he would, but not yet. Sonny didn't have the balls to kill but it was worth a try. Branford swallowed hard.

"Logical," he said. "I'll go below and get Sonny." Branford spun a plan inside his head. He'd let this crew out and have them run the ship aground. If lucky, he'd knock that thing off the fantail. He and Sonny would distract the gunmen and maybe take some out.

"Mr. Black, take a guard and see to it that Mr. Branford retrieves his daughter."

"Leave my daughter out of this!"

"A feminine quality will make the chain more efficient," Karnack sang.

Karnack touched his belt. Two guards came running with loping strides, they were becoming sluggish, getting sicker, weaker. He might have a chance; he'd knock them down the stairwell and free his crew, take the guns. In his college days he played center. He knew how to hit low and hard.

"Fine," Branford said, "Lead the way, Black."

Mr. Black limped ahead toward the hold stairwell. *Let Black go down first, stop at the mid-stair landing, spin out. Hit the gunmen. Pull one down the hole.* With luck, he'd roll a mercenary down the stairwell and take Black out. *Eat my chain reaction you bastards.* As they approached the hatch Branford made ready but he never got the chance. A blow from behind crashed down on his skull. He fell to his knees ten yards out from his trap.

He tried to stand. A rifle butt brought him low. The guards stepped over him and proceeded onward to the hatch as he lay on the flight deck bleeding. *They'll never get me downstairs…get up, get up.* He crawled across the deck. *Ground the ship.* He stated up the wheelhouse stairs and made it to the first landing. There he lost his fight to stay conscious.

FORTY

Island of discovery

Aggie began to wake. Half dreaming, a weird red light blasted her closed eyes. *What, an alien ray gun in my face?* She threw open her eyes and tried to jump up, ready to kick someone's balls. The only ball present, however, was the rising sun. Her effort didn't work out. Wrapped in an army blanket, she almost fell on her face.

"Morning slick. Breakfast's up, one minute."

"Not funny Jon!" She exclaimed thinking he saw the near-miss face plant.

"No Ma'am nothing's funny about rations."

Her eyes adjusted. He was hunched over the Sterno stove. *Thank Goddess.* Still in the blanket, she stumbled over and watched over his shoulder. Plastic packets were boiling in an aluminum pot full of sea water. The other burner held a camp-style coffee pot and it was percolating. She cast the blanket aside and sniffed deeply. The smell seemed to dissolve the salt that was caked in her nose. Coffee never smelled good before.

"I could get used to this."

He cut open each ration's bags with a pocket knife and dumped the contents in two tin mugs. He handed over a mixture of scrambled eggs, imitation bacon and mushy potatoes piled in a camp-mug. She plopped down on a sand dune to eat. He dropped two more pouches into the pot and eased up next to her with his food.

They ate two helpings each facing the sun. She inhaled all of the meal and even drank seconds of coffee. It was kind of nasty, but also comforting.

"Don't know why people say this stuff is so bad."

"Glad you liked it, Ma'am."

"You blockhead, I slept with you last night. Don't call me Ma'am, gosh."

"Nothing happened…Ma'am." Jon said with a half-faced smile. "Dreaming about it doesn't count."

She leaned over, took his scruffy black-whiskered jaw in her hands, pulled him in and kissed him hard. She pulled away slightly and nibbled on his lower lip before backing off.

"Does that count? After we get through this, Mr. Colbert, more to come, OK."

"Yes Ma…"

She stopped him with that don't-call-me-ma'am look.

"Ok…Aggie…you don't owe me nothing. Comrades in arms…I like you and all…you're a fine filly…I mean…I'd treat you proper…ah hell."

Jon's face was beet red. She knew how he felt. He didn't get to date much back home, not many girls around, is what he had said. He didn't know what to say or do, she suspected. *I better help him off the hook.* He really was shy.

"When we get home, we'll go for a burger or something. But first let's get this done."

"What're we doing?" Jon asked.

"Rescue my parents and everyone," She said.

"One problem: how?" Jon said pushing back his abused, faded hat. It was crisply black when they set sail. Mel would have approved of his new hat look; droopy, dirty, moldy brown.

Reminds me, call Mel and have her send the Calvary. She pulled the phone from her damp pocket and couldn't tell if it was dry. A day in the sun would do it. Turning it on now was risky, too soon would fry it. She stuffed it back into her pocket.

"We need information, find the weakness. Mark says there's always a weakness. We'll find it and exploit it." She said, but didn't feel confident about it.

"Reckon so," Jon said.

She put the sat-phone on top of the cabin in a sunward cup holder to dry it and got out the binoculars. The island was only a mile away across a maze of shallows, channels, and coral heads. It was more a walk than a swim. Getting wet again sucked, but what else could they do? Moon Dodger wouldn't make it over the reefs.

She used the field glass and confirmed they were north of a Cay. Grandpa's ship was anchored on the other side of the island maybe half mile southwest. The Contention seemed to float above the treetops at this distance. On the near shore, a ribbon of white sand stretched east and west. They were situated adjacent to the island's center. Beyond the beach lay a palm tree forest. A weather tower poked up through the trees. No other research buildings were in sight.

"Has to be the place we saw on the map" Aggie said.

"Back doors open but not the sky." Jon pointed at a hovering MAC.

They took turns observing the activities on Anguilla. Three silver-disk MACs darted above the trees shooting light at the ground, then elevating people in beams of light. The MACs were hunting.

"Loose ends I expect." Jon said.

"We'll swim over, sneak on. Figure out the rest from there." She heard herself say it, the logic wasn't sound and she wasn't thrilled about that, but it was a start.

She grabbed two life preservers and stuffed them into the camouflaged sack. Jon put on the surfer shorts he had found in Mark's duffel bag.

"Keep your pants on and a lot more."

She pulled a pair of Mark's jeans over her cut-off shorts and slipped on Mel's sneakers. She made sure Grandpa's little dagger still hung from her cut-off short's rope belt.

"Ain't this going to make swimming harder?" Jon said.

"It's better than getting shredded. We'll float over the channels, but mostly walk the coral."

They picked their way across the reef, swimming with the float when necessary. A MAC flew toward them when they were half way across the last spot of deep water. They ducked under the float, and shared one snorkel while a MAC shadow circled them like a hungry vulture. After it finally passed, she stuck her head out of the water. The MAC was over the beach slowly moving down the coastline. *Must be looking for somebody.* Once it was out of sight, they paddled and walked the last leg as fast as they could.

"What's it doing," She whispered?

"Containment, herding up strays I reckon. Security lockdown."

"Security for what?"

As they hit the beach, the now distant MAC turned inland and disappeared. They made a break for the underbrush dragging the float. Jon pulled the blanket from the duffel's waterproof outer pouch. He wrapped them both using the blanket like a blind. The Army green blended in. The shadow of the MAC passed over them once more. Jon pointed it out.

"Our MACs based on that; we won't look human on the infrared close together."

Using the blanket as camouflage saved them from the saucer and she didn't even think of it. Sitting with Jon, backs against a palm, wrapped in green wool she realized Jon's the Navy guy, he had to know more about 'recon operations' than she. She had listened intently for the craft yet one passed over them three more times and she didn't hear it coming at all. Jon somehow knew when it was near.

"I don't get it how do you do that?"

"Hear that?" Jon said, "Be quiet, watch there." He pointed.

The sound of birdsong reappeared. A coconut crab hauling a conch shell emerged from under a nearby palm. It walked right past their hideout. Land crabs never went near people. Jon had seen it coming first.

"MACs gone I expect," Jon said, his voice caused the crab to race off. "It's not what you hear, it's what you don't hear. Critters tell you when it's safe to move."

"I don't get it. Don't the UFOs have biological detectors?"

"Yup, I flew the same model looks like. Staying close, blanket soaking heat, confused our signature."

"And, I thought you just wanted to swap B.O." She said casting the blanket off. It was hot as hell under there. "What's next, Cowboy?"

Jon pulled his cowboy hat out from the duffel-float and placed it on his head. Salt water dripped off the brim. He looked stupid but she didn't shoot off the wisecrack that came up on auto-load.

"Split up; each goes down the tree line a spell." He said," See what we can see. We'll meet back here in fifteen minutes. If you see one come over, confuse the infrared, hug a tree."

"Sky will be so proud of me." Billy thought calling her tree-hugger was an insult. She'd never see it that way again.

They stripped off their wet, heavy clothes and shoved them under some brush. She crept seventy-five yards west reaching a tall coconut palm with climbing pegs drilled into it. She climbed up slowly through rough palm bark and leaves. The only sound came from Mel's orange sneakers squishing out water. The palm fronds at the top were especially prickly but she managed to twist her way through to the highest reaches. She spotted the tin roofs of the research station arranged in a big circle. The observation tower at the center of the compound was empty. The island was only half a mile wide.

Out to sea was Grandpa's ship, all right. Three bigger MACs hovered, wobbling weirdly around the Contention. A cigar spaceship lowered a big cylinder, like a propane tank onto the fantail without a sling. All there was is a beam of light.

She heard rustling below and bit her lower lip. Two naked little gray men with no junk and big heads stumbled out of the undergrowth. One carried a wand that it was sweeping back and forth. These two were so weird she was too fascinated to feel fear but her stomach reacted. She forced down the bile, now was not the time to get sick.

Dad was always talking about aliens. He said the grays were biological robots. From what she heard on Grandpa's ship; Po-boy's guess was right. They were machines, not people.

The little robot guy with the wand stopped and put a three-fingered hand to its ear. *It has a regular head set on!* It did a one eighty and stumbled back into the jungle. The other one didn't catch on right away. *So much for intelligent machines* It just stood there waiting for … for what? A minute passed before it turned and walked back into the jungle.

She looked toward the south and all the smaller spaceships had moved in. They hung in formation around the compound. Tesla coil sparks gone mad were dancing off the Contention's fantail. The smaller of two cigar shuttles floated toward the island. Under it, hung a bubble. *Looks like a woman inside.* Aggie shaded her eyes. That woman wore a tie-dyed sundress.

It's Mom!

She clawed her way down the tree like a honey badger. She didn't even try going quietly. It still took a little time. *Mom's in trouble!* Aggie was a she-bear cub protecting her mother. She landed on the ground with 'save Mom' screaming in her soul.

She impulsively unsheathed Grandpa's dagger and turned to run. But a little gray guy stepped out of the brush just as she dug in to take off. It had a device like an electric razor. It pointed that thing at her. She charged lightning fast like a crazed warrior. The little creature fell over backwards with her knife in its chest.

"Holy crap!"

She gasped for air while a green oily liquid pulsed out of it. She almost puked. When it raised a three-fingered hand to its headset, she stomped its spindly white arm into the sand. It didn't cry out. It had no expressions at all. She tore the headset off of it. Its eyes dimmed just as Jon ran up.

"What in the hell's that!" Jon shrank back with his eyes wide.

"Relax; just a robot, a living machine, no soul, no problem." She said it as much to quell his fear as to assure herself she didn't kill a real person. "Here recon-boy, see what you can do with this." She handed him a vintage Sonny AM/FM headset radio. "We got to go fast. Mom's in a bubble."

"Aggie, I found this here kid hiding out. You better hear what he's got to say."

"I'll listen, show me. Let's go quick."

Jon scooped up the ray gun, adjusted the headset and put it on. She extracted Grandpa's dagger and wiped the green goop off on a broad leaf. Except for the eyes, it looked the same alive or dead. It wore a silver bracelet just like the one back suit guy had on. *That's how they control them, we need the sending end.*

They trotted back toward the boy's hiding place talking as they ran crunching lime-based sugar sand. They didn't have time to sneak.

"They use Earth technology," Jon puffed. "Why?"

"They'll use whatever...something big is happening...They need everything they got."

She described what she saw from the tree as they ran. Darkness shaded Jon's face, the muscles along his jaw pulsed. *He's way worried.*

They came to the stash spot. A boy about twelve sat on the duffel bag wrapped in the Army blanket shivering. *He's in shock.* She pulled the water bottle and made the boy drink.

"His name's Ernie," Jon said.

She took Ernie hands in hers and faced him. She had to get him to calm down. "It's OK Ernie, we're here, and you're safe, OK."

"I want my, my, my Mom, where's my Dad?" He said as tears ran down his cheeks.

Aggie took him in her arms and let him cry until he ran dry.

Jon placed a hand gently on Ernie's shoulder. "It's OK Pard, we're here to help, but you gota help us too, think you can do that? Tell us what happened last night."

He told of how the UFOs had attacked all night. They abducted people and floated them to different parts of the compound and put them in bubbles. She heard his tale, confused and disjointed in the telling, but what she really needed was the dirt. What was at the bottom of it all?

"OK, so Ernie, this is really important. To help your parents you've got to tell me what you heard, what the bad guys said, OK slowly, relax. Why are they doing this?" She gave Ernie her best doe eyes.

"This man, short with long arms, like a gooney, last night, was telling the midgets what to do. He told Dr. Buckley, he was in a bubble, 'we're starting a chain reaction,' this boss man said something like, 'once all the LF chambers are in position they'd suck the life out of everyone in the whole world.' The gooney man thought it was funny."

Ernie shook so hard his teeth chattered. But he bravely pushed on.

"I think," Ernie stammered, "I think, I think, they want everybody's souls. He called it a Soul Harvest, everybody in the world."

"Crap!" She sprang to her feet. "We got to stop them! We will stop them."

"That's right," Jon said, "We need a plan. Ernie, you'll help us, right Pard?"

"Yes, yes, yes, Sir."

"That tank on Grandpa's fantail is important, "She said. "Why would they go to all this trouble to steal a ship, zigzag all the way down here? Because they need time to set it up."

"And bodies to prime the pump." Jon added.

"That's right," Ernie said. "It's twenty-five and we don't have that many grownups. Gooney man said I was too young and let me go."

"We have no time. Jon, you and Ernie, distract them. Don't let them complete the circuit. I'll swim out to the ship and unplug that thing."

"Aggie, we can't hold them long. Ernie says they got two dozen, well now twenty-three robots, working the ground."

"I counted them," Ernie said. "I like math."

"They don't think fast Jon, outsmart them. Buy me time. Use the headset. I'm going." She started toward the thicket.

"Hey lady, go down that way, there's a path goes to the harbor. We got kayaks over there."

"You're all right kid, but don't call me lady!"

She took off down that footpath a hunting she-wolf; quiet, fast and all ears. Running behind a tennis court she inspected the compound through the court's chain link slats. Several people were inside force bubbles spaced fifty feet apart. She had no time to stop.

MACs hovered above the tower holding stations in a triangle formation waiting. Maybe they'd ignore her, they looked busy. Maybe they had enough people; maybe they brought Mom over to complete the circle. She prayed to the Goddess that they were too distracted to bother with her.

She hit the beach, launched a green ocean kayak, and streaked across the water like a torpedo.

FORTY-ONE

Jon meets Moby

Aggie had gone off like a sniper's shot. It was time to use the home range advantage. That boy Ernie didn't look like much. He was just a hefty video nerd. But knowledge was power. On the prairie, jungle or city, the local boys knew every unbeaten trail.

"Ernie, this here Dr. Buckley, you say he's an astrophysicist. I reckon he'd have some ideas we can use. Take me to him quiet-like all right?"

"Yes Sir, Dr. Buckley's the smartest guy here."

"Lead on Padre."

For a pudgy doggie, Ernie was pretty darn good at picking his way through underbrush. *Kids know all the tricks.* They belly-crawled under the thickest foliage and got to the edge of the compound unnoticed. From this position, Jon figured the lay of the land.

The compound was a couple of hundred yards square ending at the beach on the opposite side. The tower was in the center and its antenna array hung skewed like busted barbwire. The other buildings, one story cement block and wood bungalows with red tin roofs, ringed the perimeter. One large structure, the meeting hall and mess, he figured, ran east outside the clearing.

There wasn't much cover between buildings. A few palm trees or landscaped plants dotted here and there. Mostly, wide expanses of crushed white-pink coral gravel. Three MACs silently hovered just above the tower set in triangle formation. Sneaking through the compound wasn't possible.

Ernie nudged Jon in the ribs and pointed. "That's Dr. Buckley."

A force shield lay twenty yards right of their position. It was up against a wall of greenery. Another bubble was thirty yards left of his position in clear space.

"There're spaced even all around," Ernie whispered, "One of us in each." Ernie's face contorted like a funhouse clown: his teeth started chattering. Jon figured that was it for the boy.

"Look Partner, I've got it now. Go to my boat where I told you, there's a red cell phone on the cabin's roof, call for help. Can you do that?"

Relief washed over Ernie's face, "I've got a paddle board at North Beach. We use it for snorkeling. Sandbar isn't far."

"Press one and this here girl will pick up, name's Melissa, tell her everything; can you do that Pard?"

"Yes, Sir."

Ernie backed out and was gone. *NSA will pick it up, they's a-hunting.* Jon backed out and wiggled to the nearest chamber. Buckley was on his knees digging gravel with bare hands, sweat running off his bald head and down his face. Jon tapped on the enclosure. Buckley bolted upright.

"Human, thank God," Buckley rubbed the sweat from his eyes with the back of his hand leaving a bloody streak. "Who are you?"

"Navy, I'm here to help."

"Dig me out. The force shield weakens underground. They'll need all stations occupied to succeed."

Jon scrambled around for something to dig with. Nothing was within reach. He ran to the nearest cottage, kicked over a knee-high wooden fence, and ripped a picket slat off it. He sprinted to the jungle side of Buckley's jail, fell to his knees, and started digging. The coral gravel wasn't thick on the edge of the lot, not like on Buckley's side. He hit loose sand right quick.

As they dug, Buckley explained, "The aliens' intention is linking each precisely placed chamber. From what I gather, this combined force creates another, stronger force. The chain reaction, as Moby called it, will destroy all life on this planet. We must stop it!"

Jon worked furiously. At two feet, the shield dissipated. Jon undercut the floor and sand collapsed into the void filling the escape hole. He frantically scooped out loose material with his hands. The air above crackled with energy. The top of the bubble lit red.

He reached deep. A flash of light burned the hair off the back of his neck.

"Stand up Earth man."

Jon complied. He faced a guy half his height with arms twice as long. He was dressed in a green jumpsuit with a silver prize-fighter's belt. A ray gun, like the dead gray's gun, was in the leprechaun's hand, which he held at knee level. Two robots, not much shorter, flanked the alien. Jon held his hands ready to draw. The alien gun was tucked in his boxer shorts. Jon didn't expect aliens knew anything about quick-draw-in gun fights, but he was fixing to teach the course.

"Earth man what are you doing? It is too late. Karnack started the generator, don't you see?" The weird midget shrugged but his arms didn't move with its shoulders.

"No, I don't see." Jon said.

The alien pointed to the sky with his eyes and that was all Jon needed. He drew and shot. The alien was launched backwards like a guy getting blasted in the movies. The spaceman dimpled the hard pack and bounced away like that time he saw a fifty-five-gallon barrel of crude fall off a train car. The two grays didn't move.

"You two, drop the guns." Jon demanded. They didn't move. Jon shot. They still didn't move.

"Don't waste time," Buckley cried. "They won't move while Moby's unconscious. He controls them."

"Out? He's dead."

"No, that's a stun gun. He's higher density so the reaction is stronger. He'll wake soon. Get me out of here."

Jon resumed digging. He gained on it. Buckley finally had room to shimmy out but he didn't move. Jon reached up to grab the man and felt a strong pull inside his chest.

Something was dragging his essence into the hole. Jon launched himself backwards falling over the sand pile he had made and knocked over a gray, too. The entire bubble glowed red energy now. Buckley was a statue.

"What the hell, come on Aggie, get-er done!"

Jon ran out into the compound. None of the grays, scattered around, reacted. Light beams emanated from the tops of the force bubbles and went in and out of the MACs like a reverse prism. The beams channeled into a central ball of light. Buckley said the chambers had to be located just so. If he couldn't get inside, he'd move one.

He jumped into a Humvee. The key was in it. He fired it up and crashed head long it into the nearest force bubble. The bubble rocked and tipped back. The red light wavered turning pink. *This'll work.* He shifted into four-wheel drive and pushed. The bubble tilted and reformed, but in a slightly different place. He rammed it again. No good. It wouldn't move any further.

He figured he'd move each one just a little. That had to slow things down. Buckley's cell was undermined, it might tip over. He slapped the Humvee into reverse. Jon turned facing backwards placing one hand behind the passenger seat. Buckley's was twenty-five yards back.

That chunky alien had revived. It came running out from behind Buckley's jail. Waving its arms, it stopped between him and Buckley. *Go time.* Jon stomped on the accelerator and dumped the clutch.

The alien shot but his stun-gun didn't do squat. Humvees are EMP proofed. Jon charged like a raging bull. The alien danced back and forth and made a fair representation of a rodeo clown. Jon had roped quicker doggies. He drove Moby into Buckley's prison creating an ear-splitting bell clang.

Jon woke in the back seat. Felt like he'd hit an iron fence post. He lay on his back, looked through the window and watched imaginary stars swirling around real lightning bolts. Why's lightning shooting at the sky?

He pulled himself up with his arms and tumbled out of the truck onto hard packed gravel landing with a crunching thud. He managed to roll onto his back. Moby was propped up like a frozen scarecrow crushed between the Humvee and the force shield...dead. Buckley's cell had moved some but stayed upright. The Humvee's ass-end was smashed. Jon tried to think. *What'll I do next? Save Aggie,* hammered inside his hurting skull.

"Oh, hell."

He knew what to do he just couldn't do it. Even the gravel shards biting his ass didn't motivate. The light-ball in the sky was growing larger. It was just too damn interesting. Jon liked how the MACs blinked off and on.

"Merry Christmas."

Moby's belt had blinking lights, too, red and green. Sudden clarity phased in. It was the only equipment the alien had on him. *It controls the robots. The belt's the key.* It wasn't damaged. The short alien took the tail-gate in his chest. Red and green lights blinked under the truck. *Got to tell Aggie — get the belt.* Jon tried to get up. Pain took him down like a cattle prod. *Damn leg's broke.* Moby wasn't the only hurting cowboy in this rodeo.

"Medic! Where's the dog-gone medic," Jon cried before passing out.

*****

Ernie grounded his belly-board on the sandbar next to Jon's sailboat just as an ugly bell sound tore through the air. It didn't belong. *Something bad happened.*

He froze with fear and wanted to crawl under the sand. Ernie lay back down on his board and let the little waves rock him. It felt like Mom's embrace. The motion was a comfort.

But something bothered him. Doing nothing was just what Mom would want from him; she always made things too easy and he was sick of easy. She never let him help. Never let him do anything slightly dangerous. Always treated him like a baby. He wasn't a baby any more, babies don't fight aliens. *I'm a man now, I'll show them.*

"Jon's depending on me, I'm on a mission."

He stood up and faced his island home. Bolts of light flew over the trees. For the first time in his life, grown-ups took him seriously, trusted him with something important. No way he'd let Jon down. Ernie boarded the Moon Dodger with an energy he never felt before. *My world's changing.* The phone was right where Jon said. He flipped it open, found the Mel key and pressed it.

"Dude, what's going on, you wouldn't believe Mark and —."

"Shut up Mel," Ernie said evenly. His squeaky voice sounded deep in his own ears. "This is Ernie, Jon and Aggie sent me to call; this is important."

"Dude they'll trace this. I got to get off."

"No, Jon wants it traced, we're in big trouble. You must tell everyone, put it on the web, and send directions to the Navy; tell everyone!"

Keys clacked in the background. This girl typed like a hurricane.

"Dude, I'm putting this out on the net live. I'm splashing it everywhere just in case, you cool with that?"

"Way cool," Ernie said.

Ernie told Mel everything, everything he saw, everything Jon and Aggie said. Mel had him activate video and point it at the scene while he talked. He narrated what the camera saw as well.

"It's up," Mel said, "It's on every server, emergency broadcast system. It's flooding the media."

"How, I don't get it, you some kind of hacker or something." Ernie could hardly believe she could do that. He was very good with computers himself. But after last night, maybe nothing was impossible. "Who are you?"

"Just a geek. Stay nerdy my friend."

This was the most amazing thing that ever happened. Nobody would believe it if he didn't show up and get it over to Mel. Ernie felt proud. He was part of history. Riding on newfound bravery he asked her.

"No really, you got this out everywhere for real?"

"The government twists things." Mel said. "I'm good at untwisting things. I'm not dumb, I see what they do. The Feds will cover this up, make it all go away. I'm not letting that happen. Google, check it out."

Ernie started the browser; he still had the phone-cam pointed home. No matter what he clicked, the UFO light show popped up live. What he just said came over, his and Mel's voice was on line with a two-second delay.

"How'd you do that?"

"Dude, I muted, just us talking. I can't tell. If I do, they'll kill you. You wouldn't believe it anyway."

He was ready to believe anything, but she wouldn't squeal and drag him down the hole. This girl was risking her life. *She better get off the phone before they find her.* "No more gabbing, Lady. I'll keep rolling, battery's low. I better save juice for video."

Mel hung up. Whatever happened, he'd stand his ground until the end. Mel, Aggie and Jon put their heads on the chopping block and this was the part he could do.

FORTY-TWO
Aggie boards the Contention

The Contention had moved to a new position since Aggie first saw it from the sandbar. It was now anchored a few hundred yards offshore but parked broadside parallel to the south beach. She'd go directly at it, but the long way gave cover. Fifty yards offshore she turned west along the beach, planning an approach as she paddled. She'd come up from behind.

A loud crash and a bell clang stopped her. She spun the boat. Red lightning bolts crackled and shot into the sky forming a spider web around a house-sized white lighting ball. MACs pulsated around it. The ball slowly turned deep red. Then it flashed. Plasma raced toward the ship and lit the fantail. That metal cylinder gizmo sucked it up. The ball above the compound was clear but becoming white again.

Running out of time.

Going west was too roundabout. She preferred the direct approach anyway. She aimed for the Contention, took off, and stroked like a chainsaw piston.

The third plasma ball arrived just as she skimmed up to the massive hull. The rope she had used before was gone. The fantail was covered in red molasses. *Goop's crawling up the hull! I can't go there.* She made for a bow anchor chain. *Chainlinks make good footholds.* Aggie cast away her boat as she grabbed the chain. It was slimy but still possible to climb.

The two forward anchor stations port and starboard were a deck below the flat top. She climbed over the anchor's eyelet port and onto the chain's maintenance platform. If she could draw them up, the ship would drift off station. *That'll screw them over.* She checked the monitor screen. *Not good, no manual override here.*

"Crap!"

She climbed a drainpipe and pulled herself over the flight deck's rail. She was exposed. Darting behind a curved vent stack, she peeked around it. None of the mercenaries were in sight. Four silver MACs were parked in succession chained to the deck. *Navy drones, no problem, but no help.*

She had to either move the ship, or go way aft unseen to shut that generator down. The ship was vibrating. The engines were idling. *Try the helm first, turn the ship, drag anchors, no telling how to unplug it.*

She broke and ran for the nearest cover, which was behind a Navy MAC. She moved down the flight line from MAC to MAC. That got her three quarters of the way to the wheelhouse. She stopped at the last MAC to scope it out.

The wheelhouse was seventy-five feet above the main deck. It would be a long zigzag stair climb to get there. She'd sprint forty yards across open space and fly up the stairs. The pilot's windows were empty. *Nobody's home up there.* She inhaled a lung full of air, crouched and bent her toes to blast off.

"Hold it, don't move."

The end of rifle barrel pressed against the nape of her neck. She rose slowly, turned and faced him. The guy's trigger-hand had that same bracelet on his wrist. He brought a radio to his mouth still holding the rifle on her.

"I have a prisoner. I don't recognize this one. She must have hidden when we locked up the others. What'll I do with her?"

"She, you have a female?" A melodic voice sang over the walky-talky.

"Yes, Sir, it's a young girl."

"Is she pretty?"

"Yes, Sir, very pretty." The guard said without emotion. The gun wavered as if he was trying to put it down. Aggie sensed some hidden force wouldn't let him.

"Do tell. I dearly love the pleasures of Earth females. It is a shame that soon there will be none left to be had. Bring her to me. There is yet time for a little foray."

The SWAT uniformed guy was joined by two others. They started toward the forward outlook one man on either side and one behind. They pushed her along but their movements were sluggish.

"Don't you guys think you're overdoing it? Aggie said.

They didn't answer, not even a faint smile. They wore Kevlar vests, face shields, side-arms and enough ammo to invade a small country. With all that gear, they should go slowly. *No, they're acting more like robots.* One guy just had sunglasses. His face skin was waxy-white, same complexion as the grays.

These men were stumbling-sick. She coiled her insides like a titanium spring. They weren't right, didn't even take her dagger. She maneuvered the group toward the rail. A plan sprung to mind; kick him in the balls and jump over the side: Anyone wearing that much weight couldn't possibly swim.

Ten feet from the stairs her move gelled. They changed to single file and walked along the rail with two guards behind and the other ahead. *A gift from the Goddess.* Two well-placed kicks were all she needed, one to drive the first rear-guard into the other; the next to push the front guy face first onto the stairs. She visualized her attack, back-kick, front kick, jump over the side.

She adjusted her breathing, relaxed her mind, and tensed her muscles. She was ready.

A glance above seized her engine. A seven-foot man with white wings was on the first landing looking down on her with a hawkish face. He stood over an unconscious man. He seemed twice her height. Momentarily shocked, she shook it off. *Need a new plan.*

She absorbed the scene. Grandpa was laid out on the landing. Blood, now dry, had dripped over the edge and down the stairs. *Grandpa's blood! Was he dead?* But he lifted his head; his face was caked in brown crust.

"Run, Aggie, run!" Grandpa yelled.

The alien tossed his head back and laughed like a bird. She couldn't move. The weirdness of it all iced her feet. The Angel guy looked beautiful but she felt something else; he's pure evil. A push from behind snapped her out of it. She started up the stair.

"You must know this intruder, Mr. Branford." He almost sang the statement.

"My granddaughter," Branford said pulling himself up using the handrail, his lip started bleeding. "Keep your filthy hands off her Karnack. We have a deal." Grandpa said, spitting blood.

"So, we do or did, but I didn't include family benefits. Should I cancel our contract?"

Aggie grabbed the guard's foot in front of her and yanked. His face crashed into the grated metal step. She back kicked, planting a blow into the guard's Kevlar crouch. Rearguard one tumbled backwards like a sack of seaweed and took the other one down. Rifles flew, one over the side the other skidded across the flight deck.

She was wound up for a fight but got none. All three solders just whimpered and didn't move. She turned. Alien laughter almost sucked the fight out of her. Angel guy had a Star Trek gun pressed against Grandpa's temple.

"They are spent. No matter. I don't need them anymore. Young lover come to me, ...or Mr. Branford acquires an additional orifice in his skull."

Karnack backed up the stars to the first deck above. Aggie stepped onto the wide upper landing good and pissed. Karnack, keeping his distance, waved his gun toward the sliding glass doors. *This guy's smart, stays out of striking range.*

She had been on the other side before. She passed through the foyer and into Grandpa's office. Two gray aliens stood on either side of Bug-guy holding guns on him. *Bug-man's a good guy!?*

Black suit guy was on the floor breathing raggedly. His hat was crumpled in one hand, sunglasses were gone. These grays were different than the others; taller, more animated. One looked at her and blinked its huge back eyes. She thought they were smarter but still robots.

"Status," Karnack said.

"Monitors suggest Moby is dead. Several chambers have been altered. The connection is still functional but less efficient."

"Suggestions," Karnack said.

"The system will hold. We must move Shuttle One to a new position in order to transfer power and relay it to Base Ship. The field has weakened. Place Shuttle

One to an intermediate position. Chain reaction is counting down. Five minutes to reaction; five additionally until singularity."

"Oh my, time grows short, doesn't it?" Karnack said. He turned to Aggie, "I'm afraid we won't have time to redeem Earth's females, young lover." Karnack cackled.

Aggie's skin crawled. *I really hate this guy.*

Both grays turned their heads in unison and blinked at her like they read her mind, or Angel guy sent them a signal. Grandpa's meat hammers balled up ready for war but a punch would cost him his life.

Karnack seemed relaxed and held the gun loosely. Grandpa's face boiled like a cooking lobster, but he didn't make a move. *Too risky, need an advantage.* She inched away from Karnack and closer to the grays as Karnack continued with business.

"Security report Base Ship?"

"Base Ship: Two Earth Government anti-MAC fighters are nearby searching." The gray said without moving its mouth. "Once you lift off with Shuttle One, the fighters will find your sea-based vessel quickly."

"How long?"

"Ten minutes to intercept."

Karnack bent low to address the guy laboring on the floor. The grays trained their guns on Grandpa. Karnack pulled the bracelet off Black's wrist.

"No sense wasting good equipment. Isn't that so, Mr. Black?" Karnack said. "You served me well. As a reward, I will allow you to die with your mind intact. Of course, you are too weak to stop me, I am quite safe."

Black whispered, "Bastard. Our airpower will stop you."

"They cannot, even if Mr. Branford sinks his own ship. The generator is shielded." Karnack waved his gun at the grays. "Take Praytis, we shall keep a hostage in case the GTO decides to intervene; ready the ship, I will be along momentarily. Keep our four-legged guest alive, but, by all means, shoot if he tries anything."

Karnack touched his belt. A little red orb flew out to the ceiling above the prisoner. A force bubble cascaded down and encased Bug-guy. She was outside the field. One of the grays floated Bug-guy out the door and onto the deck. A blue beam of light poured down. Praytis and the gray floated up and out of sight.

Aggie chopped the gun out of the other gray's hand. She scooped it up and jumped aside.

Grandpa went after Karnack—too close to shoot. She fired at the gray. It didn't move. A brilliant light flashed and Grandpa slid across the floor slamming into a wall. He landed under the same window she had used before and it was still open. She fired at Karnack. It didn't faze him.

"You didn't think I would give my androids or anyone really, a weapon that could hurt me, do you? This is tuned to stun Earth humans. My personal force skin isn't even necessary." The Angel's wigs fluttered, "it is a pity we don't have time to play. I do rather enjoy the favors of Earthling females." He pointed his gun at her pulling Black's bracelet from his belt. "Shall we put this controller to good use? Try it on."

Karnack held the bracelet out. An easy target despite his long arm, but it wasn't her best choice. She reached for it with her hand, grabbed his arm, pulled him in and let loose a front kick. Karnack dropped the gun and fell back. She bolted, jumped over Grandpa and through the window.

She cleared the window but not the deck rail. Her foot hooked it and she pivoted like a door hinge. She slammed into the knee-wall before crashing onto the service walkway below.

Footsteps rang the stairs and headed toward her. They were on the catwalk above. She flattened into a hatchway doorjamb. A human guard stopped right over her head.

"I don't see her, Sir, she must have gone under."

"Pity, this bracelet was perfect for her. Such fun we would have had. Guards, please man the foredeck."

Karnack must have leaned out of the stateroom window as his voice cut through the static buzzing all around her. The bracelet tracked past her and into the water. Boot steps retracted back the way they had come.

"Come co-pilot and let us collect the life force from this miserable planet."

Karnack's lofty voice faded. She ignored her pain and ran down the narrow service walk toward the stern. She climbed a drain leader up to the observation deck that ran along the outside of the stateroom. She climbed through the window and dropped to her knees. Grandpa was laid out, alive but out cold.

"Crap, Grandpa," She said shaking his shoulder. "I don't know how to drive this ship. You got to wake up. We've got to stop that generator."

"No time."

Aggie twisted around. It was that guy in black, on the floor but looking less waxy. He got up onto an elbow.

"I'll knock that sucker overboard," she cried. "Shoot the damn thing, whatever!"

"Can't," Black crocked. "Magnetic shielding. Stop Karnack's shuttle. Fly the remote into him, crash him, stops the process. Life Force returns to…donors." Black collapsed.

"I can't. I don't know how to fly. Besides they're chained to the deck. I need Jon!"

Mr. Black raised one hand and pointed at the sky. His arm dropped with a thud. She took the hint. In another minute that shuttle would split. *Mess over that spaceship.* She raced to the front door and up the wheelhouse stairs. Shuttle One was right over the communications tower, it almost touched it. She reached the wheelhouse and climbed its' service ladders to the highest roof.

The air over the sea was clearer. That black cloud was getting sucked into the shuttle. Three ten-foot round holes had opened under it. Black smoke poured into the fore and aft holes. The one at the center didn't suck smoke. She sprinted across the roof to the antenna tower and climbed the metal tree-trunk using broken antennas and guide-wires as handholds.

She climbed as fast as a monkey but hesitated once on top. The tower's summit was flat but only two foot around and not stable, it was a smashed radar dish. Below it was a jungle of mangled antenna made into skewers. If she fell, she'd be run through. Barbeque beef on a stick never stopped an alien before.

No choice. She bellied over the tower's edge and stood on wobbly legs. The ship pitched and yawed. She fell to her knees, stood again and tiptoe stretched. A handhold was just out of reach. She bounced up and her fingers touched a ladder rung just inside the hatchway. The ship pitched again. This time she didn't fall.

The last of the cloud was gone from the stern. That hole closed just as a jet fighter appeared skimming the water. *Jump for it!* She crouched but didn't get to launch.

A missile hit the fantail and deflected into the water exploding in the sea off the port stern.

The ship heaved on a big wave and rose. She jumped grabbing the second rung and hauled herself up…just in time. The hatchway closed with a concentric swirl taking a piece of her sneaker with it.

The shuttle accelerated. The entire thing slanted forty-five degrees. The hatchway became clear like a porthole. They were ten thousand feet up and hauling ass in the blink of an eye.

The angel guy made it easier for her. The G-force was strong like a roller coaster loop. She climbed twenty feet upward. The upper hatch was just like any ship's hatch. At the top there was no inertia. *It must be gravity shielded.* She pressed her face against a dirty porthole, nothing but boxes inside, Earth boxes, mostly canned tuna. *For a guy who hates people, he sure likes Earth food. What a dick.* She spun the hatch wheel and pushed. Boxes were stacked against the door.

"Crap!"

She put her back against the far side of the tube-way and pushed with her legs. It gave. She squeezed through the crack, maneuvered around the stuffed space and located another hatch. No porthole on this door. She tried the wheel. It wasn't locked.

She murmured a mantra. Her racing heart slowed a few beats. She touched the dagger for luck and spun the hatch wheel quietly until it clicked and broke the seal. Karnack's voice seeped into her hiding place.

"…fools, wasting rockets on grounded force fields. Nothing penetrates a reaction shield."

"Karnack, Base Ship here: a MAC killer has you on radar. It is closing."

"Hold position. Send out all my AI probes. Attack the fighters. I need two minutes."

Two minutes, holy crap! Aggie pushed the door open and poked her head out. It was a pilot room. Bug-guy was still inside a bubble; he looked right at her. She almost fainted.

It tilled its human head like a praying mantis and brought a finger to its thin lips—the universal sign for quiet. Then it pointed.

Karnack's back was to them. He was in a Captain Kirk chair. Two grays were up front on flight controls. A dozen 3-D screens floated on air. No time to lose. One screen had Bug-guy on it.

She opened the hatch and started toward Karnack. The floor suddenly dropped out. She jumped clear. Karnack spun out of his chair.

"Oh, you are a quick one; I'll show you the door myself."

"I'll bust you open first, try me."

"Why so hostile? I'm doing the universe a favor; do you know why the GTO is here? Yours is a dead planet, they are only waiting for you to self-destruct in order to reap these resources." He swept his hand. "I beat them to it. Your doom is assured, why delay it?"

He's buying time. "Come on pussy, kick me off this ship."

"I hate cats." Karnack came at her with long arms twirling like windmill blades, wingspread hacked the air. She didn't know how to defend against that fighting style. Mark flashed in her head. 'Size or method doesn't matter, use their force against them.' Karnack lunged. She dropped and swept his legs break-dancer style and popped up. As Karnack tumbled toward the open floor, she made ready to strike again.

His wings stopped him from falling; he projected them backward together as one. His legs were spread on the lip. He hung there an angelic tripod. She pulled her dagger.

"That can't hurt me, you fool. I wear Force Skin. Pull me up or we both die."

"K, I'll help you," she said.

She reached and took his belt in one hand pulling him almost upright. He retracted his wings. He was a feather weight. With the other hand, she thrust the knife into his gut, jammed it under the belt, slashed upward, and pulled back. Karnack wind-milled for balance. She front-kicked him hard using her bad leg. He disappeared down the hole. His belt remained in her hand.

She looked over the side. Karnack spiraled out of sight.

"I guess angels can't fly, who'd of thunk it? OK you gray guys, I'm in charge now. Bring this ship down, stop the generator."

The pilots didn't move, didn't respond at all. They sat there like dolls. She stormed over to Karnack's chair. "Just shut this hole will you." Nothing happened.

Bug-guy was pounding on the glass. She couldn't hear him. He made signs at his waist. *Put the belt on stupid.* She wrapped the belt around her waist and held it with one hand.

"Ok you two, let's get out of here."

The grays didn't move. Aggie saw on the largest monitor that one fighter jet was coming on fast. The orbs were shot down: She felt it. The belt enhanced her perception but she didn't know how to use it.

"Come on you guys, let's move!"

Bug-guy was really pounding on the glass. He waved her to come close. An explosion rocked the ship. It tilted hard to the left. In her mind she saw the fighter racing past and banking. *It's coming back.* She ran to Bug-guy's force shield.

"I don't know if this'll work, you saw what I did to that other guy. Don't mess with me. You can use the belt, if you know how."

He gave thumbs up. She thrust the belt at the force shield and it fell away. Bug-guy snatched it up and put it on. It locked around his tiny waist like magic.

"Evasion ninety left," Bug-guy cried in perfect English.

In the blink of an eye the craft was a hundred miles up range. She didn't really understand the monitors before she wore the belt, but now the displays made sense. The belt did something to her.

"Reverse the generator," Bug-guy ordered. "Close all hatches."

"We did it," she said, flopping down into Karnack's over-sized chair. The chair morphed to fit her. She expected it. "The chain reaction is toast, right?"

"Yes Captain."

"Captain, how am I a captain?"

"You liberated Karnack of the Systems Belt. His fleet is officially and legally yours, or what's left of it. Such are GTO rules. I'm Praytis, your First Mate. You willfully gave me control and so appointed my rank. The system's owner may delegate control."

"We better go back, make sure the people on Anguilla are OK."

"They are all right. Ship's AI enhances telepathy. Two Jets are still after us. They are closing in as well."

She looked at the display; two MAC killers were converging.

"We took damage from that missile strike." Praytis said. "We have only enough power for one more jump. I suggest we go where they can't attack. I suggest high orbit."

"I got a better idea," Aggie said. "Is it possible to reach Base Ship? Will that one fly OK?

Bug-guy touched the belt and the screens flashed all kinds of weird symbols, some she recognized, some right out of history class.

"She is fully operational. We will make it."

"Make it so, Number One."

"What, oh yes, Star Trek. I like that show, very prophetic," Praytis said. "Engage."

Out of danger, Aggie relaxed a little and had time to feel and she didn't feel like she should have felt. She wasn't sad, she wasn't disgusted. She felt hollow.

"I killed a guy, I should hate myself, but I don't. What's wrong with me? OK he tried to kill everybody, but…I'll never pass Mom's hippie exam this way."

"You Earth humans do have special marshal qualities uncommon in the wider universe."

"Just great, we're special kinds of monsters. Do we get a little yellow bus? Don't answer that."

Her shuttle traveled two thousand miles in thirty minutes. They docked inside the belly of a twelve-hundred-foot-long metal tube invisibly orbiting five hundred miles above the Earth.

FORTY-THREE

On the Cay

A massive crash woke Jon. He brought himself up to sitting position. The MACs had fallen out of the sky. One smashed the mess hall. All the force bubbles were gone. Weak cries for help blew on a gentle, warm breeze. Remembering Moby, panic kicked Jon in the chest. He ignored his leg and stood up ready to fight, but he was the only one standing.

His checked himself, a bump on the head, knee was dislocated not broken. Using two hands, he popped his knee back into place. It wasn't the first time he'd done it. Breaking horses on the ranch busted him out of joint so many times the doctor showed him how to fix it just so Doc could save himself trips out to Daddy's ranch. Doc had to make that trip all the time, but not on Jon's account.

Jon hobbled past the dead leprechaun over to Buckley.

"I'm alive," Buckley said. "Weak, I need water, I'll survive."

"What happened, where's Aggie?"

"Aggie, I don't know him. You missed the show. That big UFO took off. Two U.S. fighter jets went after it."

"Aggie's a girl. I best go see how folks are."

Buckley saw the dead alien and bolted upright wild-eyed. He pointed at the nearest gray. It was holding a gun. Buckley cried out, "alien!"

"Relax Pard; he's not going no-where. He's plumb decommissioned. A robot without a joy-stick up his ass doesn't work so good. Dog-gone, I'm start-in to sound like Aggie."

Jon limped over to it and pushed it over. It toppled like a mannequin; its gun pointed at the sky. He took the strange gun and tossed it to Buckley.

"Y'all get under shade while I see to them folks, yonder."

Jon limped his way around the compound. There weren't any dead Earth people. Three other kids around Ernie's age came out of hiding. Jon set them to bringing people water after explaining the grays were robots and weren't running no more.

Ernie showed up a short time later and reported he'd made the call. He handed Jon the phone. Jon was bushed. His knee hurt to beat all hell. It was about then he reckoned he also had busted some ribs, a tore shoulder muscle, too.

"Partner," He said to Ernie, "You'll have to take over. See that folks get plenty of water. I got to get off this leg. Round up a posse, later, anyone what's able, get them out to the ship, see if Aggie needs help."

"Yes, Sir," Ernie said smartly.

No doubt the boy was proud of himself. He ran off like a bucking colt.

Jon hobbled to a bench, sat, and stretched his bad leg out straight. He flipped open the phone and called Mel. She picked up fast like she was expecting him.

"Hi," Mel said. "Where's Aggie. I don't see her anywhere. She's not on the ship."

"Excuse me Ma'am, how'd you reckon it was me."

"Dude, watch the screen."

"I ain't no dog-gone dude."

Jon shaded the screen with one hand. A live satellite feed zoomed in on the island. Jon got a bird's eye view of his hat. Top of his shoulders was sunburned.

"Dang, how'd you do that?"

"I can't tell you. I'd have to kill you."

"Aggie's been rubbing off on you, too. Any old cow-poke can see that."

"That's enough," A women's voice cut in. "Melissa, stick to business. Where is Agatha Piper?"

"Who wants to know?" Jon said.

"President Jane Albright, your boss. The U.K. Air Force will be there in ten minutes. I want to talk to Ms. Piper. I need her report."

"Ma'am, I don't know. She oughta be on Branford's tub."

"That ship is off limits. Don't let the Brits board her. I want you…"

Jon flipped the phone shut. He didn't give a cow pie about screwing the British. All he knew was Aggie might need help and help was on the way. Let the Brits board. They can have all Branford's secret files and the MACs, too, for all he cared. He was sick and tired of secrets. Wherever help came from, he'd take it. By the looks of the ruin around him, it'd be a while before Ernie and his posse could board.

He lay back on the bench, put his other leg up and pushed his hat low over his eyes. He didn't bother looking when two of the fallen alien MACs lifted off and flew away. He saw from under his brim that the one inside the mess hall was jammed in the roof's trusses. It fired up and tried to go, but it was stuck.

Finders keepers. He was trespassing on British soil, after all, least he could do was be hospitable and let them have a spaceship.

FORTY-FOUR

Aggie in orbit

Once onboard Base Ship, she and Praytis had a long walk to the bridge. Aggie had questions. Praytis answered everything she thought of. He confirmed that grays were just androids. She was relieved. But what blew her mind was that grays are made from cow parts and human DNA. But they weren't human at all. The big surprise was human variants were common throughout the universe, but weirdly, cows were not. Cow parts are a big market industry and someone on Earth said the GTO can help itself.

She learned aliens of one kind or another had been watching Earth, and other rising planets, for millions of years. Praytis told how Earth's governments and the GTO hadn't come to terms. The GTO wasn't willing to sign the deal that the Powers wanted. Why? The top guys were monsters. She already knew that. That was understood by anyone paying attention. Biological sickness was how scum floated to the top; that was news but the insanity of the ruling elite wasn't.

Mom and Dad never stopped talking about the perils of humanity, the police state, the political corruption and all that. She soaked it up without trying. Earth's leaders were driving everyone over the cliff. It was way past time the people took over. *Daddy's right, The Man sucks.* She shared that with Praytis.

"Very astute of them," he said.

"Goddess, I hate when my parents are right."

Arriving on the bridge, Praytis introduced her to the Base Ship's intelligent computer interface. It referred to its self as Mother. Aggie sat on the bridge's command chair and the ship embraced her.

"Hi, Mother we're home."

The ship's overhead lights blinked in response, its way of laughing.

"It will take a short span of time for her to acclimate to your brainwaves and learn how to interact with you well," Praytis said. "You have not been Ram-ed conditioned. Moreover, no Earth human has ever held a systems belt. I did not think it possible. She seems to like you, however."

"What's not to like?"

"Oh, yes, I see, very well then. With your consent, I will ask for a status report." Aggie nodded. Praytis closed his eyes for a moment. "Karnack had quite a pervasive satellite system, very impressive. I see why no one caught him for so long. He was quite the spy-master."

"What about my friends?" Aggie asked.

Praytis's report flashed in her mind. Her auxiliary ships had crashed. The force bubbles and pilot control dissolved when Karnack lost this belt. His three MACs hovering over Anguilla grounded there. Shuttle Two had been shot down executing automated evasion. It rested in shallow water off a Cuban beach. *They'll think its toast but she's doing auto repair.* The high-end AI probes Karnack had sent to distract fighters had dropped out of the sky and were presently bobbing in the Gulf. Safe enough, they look like lost channel markers. They could wash up anywhere. Mother added, inside Aggie's head, most will wash up in South America.

"Finders keepers," Aggie said.

An alert popped out of nowhere. Cuban jets were racing toward Anguilla Cay. The British had jets closing, too. U.S. jets were diverted, closing in. The power dance began.

"No way, we're not going back. But we need to know..." She said. On the thought, a camera zoomed into the compound. Fear slapped her. "Those jets will blow each other up. They'll crunch the people on the ground. Where's Jon?"

A halo-screen popped up. A satellite view showed Jon lying on a bench. His pant leg was rolled up and knee looked like crap. They were safe, but not for long.

"Get the saucers airborne," she said. "Use them for distraction."

She started thinking it out. One shuttle was crisp the other damaged and the little MACs were so small. She didn't want to lose any more of them anyway. What would draw off the fighter? *How about a mother ship?* What she really wanted was to go home and be done with this mess.

"What if they didn't have a reason to fight over this junk, what if everyone knew?" Aggie said thinking out loud.

Mother understood the new boss. *Mother's really very nice.* Mother impressed inside Aggie's mind that Mother was happy to help. She made good suggestions at lightning speed and all inside Aggie's head. Foremost, Mother said they needed cover. *Self-preservation.* So, Aggie launched all thirty of her non piloted mini probes. *Spread out, get seen, and don't get caught.* Aggie had the two saucers distracting fighters take off for DC and set them to land on the Whitehouse lawn. *That'll keep them busy.*

Praytis smiled like a kid with a new toy while she thought orders. She had a sudden realization and snapped out of it: Mother ship was inside her head! Aggie jumped up, alarmed. The feeling of invasion left her. It was so weird, a little scary, but at the same time she missed the sensation.

Praytis said to her. "In the chair you are linked directly into ship's systems. Mother will not harm you."

"Far out." She eased back into the chair and embraced the ship-mind.

She never had a dog so she named one semi-smart mini probe Buddy. 'Earth people call them orbs,' Mother said. Buddy was designated a direct link responder—whatever that meant. She spoke to it through Mother's silent com. Buddy had a rudimentary intelligence. *Ok, Buddy, I have a special job for you. Go to Key West and zip around the Navy base. If they chase you, stay low...buzz Key West High School while you're at it. Clear my path. They won't shoot at a school.*

"They won't shoot at Buddy, right Praytis?"

"America doesn't have anything that will disable a mini probe," Praytis said. "Mother has Earth's military bases under surveillance. Whatever they do, we will know it."

She got out of the command chair. Telepathy with intelligent machines was getting to her. She couldn't tell what her ideas were or not. She wanted to think without voices in her head.

Her first thought was land Mother on the White House lawn, but she knew Mother wouldn't like it, it was too risky. She's big, an easy target. Besides, that cliché was covered with the saucers. They could get shot down but not easily. No, a better landing sprung to mind. A place America would not bomb because too many moneyed people lived there, a place that the media couldn't miss. She checked the viewer; her probes were raising hell. American jets were everywhere but they were not near where she wanted to go.

"Buddy's clearing our way," She said, "it's time for my grand re-entry."

"Where are we going?" Praytis asked.

"Sunset Pier, Key West," She said. "Make it so Number One."

"Aye, aye Captain," Praytis said. His smile didn't seem weird any more. "I always desired a visit there. It is a fun place. I've seen it on U-tube."

Key West's annual Earnest Hemmingway Look Alike convention was in town. A lot of journalists and writers always attended. This was going to be good

FORTY-FIVE
Troubled landing

Mother was way bigger than Aggie had thought. In space, she seemed so small. Here, she was a bundle of oil tankers tied together and laid end to end. Hanging low over the Key, she couldn't figure out where to touch down.

The State Park was too far from the action. Mother couldn't fit on the pier; the daily Sunset Festival was warming up. She was too wide to land on any road. Hovering over Duval Street, the problem solved itself. All the boats around Sunset Pier raced off like bait-fish fleeing tarpon. The place was mobbed with writers as she had hoped. Some were drunk already. She had the feeling that writers and writer look-alikes sobered instantly as Mother floated out over the water and into open view. Mother swung around slowly showing her broadside before nosing up to a cruise ship docking bulkhead. The massive spaceship stationed twenty feet above the water used its magnetic docking motors with no turbulence. Mother maneuvered in graceful silence. Lucky break, none of the usual visiting cruise ships were tied up at port.

Aggie watched from the bridge. People ran in every direction. Some toward her with notebooks and cameras, but most ran the other way like their hair was on fire. This was turning into a riot and that wasn't good.

"Hey Mother," Aggie said, "Does the com work outside?"

"*Yes Captain.*"

"Project me outside please." She cleared her throat, people outside jumped. "Crap, sorry. Hey everybody, calm down. I'm Aggie Piper, human. Ok this ship is weird, yeah, it's alien, but I'm not. I'm coming out with a real alien. OK, so, relax its cool. I'll be out in like five minutes, K."

Onscreen many people stopped and turned toward the ship. Everyone on Duval Street and around must have heard, too; a crowd began pouring onto the pier's grounds. Satisfied, she had Mother lower a gangplank. There was a service door thirty decks below the bridge on the tip of the bow.

Mother opened and a ramp rolled out. The crowd flinched but didn't scatter. *Cool.* The center of the bridge's floor opened and she knew the anti-gravity tube would take them below. She had two grays and Praytis join her. They stepped on nothing and reappeared at the bottom level's airlock. She put a hand on the hatch wheel, took a deep breath and said, "Here goes nothing."

The hatch swung out into a little airlock foyer. The outer door was already open. She told the grays to stay back and moved to the edge of the ramp with Praytis at her side. The crowd gasped. She took another deep breath. The scent of tropical flowers, fried fish, cheap beer and salt air filled her lungs. She was never happier to taste the smell of tourism.

The crowd reacted many ways. Some ran, some wailed, some fell to their knees, some laughed, but, thank the Goddess, most of them didn't leave. *No point talking yet, everybody's too loud.* She and Praytis stood by chatting and waited for the clamor to quiet down. Someone near the landing yelled a question and others joined in.

"It's fake, right? Who made that puppet? Where'd you get the blimp? Where's the TV camera?"

"Yeah, we're hard to believe," Aggie said to Praytis. "I never believed it."

"What is that Missouri expression, it is 'Show me,' I believe,'" Praytis said.

"Mother," Aggie said, "have the grays join us, oh and ask Buddy over."

A moment passed and the androids walked out onto the ramp. Buddy came streaking toward the Pier forty feet above Duvall Street ducking over and under power lines as he went Buddy was a bright orange ball of light three feet around with a Navy helicopter following a few feet above the buildings.

"Hard to fake a helicopter," Aggie said as the Navy aircraft halted mid-air to avoid running into Mother. Buddy stopped racing instantly but floated near Mother's hull and drifted down to Aggie.

Air raid sirens howled in the distance. People on Duval had got slammed with rotor wash and lots of them hit the deck. The crowd on the pier parted as police filed in. Things were getting out of control. Aggie ran to the bottom of the ramp. The cops drew guns. One pointed a shotgun at Praytis.

"Hands up, hands up!"

The cop didn't know Praytis's arms didn't go up very far so he reared back on hind legs to elevate his hands. The crowd gasped and all at once moved back in a panic stepping on the fallen to get away. One cop pissed his pants.

"Shoot, shoot," another cop cried. Many guns swung toward her friend.

"Buddy!" Aggie screamed. "Stop the cops!"

Buddy zoomed in. A burst of white light hit the crowd. The cops froze, one guy fell over. The regular people weren't bothered at all. A guy wearing a fedora with a press pass in his hatband bent over the cop and announced in a loud voice, "He's all right, just knocked out."

Mayhem became shock. The crowd stilled. The loudest sound was a woman crying, "Oh Jesus save me." Praytis proceeded down the ramp. His weird feet slapping plastic-steel with a squishy sucking sound. For Aggie, it all happened in slow motion. *Mind-melding, weird. I like it.* Some guy in Hemmingway attire vomited and she snapped out of it.

"People do like to drink alcoholic beverages here, do they not?" Praytis said as he joined her on Sunset Pier.

Dozens inched toward them. *Reporters are never on vacation.* One guy asked Praytis for an interview, and then another. All at once, a dozen voices chimed with questions. It was like a Presidential press conference.

Aggie drew nearer to Praytis.

"Crap, I'm in for it now. I made Buddy mess-over cops. That's illegal for sure. I'm in deep trouble."

"I would not worry overmuch about it now, Captain."

Aggie ignored him. "Every time I try to do the right thing, I get screwed."

"He would have killed me. None the less, we have a bigger problem. Look."

Praytis pointed to the nearest street entrance to Sunset Pier. A big guy in a white Navy uniform aggressively pushed his way through the throng. He was followed by two freaked out looking MPs.

"That's Admiral Sanderson," Praytis said. "I am in trouble, as well."

"Jon's boss, crap. We're toast."

Sanderson marched up swinging his bulk and waving his hands like a man under attack by a swamp-load of mosquitoes. "What in the hell are you doing," Roared Sanderson stabbing a finger at Praytis. "You, goddamn stupid son of a bitch, you just killed everyone on Key West. I can't let this go Praytis, you're in violation!"

"Beg your pardon, Admiral," Praytis said calmly. "I am not, reread the contract."

"You know this thing? Samantha Steward, Sun Tribute," said a woman writing on a steno pad.

Sanderson ignored her and grabbed one of the MPs by the arm. "Get on the horn. Call Base Command. Seal off the Keys. Full lock down. No one in or out, got it?"

A hand ripped the radio out of the MP's grip. Surprise flashed on the Navy cop's face. The MPs turned around slowly.

Mark Levine was jabbing a handgun into the MP's side. Both guys dropped their rifles. Mark reached in and pulled the other MP's pistol. "There's no stopping this, must be five hundred cell phones recording." Mark motioned with the gun and the MPs backed up.

Sanderson didn't see it. He had moved toward the gangway. Aggie saw and heard it through Mother's sensors inside her head.

"Goddamn it, get on the horn!" Sanderson yelled over his shoulder.

"I don't think so. I've called off your dogs," Mark said.

"Levine!" Sanderson spun around. The reporter to his right bounced away and fell on his ass. Mark held the MP's radio in one hand and a forty-five in the other. Sanderson glared at his two men. One MP shrugged his shoulders.

"It's too late for Emergency lockdown, Admiral," a pretty, dark haired Navy chick said.

"Levine, you bastard. Everyone here's going to Gitmo. You can't stop me."

The woman stepped forward. "He doesn't need to, that's my job."

"Nostrum? What are you doing here?"

"The President isn't happy with your performance," Nostrum said flashing a CIA badge. Buddy was hanging in the air nearby and Aggie saw it through him. "You haven't been forthright with the President's UFO Commission. In fact, since you took over negotiations, things have gone backwards. I'm sorry Admiral, I work directly for The President and she sends this massage: You're fired."

Mark, pulled the clip, cleared the chamber and handed the MP's gun back to him, but not the radio.

"We'll see. Officer, arrest them!" Sanderson said to the nearest cop.

The police Captain stumbled forward; his gun's barrel was sharply bent. He shoved it into the hands of a fellow officer and whipped out a pair of old-fashioned chrome-steel handcuffs.

"I don't give a rat's ass who's what," He pointed at Aggie. That girl's under arrest…interfering with police business; destruction of property…that, that thing goes too."

"I knew it, I just knew it," Aggie said. The whole thing went out over the com. "I'm in deep shit again. Praytis take Mother, she's yours. Save yourself. I'm going to jail. Take care of Buddy, OK?"

She thrust her hands forward to accept the cuffs and closed her eyes. Inside her head the crowd advanced and surrounded the cops. The Police Captain's eyes flew open wide as a dozen hands grabbed him and pulled him backwards. Mark stepped forward and pushed Aggie's arms down. He took her hands in his.

"Not this time Ags, this time you're not in trouble." Mark said gently.

Nostrum flashed a different badge to the head cop. "National Security" She said. "Unless you want to be charged for taking Sanderson's bribes, back off. I'll take it from here."

"What about Mom, Dad?" Aggie cried suddenly alarmed. The government didn't care, they'd kill witnesses. She couldn't see anything inside her head back there. Her ships had left.

"Rescue's on Anguilla, everybody's fine." Mark said. "Introduce me to your friend? I never met a living man from another world before, not that I know of."

"Go ahead," Aggie said to Praytis, "He's one of the good guys."

Praytis waded into the people and extended his hand. Mark took it, followed by Yeoman Nostrum, then the cop boss, then one tourist after the other. Someone tossed the MP's rifles into the drink. Sanderson took his men and made a quick exit.

Long after the TV cameras were set up, Praytis and Aggie stayed. They told their stories to the world and there was nothing the deep state could do about it.

FINAL LAUNCH

I t was early; only an hour after sunrise but Aggie was up way before she needed to get ready for school. She wanted to see Mom off, but really, she wanted to make sure Mom and Dad were actually leaving. Her folks resisted Grandpa's offer to use the industrialist's spare house in Washington for free. They hated taking his money, the limo, the private jet ride and the front money but Mom had business and a new mission. Sky Flower finally decided it was time to shove off—at least someone besides Aggie herself made a big decision for a change. Dad swore he'd pay it all back after his book hit the shelves. Yeah right.

New furniture in this old bait shop seemed weird but Aggie had seen much weirder things and it was nice to sit in a chair that didn't stink like fish and pot.

Mom came out of the bedroom in a Booker Sister's thousand-dollar suit. It made Aggie cringe a little; OK Sky needed to look like a lawyer to do lawyer stuff but Mom was going a little over the top: Nothing new there.

"Aggie, will you be OK while Po-boy and I are gone?"

Dad called from the bedroom, "Sonny, I'm Sonny now, how's Po-boy Piper gone-a look on the book cover?"

"Sorry dear, you are right, of course."

"Mom, you shouldn't have cut your dreadlocks," Aggie said. "Why'd you have to cut it like mine?"

"Sky, where's my good socks?" Dad called.

Sky Flower rolled her eyes but with a big smile and said, "They're on the floor in your clean pile."

"Spiked hair with red tips on a forty something woman just looks weird," Aggie said.

"I'm not the one that created this new style," Mom said, "you set the trend, the Mel-Ag is hot right now, and Washington hates it, and I want them to know who I represent, what I represent, it's the future and it's thanks to you."

"Don't remind me of the mess I made." Aggie said.

"Honey Pie, do I have a dressy watch?" Dad called.

"No Dad," Aggie said, "you never got one, just diving watches."

Po-boy came out of the bedroom hopping on one cowboy-boot clad foot while trying to pull his new, stiff, blue jeans' leg over the other foot. He had on UFO boxer shorts. That was novel, Dad in long pants, socks, boots and underwear. Aggie would have laughed but what she was about to do sucked the humor out of her. It was good Mom and Dad were too rushed to notice her mood. They barely got ready in time to make the flight.

Aggie was about to say goodbye with a well-bit tongue so she wouldn't spill her guts when a knock came at the screen door. Thank Goddess, or she'd start blubbering and blabbing. It was some army guy with a gun, the usual. Aggie opened the screen door but barred the way in. The guy had a red, round face stuffed under a safety-officer's orange helmet.

"You look like a Halloween pumpkin, why don't you loosen that chin strap, it's not hurricane season."

"Yes, Miss Piper." He said but didn't do it. "The limo is here at the gate."

"Tell them to back in. He'll never get turned around in here, never mind, O hell, we'll walk out, get some boys in here for the luggage." Dad said. "Dog gone boots; hope I don't get blisters."

"Dad, get them to carry you, the President said they're here to protect us... right. We could get a dog sled; we got the dogs of war."

"Honey you don't have to treat them so poorly; they're just doing their job." Sky said while stuffing her briefcase with homemade granola bars laced with pot.

"Yeah, nicest prison guards ever." Aggie said under her breath.

In a flurry of activity, the Pipers were gone and all Aggie got was a quick goodbye and a peck on the cheek. This was working out. Maybe today she wouldn't try outrunning her military cop escort with the Vespa on her way to school. That game was getting old anyway, but she knew not to do anything different that might tip them off. One last cat and mouse game was in order; what the heck. She was going to miss that Vespa.

*****

Over the intercom, Aggie was called to the office — she expected it. She wasn't sleeping in math class like she used to do toward the end of the day. She was too busy with her thoughts. When she reached for the classroom door it opened without her. Her Special–ops bodyguard opened it for her, but this time she didn't insult him or crack a joke.

"Come on, let's go, I was going there after class anyway, let's get it over with." She said taking off.

"Yes Ma'am."

Aggie cringed; she was sick of government assholes following her around. She couldn't go anywhere without Madam President's goons on her ass. *And I thought the President liked me.* She sped up her pace to make the guy work harder. Mr. Security was packing all kinds of weighty hardware. *I hope he gets a rash.* Graduation was in three weeks and it was unusually hot, even in the building. Too bad she'd miss it. Since Jimmy's mom was in jail, Jimmy won't have anyone there to celebrate with him, not that Mrs. Brown ever cared. Aggie decided she'd provide him with his graduation gift.

Aggie blew into the office. The receptionist stood up from her desk behind the orange counter top and shrunk back when Aggie approached.

"Oh him," Aggie pointed a thumb over her shoulder at the sentry, "don't worry, he's harmless. They removed his balls at training camp. They make better robots that way."

The look on Miss Williams' face went from white to red to green. If Aggie had X-ray glasses, she thought, she'd see that Miss Williams was biting her tongue. Everyone did that lately. It sucked.

Aggie didn't wait for the go-ahead; she simply turned from the receptionist and headed for Preggey's office and walked right in. Preggey was seated, but there was a guy in a black suit standing behind her. Aggie's guy stayed in the short hall, but she heard him click off his gun's safety.

"Thank you for coming, Miss Piper, this is…"

"Yeah, Yeah, whatever, look I'm…"

The guy in black cut Aggie off with a wave of his hand. "FBI, Miss Piper, Melissa Van Ness has gone missing, and she is still under house arrest, if you know her whereabouts."

"Oh, for Goddess sake," Aggie said with her most exasperated voice. "You guys won't let us talk; how am I supposed to know where she's at? Screw you guys, if I knew I wouldn't say. I hate you people. Get lost, or I'll have my boy fill you full of lead."

The Special-ops guy came into the room, motioned the FBI guy to leave and the FBI guy took the hint. He stopped at the door and said, "This isn't over, don't fuck with the FBI." The FBI guy marched off, steaming like hot poop.

"Thanks Sergeant," Aggie said to her escort, "I'm going to get you a fly swatter for your birthday. I need to speak to Mrs. Preggey alone, get lost, OK."

"That's Captain: Make it quick." He said backing up.

"Whatever." Aggie rolled her eyes and flipped her hand at him just to say screw you, I'll do what I want.

The security guy closed the door. It didn't matter, the room was bugged and it wasn't Mel doing the bugging. If Buddy wasn't following her around cloaked, she wouldn't be getting any straight news. She told herself, this is better for everyone, the school, her, and everyone that mattered to her.

"Mrs. Preggey, I want to make a deal." Aggie flopped down into a chair like she was at home. "I know having the goon squad all over the school sucks, and you locked me into the scholarship, politics I'm sure, but…well here it is. I quit. I'm not coming back to school, but only if you give Jimmy Brown the scholarship, or else I'll make your life hell for the next three weeks."

The look on Preggey's face was classic pop-eyed surprised but Aggie didn't crack up.

"You don't want any UFO visitors, do you?" Aggie said. "I could have Praytis keep an eye on me in school, real up close." Aggie expected her to be outraged. But Mrs. Preggey looked relieved. The woman must have aged ten years since Aggie started back at school. "What'd you think? Make a deal?"

"Miss Piper, I do believe I can make such arrangements. Mr. Brown certainly is qualified, given that he has done so well in group home since his mother's arrest, I don't see why the Board would object."

"Make it so Number One."

"Excuse me?"

"You'll read about it in Daddy's book, if this doesn't happen." She flew her hand around like a flying saucer.

This is a good beginning. Aggie got up and left knowing she'd never look back.

Out in student parking her scooter was exactly where she had parked it. The only thing different about student parking was her ride now had a license plate on it and she had a real driver's license, and, there were two guys in a blacked-out SUV parked across the street. She rolled her Vespa over there and knocked on the window.

"Give me a ride home. You're going to follow me anyway, right?"

Two guys got out of the truck and loaded the Vespa into the rear. Aggie took the back seat saying, "Home James, but once around the Key first, I need time to think."

"That's Captain James." The driver said with a hint of good humor.

"Whatever."

People in the Keys were used to weird stuff so the local excitement had died down pretty fast. They even got used to orbs and the government agents hovering everywhere. But the news was out and way out. And the world was going crazy. All she wanted was to get away but fame and security made that impossible.

News crews had flooded the island asking her the same stupid softball questions. It was easy to tell they were approved security state generated questions. She spent a week or two last winter doing boring interviews before she went on strike. The press quickly moved on because she didn't play nice. She'd ask her own questions and answer them. A book deal was offered and she refused it. Writing was Dad's dream so she passed it to him.

The visiting GTO representatives and government officials in Washington trumped her anyway. They had a lot of explaining to do. The Military Industrial Complex wasn't pleased about it, or her. The security culture was having a hard time plugging the secrecy sieve. It would take years to explain away all the illegal crap they did 'to protect' what became known as The Secret. Regular Earth people weren't happy about it. The President championed full disclosure and became the People's hero. The spies were burnt toast. Anything that took the focus off Aggie was good. But she felt she wasn't safe. Not really.

The intelligence community pressed in. Albright guarded her and didn't let the military authorities take Aggie in for 'debriefing', but they were chomping at the bit. Albright had her ex-CIA sister on Key West making sure everyone stayed off Aggie's ass but for how long? So, life got boring, and restricted, and dangerous really, really fast.

Offers for college poured in. That was one escape, but where could she go? *Nowhere on this Earth.* Aggie was an unwilling international celebrity and Mel was in the shitter. The possibility of going to college was worlds away. *It doesn't matter anymore but it matters to me.* In the face of an expanded universe, she and her dreams seemed microscopically unimportant.

Aggie was stuck home alone. She had loaned her spaceships out. Two of the three remaining MAC shuttles and the same saucers that had landed on the White House lawn were on public display at the Washington Monument Mall. They weren't going anywhere without grays to fly them.

She sent the good ship Mother to Haiti. It was Sky's idea: 'Those poor people really need the income and attention that Mother will bring.' That's why Sky split for Washington; to lobby for Haiti and sanity. Mom said Haiti was the perfect place for Earth's first spaceport. Sky had a new cause to champion. Po-boy was busy writing, or trying, he wasn't very good at it.

Aggie gave Praytis control of her fleet. He had gathered the lost AI probes, mini smart probes and Shuttle One, and took them up to Moon Base for upgrades. Turned out Karnack had enough LF stored to buy a fleet and all that wealth became hers. Buddy, with his primitive intelligence, had the persona of a Labrador retriever and followed her everywhere. *What a pain in the ass.* Buddy drew too much attention, so he had to go, too. That's what she told the Feds, but she sent him to Mother and had him fitted with cloaking so Buddy was never far away.

Aggie had nothing normal to do. She couldn't date. Forget hanging out with Mel. That required a security detail. If not for a Presidential order commuting Mel's crime to a misdemeanor, Mel would be in jail instead of on house arrest. Going to the beach was impossible. The men in black suits made her favorite beach feel like detention hall. Whenever Aggie went kids treated her like rotting bait.

Jon was in jail. No work at Mark's Marina. Mark was forced to shut down except for slip renters. Navy Security kept people away from her house, or did they keep her from leaving it? Eyes were everywhere. It sucked. That's why and how she made up her mind.

Once home after the meeting with the Terminator, Mark called right on schedule saying. "Hey Ags, come over and hit the bag?"

"Sure Mark, anything is better than watching cartoons."

"Bring your backpack; you'll need a change after. It's dusty as hell."

That sounded too much like a hint. A little flutter hit her stomach. *He better not blow it.* She put on oversized blue yoga pants, an oversized loose T-shirt and stuffed her backpack with several changes.

She strolled down her lane trying not to look anxious. Two guys in camo were out in the brush like usual. Two uniformed MPs stood at the head of her driveway. When she got to Geiger Avenue, she looked left and right and more MPs were evident. *This sucks.* President Jane had said, 'You are a National Treasure. You need protection.' *Yeah right.* Aggie didn't feel like anything special... more like a caged chinchilla waiting to get skinned.

She had a wisecrack loaded and ready to fire at the Navy guy standing in front of Mark's closed gate, but she didn't launch. *What's the point?*

Mark was at the café with his arm around some girl in an orange bikini; they we making out. She wore huge sunglasses. It was hard to see her face. But she had a hot body and especially nice long, black hair. *About time Mark got with her, everybody but them knew they were meant for each other.* There were a few locals milling around their boats making ready to launch. Mark hadn't totally closed. Regular rental slip people, who registered and posted a background certificate, got through the checkpoint.

"Hey aren't you the Pres...oops." Aggie said.

Mark grabbed her arm and held a finger to his lips. "This is Miss Goldberger," Mark said with a wink, "A close friend of mine. Why don't you show Miss. Goldberger around while I get my dojo in order? She'll appreciate what I've done with the office...smooth sailing."

Mark had tried to talk Aggie out of it, but once she made up her mind he got on board.

Mark got up and walked toward the boat shed. Aggie took Nostrum around back and into Mark's office. Nostrum whipped off her wig. She had a short spiky blond do just like Aggie's; it was dyed exactly the same, even the red streaks matched.

"We're right getting you out of here," Nostrum whispered, handing Aggie the wig. "The agencies aren't happy, they blame you." Nostrum slipped out of her swimsuit and handed it to Aggie. "Switch quick. The President wants you under wraps but Mark and I agree with you, it's better you go underground. Jane can't control them. Consider this a test, when it's time to bug out, we'll let you know. Lots of them want you dead."

"Of course, half the world wants me dead."

"Where will you go?" The spy asked.

"I'm sailing to Mooney Bay. You know the place, right?"

"Do tourists piss on the beach?" Nostrum said.

"Hey, that's my line."

Nostrum dumped Aggie's backpack and stuffed Aggie's gear into a big tourist-type straw beach bag. Everything in order, Nostrum slipped into Aggie's clothes.

"Don't worry about that Coast Guard boat in the channel, friends of ours. Once you're away I'll take the Vespa for a little spin. The guy in the red hat is CIA, don't look at him and he'll ignore you. I'll trot over to the dojo. Your Vespa look–alike is there. Count to ten then move out."

"Bitching."

Nostrum exited Mark's office. Aggie peeked. The guy wearing a red baseball cap followed. She double-checked the wig. Moon Dodger was docked directly behind the café. She dropped the bag into the sailboat and the regulars fired their motors. *More cover, good idea Mark.* Moon Dodger was ship-shape and ready for war. She started the quiet little motor, cast off and motored away without a hitch.

As she sailed south past the Navy Base, she heard the Vespa screaming down Route One. Would the President approve of her escape? Mark provided plausible deniability. Did he work for Albright? No, Mark worked for himself. But not really, he worked for his family and Nostrum was family now.

She had a steady south wind and made Mooney Bay, which was inside the National Wildlife Refuge, in record time. No one tailed. Buddy had the air covered.

The wig drove her nuts but it was worth it. A note pinned to the rudder told her what to look for. There were hundreds of sandbars around Mooney. The right one was easy to locate; it was the only one with a black cloud hanging over it.

She beached the little boat, jumped out, set the anchor into dry sand, whipped off the wig and waved it like a signal flag. A sliver metallic disk, not one of her old ones, dropped out of the cloud. It hovered two feet above the sandbar. A split hatch opened making a gangplank. Praytis waved her up.

Mel gave her a big hug and kiss, and they almost kissed for too long. Aggie wanted to keep going but she pulled back still intent on saving herself for Jon. She'd bust him out, too when she had time to make a plan.

"Feels like home," Aggie said as she took the Captain's chair. "I missed you."

"I'm glad you feel that way." Praytis said. "Likewise, I'm sure. Speaking of feeling, how do you feel about the moon?"

"It's OK, a little weird Mom worships it, but it's cool."

"No, that's not what I mean. Moon Base is on the moon," He said.

"What should I feel? I never been there, besides I had a desert island in mind."

"We have a fine intergalactic university there," Praytis said. "We can't land but I see no harm in a flyby. Most of the skiffs reported in Earth's news of late weren't official visits. Our students endeavor in, what's the expression, oh yes, joy riding."

"Systems hear anything about Jon Colbert yet?"

"We still need too…what's the expression—jail-break him, but we haven't found him yet."

"Keep looking." Aggie said.

"The GTO thought you may well accept a scholarship to Moon University, I was asked to inquire."

"Can I bring Mel and Jimmy?"

"Do Earth humans live inside a gravity-well?"

Aggie half turned in her chair and checked the alien out. He had a big grin. She looked at Mel.

"Dude, I've been teaching him Earth humor," Mel said. "Jimmy doesn't want to go but I'm in."

"More like nerd humor than Earth humor," Aggie said dryly. Aggie just needed a break from all the intrigue. She didn't want to run away, just get away for a little while. Make plans in case she wanted to take off for real. She still had Earth school solidly in mind. "It can't hurt to visit, right?"

"Shall it be the moon, then?" Praytis said.

"Make it so Number One."

Aggie and Mel zipped off to the moon, but it wasn't the end, it was the first crack in a secret knowledge dam and the dam keepers weren't pleased. Aggie's dream of attending college was at hand, and everyone offered scholarships but whether Earth or moon it wasn't free, not really.

The cost of her leaving Earth unannounced would cause problems if the butt head Feds knew about it. The people in power would crap a brick. Aggie's parents, Mark and his new lover would face a shit storm over this little adventure if they got caught. She'd make this a short trip. She felt like dividends and unexpected adventures were just ahead, but now wasn't that time. Eventually, once the smoke cleared, she'd pour down benefits on all the people of Earth. That was her big idea. She didn't know how yet, maybe after college she'd know what to do.

She wasn't ready to make up her mind about anything. A quick, secret trip was all she wanted right now, just a way to test the waters, feel things out, just this one time, but things didn't work out that way.

*****

Sanderson was back at his desk deep below Key West, it was the best place for anyone dodging red laser dots and crosshairs. New enemies and former allies were dogging his ass. The President wasn't least among his problems, but she was handled for now. Things were improving. His old olive drab rotary phone rang and right on time. He picked it up gingerly.

"Sanderson here, are they away…Good, good, and the Van Ness girl is with them…Excellent, keep me posted."

Sanderson eased the antique phone back into its cradle like a newborn baby. Things were looking up. The game wasn't over yet and he was still a player.

THE END

ACKNOWLEDGEMENTS

A lot of people went into making this work of fiction. I'd like to thank my beta readers, Kathy Rosco, Lisa Cross, Pat Anderson, Dean LeVar and Cecelia Faiga. Thank you, Pattie Giordani, for line editing and proof reading. Thanks to Gayle F. Hendricks my formatting guru along with many others including the Lehigh Valley Writers Group (GLVWG.org) whose members have seen my works in progress and given me much needed constructive criticism along with supportive encouragement. Special thanks to my longtime friend, mentor, and editor Angel Ackerman for help on many of my writing projects and her husband Darrell Parry who worked with me on my cover art. My greatest thanks are to Lisa Cross, my partner, who puts up with my writer's life and was instrumental as a story critic, spell checker and reader. Without her emotional support, I could not write.

ABOUT THE AUTHOR

Rachel Thompson, writing fantasy and sci-fi as R.C. Thom, began her writing career after surviving a devastating motorcycle accident in 2003. She has since published non-fiction pieces in newspapers and magazines along with a handful of short stories. *Soul Harvest* is her first published novel. The sequel, *Aggie in Orbit* is available now. *Aggie in Space* is in process. Her short story anthology, *Stalking Kilgore Trout* and high fantasy novel, *Dragon Fire,* are also for sale now. Her novel, *Book of Answers.* will be release in 2019. Email her at rc@rcthom.com, or humanrights4all@aol.com and visit her website at rcthom.com.